He told me he would treat my heart with great care. He was lying, of course, for it was all a very clever, skillful seduction . . .

The night I met Lord Vincent Sinclair, son of the Duke of Pembroke, was the night I lost control. I never imagined that I, Cassandra Montrose, could engage in such wicked, wanton behavior with a man I hardly knew. But in that fateful moment, alone in his coach, the passion I felt for him was undeniable, even though I knew that after my surrender, I was unlikely to ever see my lover again.

Until a fateful secret brought me to his door. . .

I always believed my pride would prevent me from becoming any man's mistress—especially a rogue like Vincent, who cares for nothing but his inheritance. Yet I have a very good reason to remain in Vincent's life. If only he did not tempt me so . . .

By Julianne MacLean

The Mistress Diaries
In My Wildest Fantasies
Surrender to a Scoundrel
Portrait of a Lover
Love According to Lily
My Own Private Hero
An Affair Most Wicked
To Marry the Duke

If You've Enjoyed This Book,
Be Sure to Read These Other
AVON ROMANTIC TREASURES

In Bed with the Devil *by Lorraine Heath*
How to Propose to a Prince *by Kathryn Caskie*
Never Trust a Scoundrel *by Gayle Callen*
A Notorious Proposition *by Adele Ashworth*
Under Your Spell *by Lois Greiman*
The Devil Wears Tartan *by Karen Ranney*

The Mistress Diaries

Julianne MacLean

An Avon Romantic Treasure

AVON
An Imprint of HarperCollinsPublishers

This is a work of fiction. Names, characters, places, and incidents are drawn from the author's imagination or are used fictitiously and are not to be construed as real. Any resemblance to actual events, locales, organizations, or persons, living or dead, is entirely coincidental.

AVON BOOKS
An Imprint of HarperCollins*Publishers*
10 East 53rd Street
New York, New York 10022-5299

ISBN-13: 978-0-7394-9821-7

Printed in the U.S.A.

Acknowledgments

Many thanks to Deborah Hale for all her help in the plotting stages, and Michelle Phillips, my cousin and friend, for reading the early draft. I especially want to thank my editor, Erika Tsang, for her insightful comments about Vincent, which inspired me greatly during revisions. Thank you to my husband, Stephen, for all the support and hard work producing the video trailers for my books. Finally, a huge thank you to my young daughter, Laura, for her creative contribution to this book—Letitia's birthmark. Thank you for brainstorming with me.

The Mistress Diaries

Prologue

I have always considered myself a woman of high moral fiber. How then could I have done such a thing? Where were my values and principles? But of course I know the answer to those questions. It was without a doubt the blinding intensity of his charm, which made me forget everything I believed in.

—from the journal of
Cassandra Montrose,
Lady Colchester,
May 14, 1873

Lord Vincent Sinclair kicked open the door of the sumptuous London hotel room with staggering brute force and carried Cassandra Montrose, Lady Colchester, over the threshold.

Already delightfully tousled and flushed, for he had kissed her senseless in the carriage the entire way there, Cassandra laughed and wrapped her arms tighter around his neck.

"I cannot believe we are doing this," she said. "How shall I live with myself in the morning? You are a very bad influence, Lord Vincent—a rake of the highest order."

He grinned and kicked the door shut behind him, then carried her across the rose-scented room in a glorious fluttering of silks and lace. He set her down by the enormous mahogany bed draped in crimson and gold velvet.

"How wonderful that you are aware of my most distinguished reputation, darling. Now I can be sure there will be no unrealistic expectations in the morning, no tears or broken hearts." He grinned flirtatiously, his eyes smoldering with wickedness. "In that regard, I suppose I should warn you now. I am not the kind of man a woman should pin her hopes on."

She raised a mischievous eyebrow. "As I said, a very bad influence indeed."

Pulling at his white cambric bow tie and unbuttoning the top of his shirt, he smiled with devilish intent. "I quite assure you, Lady Colchester, I have not yet *begun* to be a bad influence. My best is yet to come."

"I don't doubt it."

He paused a moment just to look at her, then slowly removed the mother-of-pearl combs in her hair and slid the pins from her upswept locks, tucking them into his breast pocket with a confident glimmer in his eye.

Cassandra's heart drummed with anticipation as her hair came loose and fell onto her shoulders. She had never imagined she would ever be so bold, so brazen, as to leave a ball and dash off into the night with a darkly handsome stranger she had only just met, a reputed rake and heartbreaker. But she supposed life was full of surprises—and not all of them as exciting as this one was turning out to be.

For that reason alone she deserved this night of pleasure, didn't she?

Yes. One night of passion before she went forward with her life. It was more than she ever would have imagined for herself earlier that evening when she had almost resigned herself to a loveless marriage for the second time in her life.

Almost.

Vincent took her face in his hands, ran his thumbs lightly over her cheeks and gazed into her eyes with urgency. "I couldn't help myself," he said. "You put a spell on me, and when the night was coming to an end, I knew I couldn't part from you. I had to steal you away."

He took her into his arms and held her for a brief, breathtaking moment before he lowered his mouth to hers. The kiss was deep, damp, and tasted of champagne, and the intimate stroke of his tongue was so gratifying, so stimulating to her senses, she wondered how she was ever going to survive the multitude of pleasures to come.

He slowly turned her to face the bed, then began to unfasten the tiny pearl buttons at the back of her gown. Cassandra shivered at the sensation of his skillful fingers working down her back, and when he slid the lace neckline off her shoulder, she melted, for his hand was warm as it brushed lightly over her skin. He touched his lips to her nape, and her entire being trembled within.

With measured proficiency, he turned her to face him again and began to undress her, keeping his eyes fixed on hers the entire time.

As she met his penetrating gaze, she distinguished something dark and cynical in his eyes—something almost dangerous. It was as if he wanted her to see it and to know that he was not to be romanticized. *This is not love,* he seemed to be telling her. *Nothing will come of it. This is just one night.*

Strangely, however, she was not deterred. She had no reservations about what they were going to do. She wanted only to experience the sexual act as it was meant to be experienced—with a man who knew exactly how to awaken a woman to real pleasure.

Carefully, he dealt with the clasp on her priceless jeweled necklace. He peeled her gloves from her hands, laying soft kisses on her wrists, then knelt before her and removed her satin slippers and silk stockings, one leg at time.

Whenever he bared more of her hungry, yearning flesh, he laid a kiss in that place and touched her with teasing, featherlike fingers that made her ache and burn for more. It was the most exquisite undressing of her life.

At last she was standing naked before him, openly, without shyness or modesty, aroused by the cool air on her feverish body. She had never felt so beautiful, so feminine, so erotic.

Nor had she ever felt so reckless. It was outside anything she had ever done, and she prayed she would not burn in Hell for it—for giving in to her sexual desires so heedlessly with a man she barely knew, without a care for the consequences. But the fact of the matter was, she cared for nothing at this moment but her own pleasures.

What was it about this man? No wonder he was famous for his seductions.

Sliding a hand down the plush line of her hip, she reveled in her arousal while he swept his gaze appreciatively from her eager eyes to her full breasts, then down her long, slender legs. There was a dark hunger in his expression as he began to remove his own black and white formalwear—his jacket, his white tie and white waistcoat, his trousers and underclothes. He tossed everything to the floor, even his heavy pocket watch and cuff links, then stood nude by the bed, his strong, muscular body gleaming in the golden lamplight.

Cassandra was mesmerized. All she could do was stand and wait, breath held, for him to touch her.

Gazing into the blue depths of her eyes, he stepped forward. The tip of his erection pressed into her stomach, and her heart quickened with need. Were they really going to do this? She was trembling with anticipation.

He took her upper arms in his hands, then covered her mouth with his. The kiss was fierce, deep and insistent.

A moment later he was easing her onto the bed, their naked bodies entwined intimately on the soft crimson covers. His skin, hot and smooth, burned into hers, and her breasts rose and fell with the tremulous pace of her breathing.

"You have bewitched me," he whispered as he dropped hot kisses down her quivering belly. His fingers worked over her naked hips, down her legs, and slid back up to stroke her sensitive inner thighs. "I knew from the first moment I saw you that I had to have you."

"I felt it, too, just as I feel it now. I can barely comprehend it. All I want is to give myself to you completely. I want nothing else. It makes no sense when we have only just met."

Bold words, all of them, and foolish, when she considered what she knew of this man—that he was the wildly disreputable son of a duke and could send the blood rushing to her head with mere kisses alone. But she couldn't think straight when he touched her, couldn't breathe, couldn't fathom anything outside of this blissful need to be close to him, even if it was only for one night.

"How is it possible I have never met you before now?" he asked, poised above her, still looking into her eyes. "Where have you been hiding?"

Her tone grew serious. "I told you when we danced. I only just came out of mourning."

Her husband had been dead for exactly one year.

Vincent brushed a finger lightly across her cheek and over her moist lips, swollen from his kisses. "You have been lonely, then?"

"Very." It was God's own truth. She had been lonely since the day she realized her husband had never loved her, for there had always been another—his mistress, the great love of his life.

"Did you love him very deeply?"

No one had ever asked her anything like that before, and she blinked up at him, not quite sure how to answer. There had been moments, terrible moments, when she'd known nothing but misery.

Vincent closed his eyes. "No, do not answer that. It was wrong of me to ask, and I shall only be jealous of the man who was first to have your heart."

"There is no need for jealousy," she told him, understanding more with every passing moment why he was such a renowned master of seduction. He knew exactly what to say, how to feed a woman's desire for intimacy. "My heart is yours tonight. As is my body."

He opened his eyes again and laid butterfly kisses on the tip of her nose, her eyelids, her forehead, and down her cheek.

"Then I shall treat your heart and body with great care." He took a nipple into his mouth, flicked his tongue over the aroused, pebbled tip. "And I shall treat *this* with great care." He moved to the other rosy nipple and continued to drive her mad with lust.

Soon he was kissing her body, using every refinement of his warm, masterful tongue to push her to the edge of heaven, into an overwhelming sensual madness. His hand moved between her legs, and he pleasured her there until her excitement swelled to a perfect, mounting climax. She heard herself gasp with fright, for she had never known such exquisite indulgence. Her husband had certainly never taken the time.

She threw her head back and gasped, while Vincent braced himself on two strong arms above her. "Let me inside you," he whispered.

Shameless, her hands came up to stroke the hard muscles of his chest. "Yes." She spread her legs wide and, obsessed with longing, hands trembling, took hold of his firm buttocks.

He paused to look down at her, his dark, passionate gaze roving down her nude body. She could not wait another moment. Thrusting her hips upward, she let out a moan while he drove himself in. She felt a great surge of pressure stretch and fill her, hot and fiery, slick and wet.

He went still, deep inside. His voice was low and controlled. "Tell me, Cassandra, is this a safe time?"

She gazed up at him, distracted. All she knew was her desire. "What do you mean?"

"If it is not, I will take care not to cause any unwanted accidents, but you must tell me now."

She could barely think. A mighty hunger was escalating inside her. "There is no need to worry," she replied. "I cannot . . . "

All at once the words became scrambled in her brain. She closed her eyes and breathed slowly, tried to remember her life outside this room, then somehow summoned the courage to speak the truth—to bury the feelings of failure and inadequacy she had known in her marriage.

"I cannot have children," she explained. "I am barren."

He lay motionless inside her, staring down into her eyes. "You are a beautiful woman, Cassandra. Do not ever forget that."

She understood that the sentiment was meant to comfort her, to offer her some solace from her self-recriminations. He was indeed a master at this. She softened warmly inside.

He began to move. She lay her head back upon the bed, gazing up at the strong lines of his jaw and his powerful dark eyes, heavy with desire as he made love to her in the dim, golden light.

It was magnificent, all of it, and she wondered if this was the kind of love the poets wrote about.

But no, it could not be. He was a man with a reputation, a seducer of women. This was only one night. She could not allow herself to become carried away by romantic notions. It was sexual pleasure, physical release, nothing more.

Soon the vibrations mounted, and she watched, listened, and gloried in the sensation of Vincent's climax coursing through his strong, throbbing body, then flooding into hers. She felt the hot, frothy gush of his seed as she had felt her husband's when they were man and wife—but nothing about this night could compare. Something had sparked inside her from the beginning, the first instant she locked eyes with him in the ballroom. It was pure magic, like nothing she had ever experienced, vital and intoxicating, and it could have gone no other way. She simply had to have this night with him.

He groaned with the savage force of his completion, then relaxed and lay heavy upon her. Cassandra closed her eyes and held him tight, blissfully aware of his heart beating against hers while she hugged him to her.

God help her, she did not want to let go. Despite her determination not to be swept away by romantic notions, she wanted to hold onto him forever, to feel this incredible, astonishing intimacy, this crushing closeness she had never known before this moment.

She sucked in a breath, and her body shuddered its release. A single tear squeezed from her eye and dropped across her temple, seeping into her hair.

She had not expected to feel like this, not with a rake like him. She was overcome. There was a strange, aching pain inside her heart that was both beautiful and terrifying. She felt very foolish.

Gently, he withdrew and rolled onto his back beside her. They both stared up at the ceiling in silence.

"I was not expecting anything like this tonight," he said in a low voice, as if having read her thoughts. "I was not even going to attend the ball. I had been invited elsewhere."

He sounded surprised and bewildered. His dark brows pulled together in a frown.

"I did not expect it either," she said, her voice faint and shaky. "I've never done anything like this in my life. It might be common for you, but . . . I don't know what came over me."

He turned his head on the pillow to look at her. "There was nothing common about it. You're very . . ." His eyes dwelled curiously upon hers, as if he didn't quite know how to finish what he'd started. "You're very unique."

She faced him and rested a cheek on a hand. "So are you saying that what we did tonight was special? Because I confess that when we left the ballroom together, I was under the impression you did this sort of thing all the time." Then something made her lighten her tone and touch him playfully on the shoulder with the tip of her finger. "Meet ladies at balls and whisk them away to your carriage, kiss them until they're dizzy with pleasure, then carry them off to your bed."

"Your impression was correct," he replied, his darkly flirtatious countenance returning. "I do this sort of thing all the time, at every possible opportunity. Do not forget it, darling."

She certainly would not.

"But truly," he said, rolling onto his side and

pulling her close, "it's been a long time since I've had a night such as this." It was music to her ears. "I hadn't thought myself capable of it."

"Why not?"

His eyes narrowed with scrutiny. "I am afraid it's a long and depressing story and I couldn't possibly bore you with it. Besides, I don't want anything to spoil this perfect night."

She inched closer. "It has been perfect, hasn't it?"

He sat up and rolled onto her again. She wrapped her legs around him.

"Promise me," he said, "that you won't rise from this bed in the morning and feel guilty for what we did, then leave London in shame to hide away in the country and punish yourself. I want to see you again."

Did he mean it? No, surely not.

"I want to see you again, too," she cautiously replied, "but I . . . "

His head drew back. "You what?"

She hesitated, for she was not even sure she knew what tomorrow would bring. She had come to London to meet a man who had expressed interest in her as a wife, but in the first moments of their meeting, she knew she could never love him. So, without the joys of motherhood to make such a union worthwhile, what would be the point, except to be provided for? Surely she could find another way to do that. She would not be averse to becoming a governess or a lady's companion . . .

"It's rather complicated," she explained. "You see I came to London because my late husband's cousin and heir, the new Lord Colchester, has been making arrangements to see me married again."

He frowned. "Already? But you only just came out of mourning."

"As I said, it is difficult to explain. Lord Colchester is an impatient man."

Impatient and despicable.

"But you are not betrothed *yet*, are you?" He stared into her eyes. "Tell me I did not just make love to another man's fiancée."

"No, no, it's nothing like that," she assured him. "But there was a man at the ball this evening who had been corresponding with Lord Colchester and was making inquiries about me."

"Who?"

She paused. "Clarence Hibbert. Do you know him?"

Vincent's eyebrows lifted. He laughed. "Clarence Hibbert? For *you*? Good Lord, you must be joking."

She found herself chuckling as well, when she had never seen humor in any of this before. But she supposed it was true. Mr. Hibbert was small, plump, and balding, and he was a complete featherbrain. A rich featherbrain, mind you, but still a featherbrain.

"Joking or not," she said, "I think I might have spoiled my chances with Mr. Hibbert when I ran off with you."

"Thank God for that. He's all wrong for you, Cassandra. Not only is he a bumbling idiot, he's almost three times your age. A woman like you needs a strong, young, robust man with plenty of energy in his body and a good deal of activity in his brain." He grinned and slid his hands under her bottom, then pulled her tight against his hips. He was already growing firm again. "You weren't truly considering him, were you?"

"Only until the moment I met him."

"Ah." He slid his palm from her waist to her breast and stroked her erect nipple with his thumb.

"The fact of the matter is," she explained, tipping her head back when he began to kiss her neck, "I cannot continue to be dependent upon Lord Colchester. He will wish to marry one day, and I need to move on with my life."

"So you will continue in your quest for a husband."

She wet her lips. "Or perhaps I will find some other situation. I might try to find work as a governess."

He stopped what he was doing and looked at her. "*Work.*" He spoke the word as if it were a concept uttered in a foreign tongue. "But Cassandra, you are a lady."

"A lady with very few options available to me. I cannot live on social position alone."

"But your husband must have left you an inheritance."

"Indeed, he left me a very generous one in his will, but unfortunately the money did not exist. He spent everything on his mistress. There was nothing but debts."

Vincent's eyes narrowed with unease. "Do you not have family who can take you in?"

All at once she wished she had not confessed any of this. The whole night had been so magical, and now she was spoiling it with the realities of her dismal life. "That would be a last resort," she said. "They are not welcoming people."

Cassandra took his face in her hands, then pressed her lips to his, wanting only to recapture the magic. "Please, let us not talk about this anymore. I shall be brilliantly happy with my future, whichever path I choose. I am a free woman with a will of my own."

She reached down and began to gently squeeze and stroke him.

He let out a husky groan. "My God, you are incredible. You make me feel so . . . " He did not finish the thought. He merely dipped his head and closed his eyes.

She blew softly into his ear and whispered, "Tell me, Vincent. How do I make you feel?"

"Alive."

He laid kisses down the length of her neck, across her shoulders and breasts. Fire ignited deep inside her.

"Poor Hibbert," he said. "He doesn't know what he lost."

"And you cost me a husband, you naughty man. You shall have to make it up to me, you know."

He inched downward, his tongue continuing to pulse gently across her belly. "Then perhaps *I* shall marry you instead."

Knowing better than to take him seriously when he was a known libertine and they were both tangled in the persuasive pleasures of erotic sensation, she shook her head at him. "That wasn't exactly what I had in mind."

"No?"

"No. And you shouldn't tease a lady about something like that, Vincent. As a gender, we take marriage very seriously."

"What if I was not teasing?" he asked. "What if I mean to have you all to myself, forever and ever, till death do us part?"

She fought to keep her head—because he could not possibly mean it—but desire was clouding all hope of reason. "I hadn't realized this night was quite as perfect as all that."

He rose up on both arms and shifted his hips, easing himself into her pliant, heated warmth. "Believe me, it was."

"Then let us see where it goes," she suggested, wondering if it was possible for a woman to die of utter happiness.

"I already know where it's going," he declared in a low, gruff voice. "At least for tonight." He reached over to turn the key in the lamp, and darkness enveloped the room.

In the morning, Cassandra was startled awake by a bright, blinding beam of light cutting through the crack in the drapes. She blinked and squinted and sat up, hugging the sheets to her chest.

She was alone in the room, naked, and her head was aching from too much champagne the night before. What time was it?

She glanced at the pillow beside her, trying to make sense of her surroundings and situation.

Oh yes, the pleasure. The sensations. His body in the night . . .

She looked around the quiet room. Her gown was in a neat pile upon the chair. Her jewels were still on the dressing table where he had set them. His clothes, however, were gone. There was not a trace of him anywhere.

She swallowed uncomfortably as she imagined him creeping out of the room, making his escape in the predawn hours—which he had no doubt done many times before with countless other women just like her. He had left nothing behind but his scent on her skin, which would not last long, and—*good God*—a stack of money on the bedside table.

A heavy, sickening lump settled in the pit of her stomach. She had never been an irresponsible woman, yet she had behaved recklessly with a wicked, albeit charming, rake. He had admitted openly that he was not to be depended upon, yet she'd spent the night with him regardless. For a brief time at the height of their lovemaking, she had even imagined it was something more, something very magical. Not just for her, but for him, too.

It had been nothing of the sort, of course. He doubtless made all his lovers feel that way. It was why his path was littered with broken hearts.

She cupped her forehead in a hand and squeezed her eyes shut. What in God's name had she been thinking? Had she had that much champagne? She hadn't thought so, but how else could she possibly explain her behavior? It had been so outside of her usual caution and propriety.

Tossing the covers aside, Cassandra sat up on the edge of the bed. She rose to her feet and padded quietly around the empty room, knelt down to pick up her scattered underclothes, and chided herself as she dropped to her knees in search of a stocking under the bed. It was all so very humiliating.

Perhaps the worst part of it all was the fact that she was now fighting tears, which were pooling in the corners of her eyes. Lord help her, she was disappointed. She was hurt because he was gone, when it had all seemed so wonderfully perfect.

Oh, she would never forgive herself for being so naïve. She pulled the stocking out from under the bed and sat back on her heels, praying to God that she would never have to see that rakish Lord Vincent again. She would simply do her best to forget that this night ever happened.

Chapter 1

One Year Later

No doubt this will be the most trying experience of my life, but I must endure it as best I can, for I have made up my mind. I cannot put my own needs first. I must do the responsible thing.

—from the journal of
Cassandra Montrose,
Lady Colchester,
May 12, 1874

On the day that Lord Vincent Sinclair returned to Pembroke Palace after a tedious week securing a fiancée in London, cold hard raindrops were dropping from the clouds like overturned buckets of nails.

With his future bride sitting proudly beside him, he sat back in the rumbling coach and rubbed a hand over his chin. He looked out the rain-soaked window at his majestic family home in the distance, in all its arrogant, pompous glory. Miles away, high upon the hilltop, it gloated, preened, and reveled in its own lofty magnificence. In Vincent's mind, however, those impressive stone towers and turrets and the ostentatious triumphal arch at the entrance could not disguise the wretchedness in its foundations, for it was built upon the ruins of an ancient abbey whose walls had been knocked down by betrayal and the grisly murder of one of his ancestors.

Of course, that was a long time ago. Now it was a distinguished, dazzling palace. A house of dukes. And hardly anyone knew the intimate truth about the Pembrokes—that brotherly betrayal still breathed behind the tapestries, and a secret madness lurked in the dark, subterranean passageways.

He turned to look at his fiancée—Lady Letitia Markham, eldest daughter of the Duke of Swinburne—but found himself staring only at the back of her head, for she was sitting forward on the seat beside him, peering out the other window. He noted the excessive details of her elaborate hat—the silly lilac bows and ribbons and the complicated wreath of cherry blossoms, all of it secured over a dozen shiny black ringlets and scented with strong, somewhat sickening perfume.

At least she was a beauty, he thought as he turned and looked out his own window again. If he was going to be dragged like a dog into marriage, it might as well be pleasantly done. Letitia was tall, slender, and graceful. She had the face of a goddess, so if nothing else, she would be pretty to look at on their wedding night when he was fulfilling his husbandly duty by depriving her of her virginity.

He glanced at her again, looked her up and down with indifference, then returned his detached gaze to the view outside the window. To be honest, he wasn't even certain she was a virgin. Not that he cared. When it came to his duty to his family, he cared for very little. He certainly cared nothing for the woman beside him. She was shallow and self-absorbed and interested in nothing more than his social position as a Pembroke and his fantastically enormous fortune. She certainly did not love him.

But that was hardly a problem, he supposed, because he was a man who lived for pleasure—drinking and whoring, seducing beautiful, willing women who matched his own fervor in the wild quest for debauchery. He was disreputable and depraved, made no apologies for it, and Letitia, thank God, understood all of that. There were no preconceived notions of romance between them. She even seemed rather contemptuous of sentimental affections, which in all honesty made this woman his perfect match.

But that was beside the point. What mattered presently was that his father had already given this particular woman his stamp of approval, which was at the root of all this insanity. Vincent had gone to London to fetch Lady Letitia and propose, with the full intention of marrying her before Christmas, because his father demanded it. If all four of his sons were not husbands by then, he had made clear, they would *all* be disinherited.

The upside was that they would each be awarded five thousand pounds on their wedding day, just for saying "I do." The duke had deemed it so in the will—along with the stipulation that he must approve of each new bride of Pembroke. That was reason enough to go through with it, with this woman in particular. The money would secure him a residence far away from the palace so he would never have to return here again.

And of course, how could he forget? There was also the family curse that needed to be thwarted by four marriages, or heaven forbid, the entire palace would be swept away by a torrential flood.

Bloody madness, all of it. Bloody ridiculous madness, with nothing to be done to change it. The doctors and solicitors had deemed the duke sane at the time the will was drawn up, so there it was. Unalterable.

Exhaling sharply, he leaned closer to the window to look up at the ominous clouds in the sky and the rain that showed no signs of letting up. His father was probably in a panic today if the fields were flooding, which they most certainly were. The coach had driven through half a dozen puddles the size of fish ponds on the way here.

Dreading the senseless drama he was sure to come home to, Vincent turned to look at Letitia again, and hoped her arrival and talk of wedding plans would distract the old man from the weather.

As for himself, well, he meant to do his duty and be done with it, then God willing, he would be free to live as he chose. How difficult could one wedding be? he thought as the coach swerved wildly in the slick mud. Surely no more difficult than accepting the fact that his father was stark raving mad.

"Tell me," Letitia said, turning her ever so pretty head toward him, as if she had sensed his eyes upon her, "how soon will I get to see the necklace? I must be wearing it when we make the formal announcement."

He looked at her impatient brown eyes and tiny upturned nose, and wondered why he had felt compelled to offer that particular jewel when he proposed. It was the famous Pembroke Sapphire—a sparkling emerald-cut stone the size of a continent. It had been the engagement gift presented to his great-grandmother by the fourth Duke of Pembroke.

Another woman had worn it more recently, of course. Another fiancée three years ago. But she had not lived to see her wedding day.

He reflected upon his own infinite bitterness with a perverse touch of amusement. "I will speak to Mother about it the instant we arrive." He patted her hand. "She has been keeping it safe for you, darling."

Letitia lifted a delicately arched brow. "Well, I certainly hope so. From what I understand, it is a jewel to be reckoned with."

"As are you," he casually replied.

"Yes. As am I." She turned her eyes proudly toward the window again, leaving him to stare at all those ridiculous ribbons and flowers.

They pulled up in front of the palace, and two footmen came dashing down the stairs with umbrellas. Letitia's mother, seated across from them, stirred from her slumber and murmured, "Have we arrived?"

"Indeed we have, Your Grace." Vincent stepped out first, undaunted by the wind and violent downpour and the sharp, stinging raindrops on his cheeks, for he found it all rather poetic. It was the perfect backdrop for his arrival.

He offered his hand to Letitia's mother, the Duchess of Swinburne. She stepped out of the coach and was quickly ushered up the stairs by a footman, who struggled in the violent, blustery wind to hold an umbrella over her head.

Vincent offered his hand to his betrothed, who emerged from the carriage with a scowl.

"I am so sick of this putrid rain," she said. "Look what it has done to my shoes. It had better dry up before our wedding day, or I swear to you, Vincent, we will have to postpone. I refuse to walk down the aisle with mud on my gown."

He took the umbrella from the second footman and sheltered his spoiled future bride from the wind and rain. "We shall postpone if it pleases you."

He really didn't care, as long as they were married by Christmas.

Again she raised an eyebrow at him. "I knew I picked the right brother."

She was referring of course to his older brother Devon, who had recently considered her in his own search for a bride but had chosen another. Much to Letitia's dismay.

She was also acknowledging the fact that he was bending to her will, for she was the kind of woman who liked to have her own way.

He really didn't care about that either. He would bend all the way to China if it would secure his inheritance and get him his five thousand pounds. After that, the bending would, of course, come to an end.

Together they hurried up the steps and found dry cover under the enormous portico and clock tower. Vincent lowered the umbrella, while his fiancée wiped a gloved hand over her skirts.

"I swear, Vincent," she snapped. "This weather . . . "

He was growing tired of the subject, and quite frankly, tired of her. It had been a long coach ride from the train station.

"The sun will be shining soon enough." Turning, he handed the umbrella to the footman and offered her his arm.

Letitia's mother had already gone inside and was meeting his own mother in the grand entrance hall. The two duchesses were laughing about something, and their voices echoed off the high frescoed ceiling. They both stopped and turned when Vincent and Letitia swept through the door on a tempestuous gale that whipped at her skirts then died away as the doors swung shut behind them.

"Vincent, welcome home," his mother said, crossing the marble floor with hands outstretched to greet him. She wore an amber silk day dress, and her golden hair was knotted elegantly. She was without question one of the most beautiful women in England, despite the fact that she had just celebrated her fiftieth birthday. Tall and slim and blessed with an inherent warmth and charm, she was adored by everyone who made her acquaintance, and was famous throughout England for her kindness and charity.

"Hello, Mother." He kissed her cheek, then turned to the dark beauty at his side. "You remember Lady Letitia. It is my pleasure to present her as my betrothed."

Letitia curtsied. His mother took her future daughter-in-law's hands in her own and kissed her on the cheek. "My dear, welcome back to Pembroke. We are delighted to see you again, and under such happy circumstances."

"Thank you, Your Grace." Letitia glanced at Vincent and inclined her head as if to remind him of something.

He stared at her for a cool moment before he turned his eyes back to his mother. "It was very generous of you, Mother, to offer Great-grandmother's necklace. We are touched beyond words."

His mother's lips parted slightly as she blinked up at him, and she appeared uncharacteristically flustered, but soon recovered herself. She spoke with poise and graciousness, as always. "And I have been beside myself, waiting to see you wearing it, Lady Letitia. I shall have it sent to Vincent's rooms immediately."

His mother looked up at him again with a measure of concern, and he wondered if she had changed her mind about the necklace.

But no . . . it was something else. Perhaps his father was especially fretful today. This kind of weather always made him anxious.

Before he had a chance to inquire, his brother Devon appeared under the keystone arch at the back of the hall and stared at him as if he had just shot the butler.

Vincent felt all the muscles in his neck and shoulders clench slowly like a fist.

His raven-haired brother, with eyes as blue as an October sky, had returned from America little more than a month ago, after being gone for three very congenial years. Vincent was not yet accustomed to seeing him back in the house, striding around as if their personal war had never occurred. And his brother had taken charge of the estate as if their father had already handed over the title.

"Devon," he said flatly. "How good of you to greet us. You remember Lady Letitia, I presume."

Of course his brother would remember her. She had thrown a tantrum in his study not long ago, screeching at him and slapping his face. It was the day she learned he had proposed to another woman.

It was one of the few decadent pleasures of the day, Vincent supposed, to bring Letitia back here and present her to Devon.

His brother's gaze shifted to Letitia, as if he had only just then become aware of her presence. She glared at him for an icy instant before he strode forward and spoke with polite reserve. "Welcome back to Pembroke, Lady Letitia."

She smirked and slipped her arm through Vincent's. "Thank you, Lord Hawthorne. I am pleased to return, especially now that I am engaged to your very charming and handsome younger brother."

"My congratulations to you both." He turned his cool eyes to Vincent. "But I must have a word with you. Now, if you please."

It was not lost on Vincent that their mother was biting her lower lip. "I presume it is a matter of some importance," he replied.

"Yes, we have a rather urgent problem."

Just then their younger brother Blake appeared at the top of the stairs. "Vincent. You're back . . . "

An awkward silence ensued. It seemed to Vincent that the scene had become rather theatrical, so he slid his arm free of Letitia's possessive grip. "If you will excuse me, darling. Obviously there is some colossal household matter that requires my attention."

Her cheeks flushed red with what appeared to

be annoyance. She was growing tired of waiting for the necklace, no doubt.

"Of course," she said tersely.

His mother moved forward to distract the two ladies. "Allow me to escort you both to your rooms, where I am certain you will enjoy the spectacular views of the lake." She nodded at a footman to inform the housekeeper.

Wondering what was so bloody important that it could not wait until he had a drink, Vincent broke from the ladies and followed the brother he so deeply despised into the library.

"I beg your pardon?" Vincent said as Devon handed him a glass of brandy. "Did I hear you correctly?"

"Yes."

"You are telling me a baby was brought here. To the house. This morning."

"Yes."

"And the child is alleged to be mine?" His body went utterly still as he comprehended this most shocking news, which in no way could be true. "This is beyond even you, Devon. You cannot be serious. Is this a joke?"

"Am I laughing?" his brother replied. "Do I appear amused, even in the slightest?"

No, he most certainly did not.

The possible legitimacy of his brother's pronouncement and all its implications struck Vincent hard, but any immediate anxiety was smothered instantly by denial, for he had always been careful. Exceedingly careful. It absolutely could not be true.

He glanced down at the brandy in the glass, stared at it for a moment, swirled it around, then without taking a drink set it on a table. He crossed to the window and looked out over the vast estate to the horizon, blurred by mist and clouds. Everything inside him was churning with shock and unease and a tumultuous mix of emotions he could not even begin to fathom. All the while his intellect was measuring the predicament with heightened precision and clarity.

He thought of all the women he had bedded over the past year. He tried to picture their faces, but most were blurred images, flashes of memory. A laugh here, a kiss there—all insignificant, forgettable encounters. Only one stood out in his mind, like a lone portrait in a fine gallery. Of that night he remembered everything.

But it could not be her.

"How do you know this woman is telling the truth?" he asked, not yet ready to believe it, for there were many reasons a woman would stoop to such tricks. Wealthy and powerful, the men of Pembroke were each in their own right a tempting prize. Setting a trap such as this would be all too easy where he was concerned, for the whole of England knew of his reputation, and certainly the women he slept with were not known for their morals and principles.

Except perhaps for that one particular woman, on that one particular night. She had been different from the rest. But it was not her.

"That is the problem," Devon said. "We have no way of knowing."

Vincent walked to the sofa and sat down, then planted his elbows on his knees, bowed his head and squeezed his hair in his hands. "Christ, what timing."

"It was bound to happen sooner or later," Devon said. "You're a man who enjoys his pleasures with women of loose morals. You are notorious for it."

He lifted his head. "I always take precautions. I've been careful."

"Evidently not careful enough. It doesn't take much, you know. Just one moment of weakness or forgetfulness."

Vincent glared at his brother with unadorned loathing. "I know how it works, Devon, and I don't need a lecture from you, of all people."

The reminder was enough to silence his brother, for they both knew that Devon had experienced his own moment of weakness three years ago. That precise lack of control over his passions had cut and mutilated their friendship forever—all because of a woman they had both loved. A young woman named MaryAnn, who was off-limits to Devon because she was engaged to Vincent, and he had loved her with all his young and foolish heart.

But Vincent did not need to think about that. She was dead and buried.

Devon picked up Vincent's brandy, handed it back to him, and sat down in the opposite chair. "You're going to have to speak with this woman and find out if the child is yours."

"Speak with her." Vincent frowned. "She is here?"

"Yes. She is in the green guest chamber in the south wing."

Vincent stared down at his brandy, then downed it in a single gulp. "What is her name?" he asked, grimacing as the alcohol burned a scorching path down his throat.

"She is guarding her identity quite doggedly I'm afraid. In fact, she doesn't even want to be here. It wasn't her intention to see you. She only meant to ensure the infant was cared for."

Vincent felt a sudden pressure inside his head. "She hasn't asked for money?"

"No."

"You're sure?"

"Yes, I'm sure."

He frowned. "What happened, exactly, when she arrived? And who knows about this?"

"She came at dawn on foot and knocked on the servants' door. She explained herself to Mrs. Callahan, then asked her to deliver a letter to Mother. The letter states the child is yours but that the mother can no longer care for her because—"

"The child is a girl?"

Devon paused. "Yes."

Vincent tipped his head onto the back of the sofa. "Go on."

Devon continued. "Unfortunately the woman in question was long gone by the time Mother read the note. Mother went immediately to fetch the child, who was with the housekeeper, and brought both the infant and the note to me. I woke Blake, and we went out on horseback searching for her. She wasn't difficult to find, as she was not well and hadn't gotten very far."

Vincent looked up. "Not well, you say."

Devon answered the question with a grave nod.

He sat for a long time, still trying to make sense of his emotions, which were beginning to assert themselves with astounding force. He wanted to leap out of his chair, dash out of this room and go see the woman and child for himself. He did not act so hastily, however, for he knew he must keep his head. He could not permit himself to ignore the possibility that this was in fact a trap. That it was another man's child, not his.

"So Father is not yet aware what has occurred?" he asked.

"We did not believe he could cope with the news just now."

Vincent rubbed a hand over his thigh, contemplating the situation. "I agree with you on that point at least. It is difficult to predict how he would react. We should keep this from him, at least until I have a chance to speak with the woman, whoever she is." He stood. "I will go now and deal with her."

"I don't see how you have any choice, Vincent. It appears your recklessness has finally caught up with you."

Vincent glared heatedly at his brother. "Spare me the self-righteous babble, Devon. You're no saint yourself, and you know it."

He turned and left the library.

Mounting the stairs with one steady, sure-footed step at a time, he resolved to keep a vigilant head when he met this woman, for she could easily be a fortune hunter, and if she was, he would have to draw her out.

If on the other hand the child was his . . .

Something inside him lurched involuntarily. What would he do? Give her money, he supposed. Remind her that he was a callous, irresponsible rake with a heart of stone. Send her on her way.

He walked faster down the central corridor,

tense and impatient, irritable in his discomfort. He encountered no one on the way, and even if he had collided head-on with someone and knocked them flat on his or her back, he would not have stopped, for all he knew was his agitated need to see this mysterious woman, to learn her identity and circumstances, and to ascertain if he was in fact a father.

He would know, wouldn't he? Something in him would sense the truth, would recognize his own flesh and blood.

It was quiet as he strode through the gallery, past the potted tree ferns, around the corner, and at last down the south corridor. The doors to all the rooms were shut. He did not even know which one was the green guest chamber.

Heart pounding with impatience, he tried them all, gripping the knobs, shaking and rattling the doors that were locked until he found himself stepping into a bedroom.

Suddenly, he stood on a soft oval carpet, facing a window with drapes drawn to keep out the day-light, staring at a woman asleep in the bed.

Chapter 2

He once told me he would treat my heart and body with great care. He was lying, of course, for it was all a very clever, skillful seduction.

—from the journal of
Cassandra Montrose,
Lady Colchester,
December 2, 1873

Vincent stood in the dimly lit bedchamber, not quite sure if any of this was real. He blinked a few times. Was he seeing things? No, he was not.

It was *her,* no one else. It was Cassandra Montrose, Lady Colchester, his fiery lover from that incredible night a year ago—the one he had worked so hard to forget. The one who claimed to be barren.

He noted with more than a little discomfort that her face was pale and gaunt, her lips dry and chapped. Dark circles framed her eyes. What the devil had happened to her?

All at once his heart seemed to pound out loud like a bass drum in an empty opera house. Lady Colchester startled awake at his presence and stared at him.

God, those eyes. They, at least, were the same—still full of confidence and intensity, so utterly captivating that they knocked the wind out of him, just as they had that night in the ballroom.

Bloody hell. Of all the women he had bedded, why did it have to be this one?

Sucking in a breath, he gazed quickly about the room.

"You are looking for your daughter," she said.

There it was. The voice he had also driven from his memory—that low, husky, sensual cadence.

"If she is in fact mine," he replied harshly, remaining faithful to his vigilance, relaxing into more familiar behaviors, and reacting only to the fact that she had lied to him about not being able to conceive. "I am here to ascertain the truth."

Those overwhelming eyes narrowed. She wet her lips and spoke with quiet restraint. "A very kind woman came and took her to the nursery so I could get some rest. She said her name was Rebecca."

"She is my brother Devon's wife, Lady Hawthorne."

Cassandra folded her hands on her lap and stared at him in silence.

He studied her in return for a long moment as everything came rushing back at him—the memory of how she felt in his arms that night when they danced, the sound of her teasing laughter in the carriage, the scent and flavor of her clean skin when he tasted her with his lips and tongue while he undressed her. It was a remarkable night, he could not deny it, but he had not been looking for that. He had not wanted anything so profound. He was not capable of it, not then, not now, and she had known it. He'd made it very clear. He *always* made it clear to the women he took to bed.

"So it really is you, then," he said.

She laughed bitterly. "I am not sure who you mean exactly. If you are referring to the woman you made love to a year ago, then yes, I am she. Though I am quite aware of the fact that I am not the only one you shared a bed with during that time, so maybe you are still just as baffled as you appeared to be when I woke up to find you gaping at me just now. I could be anyone, really. Couldn't I?"

"I remember you, Cassandra." He remembered every bloody thing about that night, much to his dismay.

Her eyebrows lifted. "You remember my name! Indeed I am impressed! It was so long ago, after all. So brief and unimportant and inconsequential."

His brows pulled together in a frown. "Obviously it was not entirely inconsequential. You had a child."

Anger was suddenly boiling up inside of him, but for a terribly surprising reason, which shook him inwardly. Why hadn't she tried to contact him before now? She had communicated nothing. For the past year he had been completely ignorant of the fact that they'd conceived a child together.

Which incidentally *never* would have happened if she had been truthful about her ability to have children. He never would have allowed himself the luxury of climaxing inside of her without protection.

Yes, he remembered that all too clearly as well. In fact he had remembered it a number of times over the past year. It had left him dissatisfied with every meaningless orgasm since. And none too happy about it.

"I hope you don't think I am going to get down on my knee and propose to you," he said, "because I am not."

"And what a dream come true that would be—to become your Lady Vincent." She scoffed. "Rest assured, sir, that particular blessing was the last thing on my mind when I decided to come here."

He paced around the room. "And what *was* on your mind, exactly?"

"Didn't you read the note I left, before your

brothers came riding after me as if I were an escaped convict?"

"No, I have not yet seen it."

She looked away. For a long time he watched her. She seemed too angry to speak.

"You look different," he said.

"Yes, I know," she replied. "Poverty has that effect on a woman."

Experiencing a chill from her tone, he strove to keep his voice steady and find out exactly what had happened to her since they'd parted. "My brother said you are not well."

"Do I *look* well to you?"

"No, you do not. Tell me what has happened to you."

She paused, staring at him. "I wouldn't think it would be that difficult to guess at. A number of weeks after the night we spent together, I was surprised to discover I was pregnant. Obviously, it was the stuff of scandal, and my late husband's heir was more than happy to have an excuse to call me a whore and turn me out into the street with nothing, just to keep himself out of it. It was all he wanted anyway, to be rid of me. So I had no choice but to go home to my family, but they were appalled by my disgrace and immediately disowned me. After that I managed to survive on my own by working in a hat shop. I am still employed there. For the time being at least."

He strode forward, closer to the bed. "Why did you not come to me? I would have taken care of things."

"'Taken care of things.' I don't even want to know what you mean by that. Though I suppose it's something you've had to do more than once in the past."

"I would have provided for the child," he clarified.

She shook her head with skepticism. "She has a name, you know. Not that you would even care to know what it is."

"You are quite right, I don't care."

Before he could truly contemplate his initial instinct to be cruel, she heaved forward and coughed violently into a fist.

Vincent crossed the room in a single pulse beat and pulled a clean handkerchief from his breast pocket. He put his hand on her thin shoulder while she coughed, eyes tearing, her body shuddering as she fought for air. When she finally regained control and could manage a clear breath, she reached for the handkerchief he offered and wiped the tears from the corners of her eyes.

"You're very ill," he said, cupping her scorching hot forehead in his hand. "Have you seen a doctor?"

"Yes. I do not need to see another. There is no point."

He was cross with himself for not realizing earlier how ill she was. "So that is why you came here? Because you need care?"

She hesitated. "I did not come for myself. That is what I wrote in the note to your mother. I had to make sure my daughter would be taken care of. She will need a home. Do you understand me, Vincent? Do you?"

She leaned back on the pillows again and stared at him intently with grim, sober resolve.

Good God, he did.

For a long moment he studied his onetime lover, then felt the remnants of an old familiar pain he thought he would never have to feel again, that he had banished completely, but evidently it was still buried in the deepest realms of his being.

He glanced at the clock on the mantel.

"I am going to summon the palace physician." He moved around the bed and tugged on the velvet bellpull, then went to the door and waited in the corridor until a maid appeared. "Go and tell Mrs. Callahan to send for Dr. Thomas," he instructed the girl. "Tell her he is needed for our guest, not the duke. Be quick about it."

"Yes, milord." She turned and ran in the other direction toward the back stairs.

Vincent returned to the guest chamber, where Cassandra was resting quietly, her arms folded on top of the covers, her eyes turned toward the window. He moved around the room, watching her, comparing how she looked today to the way she had looked when he first met her in that fateful ballroom. She had charmed and beguiled him with her expressive blue eyes. She had been all smiles and confidence, flirting and laughing with him as they danced.

There was no laughter in her eyes now. There appeared to be very little of anything but defeat, mixed with a single-minded resolve.

He could not accept what she was trying to tell him.

"There is no point in sending for your physician," she said. "I already know my fate."

"I want a second opinion."

She inhaled slowly and deeply, and he could see this was exhausting for her. "Fine," she said. "Get a second opinion if you must."

He felt a surge of anger swirl inside his gut again, the same anger he had felt before. "You should have told me about this," he said. "How could you have kept it secret?"

She shot an exasperated look at him. "I did tell you! I sent you a letter explaining everything, including how to contact me, but you ignored it."

God, the letter. He remembered receiving it. He had not opened it because he did not wish to see her again. He had not wanted a repeat of that night. He had not wanted that kind of passion. As a result, the letter sat on his desk unopened for days.

And then he burned it, as he burned all of the letters his lovers sent to him.

"I never read it."

"But you did receive it," she said with deliberate accusation.

He raised both hands to confess what was an unalterable fact.

"I hate you."

"That's rather harsh, don't you think? You cannot crucify me for not opening one letter."

"I also tried to see you. Your butler was unpardonably rude to me. It was more than clear he was under strict orders to turn all your female callers away. He would hear nothing of what I had to say. He shut the door in my face."

Vincent could only shrug, for he could not deny the truth. His butler had learned the importance of preventing false hopes where ladies were concerned, and for that he had no regrets. It was quicker that way. Some would say kinder.

"And not long after that," Cassandra continued, "I saw you in the park with a woman. She slapped your face and ran off in tears. I watched you turn and walk away without a single glance over your shoulder. Without compassion or remorse. That was when I decided to manage my future on my own. I wanted nothing to do with you." She paused. "Let us not even mention the money you left on the table that morning."

The money. He had forgotten about that. Though in his defense, he had not meant to degrade her. He'd only wished to leave something behind to see her safely home.

"I did not mislead you that night," he said. "You knew what kind of man I was. I made it very clear I was not to be depended upon."

"I am not claiming otherwise. I learned my lesson, and I have accepted the consequences of my actions. I am not here to discuss the night we spent together or plead with you for your affections or anything of that nature. You already know that is not why I came."

"Yet you seem very angry about it."

She was clearly struggling to curtail the emotion in her voice. "I suppose I am, in some ways. I am angry how all of this has turned out." She gestured toward him with a hand. "I did not ever wish to need help from a rake such as yourself, who feels nothing for the women he makes love to. I hate that I had no choice but to come here. I hate that I cannot be a mother for my daughter. I hate that I am ill." She was quiet for a moment. "Would you open the drapes, please? It is dreary in this room."

He crossed to the window and threw the curtains open. "How is it that I am the one on trial for amoral behavior today," he asked, "when you were the one who claimed you were barren? Do you remember that? It has been a year, Cassandra. How do I even know the child is mine? You were not a virgin. You leaped into bed with a stranger."

"You were the only one," she assured him.

He frowned. "How do I know you are telling me the truth? You lied once before."

He was no stranger to the lies and deceits women were capable of.

"I did not lie," she said. "I was merely mistaken. I was just as surprised to learn of the baby as you are now." She shook her head. "Not that I care what you think of me. I only care what your mother, the duchess, will think, for it is my hope that she will accept my daughter and raise her. I have no illusions. I don't expect *you* to be around much. Everyone knows you prefer London to the country, and that you are completely unreliable. So in that regard, at least I will know my daughter will have very little influence from you. She will at least have some hope for a future, with your kind and gracious mother as her guardian."

For the first time since he'd entered the room, he was at a loss for words.

Cassandra turned onto her side, facing away from him. "Maybe you will find all of this easier to believe," she said, "after you've seen your daughter."

His daughter. He had not yet truly conceived of it.

"Why don't you go and do that now, Vincent, because I am tired. I do not wish to continue this conversation, and I must know if your mother will accept and raise her. Promise me you will at least try to consider the truth—that she is yours."

He stood motionless, deliberating over everything she had said, shaken by the tone of pleading that had just entered her voice.

Balancing the sudden weight of an unimagined future and all the responsibilities he had not asked for, he said simply, "I will consider it."

Then he turned and headed for the nursery.

Chapter 3

I fear that when I say goodbye to her and kiss her for the last time, my heart will turn to dust and my soul will disappear from both heaven and earth forever.

—from the journal of
Cassandra Montrose,
Lady Colchester,
May 12, 1874

Vincent entered the children's wing and stopped in his tracks when he heard the sounds of muffled female laughter on the other side of the nursery door. His sister-in-law Rebecca had brought the infant here, but by the sound of things, she was not alone.

Tipping his head forward, he listened at the door, but then heard only silence in the room, along with the heavy beating of his heart inside his chest. Everything about him felt heavy, here in the corridor, outside the nursery. He paused a moment to steady himself.

So much had happened in the past half hour. Cassandra was back in his life when he had honestly never expected to see her again, not since leaving her that morning without a word, without even saying goodbye.

He still remembered her sleeping soundly in the dawn light when he paused at the door at six in the morning, doubtful and disconcerted, shoes in his hands, his jacket draped over an arm. They'd had an extraordinary night together, talking freely and making love. By the end of it he had felt joyful and alive, out of control, stunned by the power of an explosive infatuation. He'd known he was in danger of falling head over heels in love, but had not wanted that. He still did not want it. He would never want it.

Yet on that morning a year ago, he'd hesitated at the door of the hotel, grappling with the possibility of staying. He could have returned to the bed where she was stretched out on her belly, nude and vivacious, her plump bottom and delicious pink thighs tangled delightfully in the rumpled sheets. He had no idea how long he stood there with his hand on the doorknob. His desire for her had not waned, though he struggled to repress it then and in the following weeks.

Now, a year later, he was standing with his

head resting against a very different door, and on the other side of it there was a child—a tiny infant she had given birth to nine months after that incredible night.

He could not go on denying the truth. The child she had brought to Pembroke Palace was his own. Somehow he knew it, as he'd imagined he would. He had a daughter, and he had been deemed unfit to be a part of her life.

Because he was a degenerate rake.

He suddenly felt sick to his stomach, which was unusual and surprising, for his reckless manner of living had never bothered him before. After what happened with MaryAnn, after that excruciating betrayal and the horrible grief that followed her death, he had promised himself no regrets where women were concerned. No genuine feelings or affections. No vulnerability. He had simply not been capable of any of those things. His bitterness had turned his heart to stone, and he preferred it that way.

A part of him did not want to open this door. He did not want what was on the other side. He liked his life the way it was. He did not want it to change. He would do his best not to let it.

Opening his eyes, he steeled himself and knocked.

Rebecca called out from inside. "Come in!"

He took hold of the cool brass knob, pushed the

door open and stepped over the threshold. The room was bathed in the bright cheerful light of day, despite the fact that it was still raining outside. In the far corner, a nursemaid was folding baby clothes.

In the center of the room, Rebecca was sitting on a colorful red blanket on the floor with his sister Charlotte. Between them, arms outstretched toward the ceiling and little legs kicking wildly, was the baby in a tiny white gown.

His blood began to rush through his veins. His thoughts were dashing around suddenly, untouchable.

No one said a word. The only sounds in the room were the raindrops striking the window like hard pebbles, and the soft rustling of a small white skirt, flapping and fluttering around those tiny little legs.

Though his eyes were fixed only on the child, he was aware of both women staring up at him with wide eyes. He sensed their trepidation.

"Vincent," Rebecca said uncertainly, rising to her feet.

For the first time since entering the room, he took his eyes off the baby and looked into those of his sister-in-law.

She spoke carefully. "Come closer and see her."

It all felt like some kind of strange dream—

his brother's wife leading him across the room toward the blanket.

He stood tall, looking straight down at the babe, who had black hair to match his own, beautiful brown eyes, and pudgy, soft-looking cheeks.

"I suppose this is quite a surprise to come home to," Rebecca said in a rather light conversational tone, considering the awkward circumstances. He understood she was making an effort to ease the tension in the room.

He squatted down on his haunches.

The infant was still kicking, then he heard her baby voice for the first time—a string of happy gurgles and giggles. Instinctively he offered his forefinger, and she gripped it in her chubby little hand and squeezed.

"Would you like to hold her?" Rebecca asked.

He glanced up briefly, and without a word slid his arms under the babe, cradled her head in one very big hand, and scooped her up as he rose to his feet. She weighed next to nothing.

"She's a Sinclair," he said with authority, his voice deep and low.

"Yes, she is," Charlotte replied with a smile, as if to encourage his acceptance of the child. Yet at the same time there was a profound depth of meaning in her accord, for she—his half sister—was only half Sinclair. She was golden-haired like their mother and carried none of the duke's traits.

Holding the baby in his arms, he turned his back on Rebecca and Charlotte, who remained seated on the blanket. He walked to the window, so the light could shine in on his daughter's face.

She was alert and intelligent looking, very aware of him, and curious. She reached her little hand up toward his nose.

"Hello there," he said.

But what should he call her? He *did* want to know.

"Her name?" he asked, almost in a panic, turning quickly to Rebecca and Charlotte.

"Her name is June Marie Montrose," Rebecca replied.

He turned his back on them again and faced the window. All at once it felt as if they were the only two people in the universe—he and little June Marie Montrose, who was reaching out again with her pudgy little hand and taking hold of his chin.

Good Lord, how could he even comprehend this? There was a tiny person in his arms. She was so very small. Her movements were astounding. He threw his head back and laughed.

"Do you see that?" he asked, turning, seeing the shock on his sisters' faces. "See how she kicks? She wants to go places. She'll be crawling before we know it."

Charlotte and Rebecca both laughed and agreed,

their relief obvious. Clearly, they had been worried he would shun the child. With good reason, he supposed, as he turned toward the window again. He had expected to do just that less than five minutes ago.

But how everything could change in the blink of an eye, he realized with a powerful burst of emotion.

Who would have thought? It was staggering. Earth shattering. He could not stop looking into those deep brown Pembroke eyes, which seemed to reflect his own.

He could not believe it. He, Vincent Sinclair, was a father.

At half past four the Duke of Pembroke entered the drawing room where Lady Letitia was seated with her mother, the Duchess of Swinburne. The ladies were sipping tea while they awaited the overdue arrival of Letitia's fiancé—and more importantly, her engagement gift, the Pembroke Sapphire.

The duke was dressed with impeccable style in a black velvet jacket and trousers, a clean white linen shirt, and a green and gold paisley tie made of the finest Italian silk money could buy. From the ankles up he was the very picture of elegance and grace.

If one were to look down, however, one would

discover that his feet were bare. And if one had the advantage of seeing through the fine fabric of his jacket and trousers, one would know that beneath it he was dressed in a bright blue sea bathing costume.

The ladies stood up as the duke came to stand in front of the fireplace. He bowed slightly at the waist. "Greetings, Duchess," he said to Letitia's mother. "And my compliments to you, Lady Letitia. Welcome back to the palace, this time as a future bride of Pembroke."

Letitia smiled and curtsied. "How wonderful to see you again, Your Grace. It is a pleasure to return so soon."

"Ah yes, pleasures, pleasures." Eyes never leaving Letitia's tall, exquisite form, he walked around the tea table to stand before her, almost in a dazed stupor. "My word, it is remarkable. Why had I not noticed before?"

"Noticed what, Your Grace?" Letitia's mother asked.

His eyes lit up. "You are the very image of the first Duchess of Pembroke—a famous, dark beauty who gave the first duke eleven children. And you are just as comely as you were the last time I saw you. What was it, a week ago?"

"Nearly a month," she replied.

"A month. You don't say." He gazed with fascination at her long-lashed brown eyes and creamy white skin, then took hold of her hand and raised it to his lips. "I dare say, my son is a lucky man. If I were younger, he would have his work cut out for him."

She laughed. "You are too kind, Your Grace."

He laid a kiss above her knuckles, then stared, transfixed, at the back of her hand.

Letitia glanced uneasily at her mother, tried to pull her hand away, but the duke yanked it back.

"What is this?" he asked, rubbing a thumb roughly over the discoloration on her skin, as if it were a smudge of dirt.

"It is nothing, Your Grace." She tried again to pull her hand free of his, but he would not have it. He yanked it back a second time, as if they were playing some childish game of tug of war.

The duke's cheeks took on a bright red hue, his eyes locked upon hers, spellbound, as he awaited her reply.

"It is a birthmark," she finally explained. "I've had it forever."

Without letting go of her hand, the duke sank onto the sofa cushions, looking as if he'd just been informed of a death in the family. "A birthmark . . . " He rubbed a hand over his face.

Letitia looked frantically at her mother.

"It is really nothing," the duchess said, stammering slightly. "Most of the time the mark is hidden, as Letitia is always wearing gloves when she is out—at balls, driving in the park, what have you . . . "

"No!" the duke shouted. "You shall not wear gloves, Lady Letitia. Never in this house. Do you understand me?"

Mother and daughter looked uncertainly at each other and nodded.

The duke inspected the birthmark again. He stretched her arm and almost pulled her off her feet so he could see the mark with the window as a backdrop.

"But where is the sapphire necklace?" he asked, sounding incredulous.

"Adelaide had it sent to Lord Vincent's rooms shortly after we arrived," the duchess told him. "We have been sitting here waiting for him for the past half hour."

The duke's bushy gray eyebrows lifted as he rose to his feet. "I do apologize. My son can be tardy, and he obviously does not recognize the magnitude of this event. You must have that sapphire around your neck, Lady Letitia. You know that, do you not?"

"Yes, of course, Your Grace," she replied.

"Good. Then I shall go and find out what is keeping him."

He left Letitia and her mother standing in the

drawing room staring after him in silence, blinking their eyes, bewildered by what had occurred.

Letitia sat down and picked up her teacup. "Crazy old man."

"At least he is bringing the sapphire."

"Oh, do shut up, Mother."

Chapter 4

I will always wonder what my life might have been like if I had married a man who loved me with undying passion. Perhaps I might not have been so vulnerable to the attentions of a rake.

—from the journal of
Cassandra Montrose,
Lady Colchester,
February 9, 1874

After spending a full hour in the nursery with June, Vincent returned to the green guest chamber, where Cassandra was awaiting his decision about whether he would accept her child to be raised at the palace.

He knocked and opened the door, but was startled to find his mother already in the room, seated at the bedside. Cassandra was sitting up.

She took hold of his mother's hand, bowed over it and kissed it several times.

Vincent stood quietly, watching them. His mother glanced up at him, then kissed Cassandra on the forehead. She approached him at the door.

"You wish to see Lady Colchester now?"

"Yes," he replied. "If you will excuse us."

"Of course."

She left the room, but he followed her out into the corridor. "Before I speak with her, Mother, I must inquire, does Father know about this yet?"

"No. He has always been very . . . " She paused and cleared her throat. "He has always been very strict about this sort of thing."

Vincent was more than aware of that fact. The duke had never in his lifetime accepted responsibility for any of his own illegitimate children, and there had certainly been a few of them brought around over the years.

The fact that the twins—Charlotte and Garrett—had grown up here at the palace, passed off as the duke's own offspring, was a wonder of epic proportions. The only reason the duke had permitted it was because, in the first four years of their young lives, he believed they were his. Later, when he learned the truth, it would have put a black mark of scandal upon the dukedom if he had rejected them, and he was always taking great pains to protect his dynasty.

Consequently, no one outside the palace walls knew the secret of his mother's one adulterous transgression. She was still the famously moral duchess, loved and adored by all. Charlotte and Garrett had not been turned out. They continued to live at Pembroke. Not that it made much difference about their treatment once the duke knew the truth. The only child who ever mattered to him was Devon—his eldest son, his perfect heir, the son who could get away with anything and everything and never meet with punishment.

As for Vincent, when he was a boy, he had always considered himself quite grand and auspicious on the rare occasions his father actually remembered his name.

"Let us continue to keep it quiet for now," he said, sweeping those old memories aside.

"Yes, Vincent. I agree that is best. Your father, I regret to say, would not be very understanding about Lady Colchester's predicament."

Vincent nodded and returned to the green guest chamber, where Cassandra was watching him from the bed, waiting in silence for his decision.

He paused a moment, wondering how Letitia was going to react to all of this. Truthfully, he had not given his fiancée a single moment's thought since he learned Cassandra was in the house, and it was not difficult to sweep her from his mind yet again as he approached the bed where the mother of his child lay waiting for him.

It had been a full year since the incredible night of passion that changed Cassandra's life forever. Since then she had been turned out of her home, become a disgrace to her family, struggled against poverty and the unforgiving judgments of others. Now she was about to face the unthinkable—the ordeal of giving up the daughter she loved more than anything in the world to a man who possessed no heart.

She was uncomfortably aware of Vincent's physical presence as he entered the room—his dark, striking coloring, the manner in which he carried himself, so proud and tall and confident. He was devastatingly handsome. There was no denying it. It was the reason she had lost sight of her good sense a year ago and fallen into disgrace. But all of that was pointless to think of now. This is what it had come to. She had no choice but to accept it.

Vincent settled into the soft upholstered chair by the bed and lounged very low in it. He raised a booted foot, rested it on the edge of the bed, and tapped a finger on his knee.

"Well?" she said, curiosity drumming inside her heart. "Did you see her?"

"Yes."

"And do you believe me now?"

"That she is mine?" He kept her in suspense for a moment or two. He truly was an unfeeling scoundrel. "Yes, I do."

Cassandra relaxed slightly on the pillows. She took a moment to digest his reply before speaking. "What made you believe it?"

"I just knew. Call it instinct if you like."

Feeling the intense heat of her hostility begin to cool somewhat—for at least she would not have to argue with him about it—she turned her gaze to the window. Her voice remained aloof. "She has your eyes."

"To your great disappointment, obviously."

"No. I am glad. It is a blessing."

"Why?"

She looked at him. "Because when your mother held her in her arms this morning, she saw *you*, which was all that I prayed for. You see, I believe your mother is a great woman, and in case she hasn't told you yet, she has just agreed to take June and raise her as a Sinclair, with or without your acknowledgment that she is yours. She has promised to come up with a family connection somewhere to explain her. She will likely be raised as a cousin."

It was more than she ever could have hoped for. June's well-being had been secured.

He inclined his head at her. "True to form, my

mother has beaten me to the punch. I suppose I should know by now never to underestimate her. She has the heart of both a saint and a lion. She is deeply devoted to her children, and we all adore her for it."

"She has beaten you to the punch? So you were going to tell me that you, too, agree to accept June?"

He nodded only once and held his head high. "She will want for nothing. I will see to it personally."

Cassandra chuckled to herself. "You'll see to it 'personally'? I believe I am witnessing a miracle today. You are agreeing to make a commitment—though it will no doubt be a temporary one as soon as the novelty of fatherhood wears off. But at least I have your mother's word for the long term. That is all I need."

He dropped his booted foot to the floor with a heavy thump and sat forward. "Why do you find it so surprising that I would wish to have some involvement? You didn't think you could just drop the child off at the palace and that I would stay out of it, did you?"

"You seemed very determined to stay out of it when you first walked through this door an hour ago. You did not even want to accept that she was yours."

She could not even comprehend how any parent

would not care to know his or her own child. It was going to break her own heart into a thousand pieces when the time came to say goodbye—even though she knew it was for the best.

"That was before I saw her."

She tipped her head mockingly. "And let me guess, you fell instantly in love and found your integrity and honor as a gentleman. You have discovered your soul at last. Is that it?"

"Hardly. You know I have no soul. But that is not the point. The child is mine, she has my eyes, so I will accept my responsibilities."

She sat back. "Ah. What a delightful, loving father you will make—accepting your responsibilities."

He looked at her with challenge. "What if I mean to make a go of it? What if I intend to dote upon my daughter and give her the moon and the stars on a silver platter? You didn't see me in the nursery just now. I was cooing and tickling."

She was surprised by something darkly flirtatious, which she could feel emanating from his eyes as well as her own, and was reminded of the woman she had been that night in the ballroom. She remembered how her mood had exploded like fireworks in the sky when he looked at her with that dangerous smile. She remembered how desperately she'd wanted to be wicked and run off with him into the night.

But then she remembered what had brought her here, and her heart sank in defeat. She had been to hell and back over the past year, struggling to make a home for her baby on her meager earnings from the hat shop. She'd had no one to confide in about her fears and frustrations, and now she was ill and was going to lose the battle she had been fighting so valiantly until now. Very soon she would not be able to care for June. She had no choice but to give her up, even though it was going to break her heart.

"I am afraid it would take more than a few minutes of cooing and tickling," she said, "for me to believe that you have discovered your integrity."

Vincent lifted his boot and set it on the edge of the bed again. She grabbed hold of the leather toe and shoved it off with impressive strength, considering how ill she was.

The corner of his mouth curled up slightly. "I had no idea your bitterness toward me was so passionate. I confess I am feeling somewhat aroused."

She felt her cheeks flush with fury as she sat back against the pillows. "I pity your fiancée."

"Ah! I wasn't sure if you knew about my charming future bride, but I suppose news does travel fast here at Pembroke. It is those damned inconvenient subterranean passages. I've been saying for years we should fill them in or block them off or something."

She ignored his digression. All she could think about was how foolish women could become—herself included—when he turned on that wicked charm. Even now, the devilish look in his eyes was making her heart race like a bandit.

"The poor woman is no doubt hopelessly infatuated with you," she said, "and dreaming of her fairy tale wedding, unfortunate, naïve creature. She will be in for a rude awakening the morning after your wedding night."

"I assure you," he said, "Letitia is not naïve."

They were quiet for a few minutes, separate in their own thoughts. Vincent was tapping his finger on the armrest.

Cassandra spoke first, and managed to do so in a softer voice, for she knew there was no point in fighting with him now. It was over. All of it. He had agreed to accept June as a Sinclair. Her daughter's fate had been decided. That was all she'd wanted.

"You are very appealing when you choose to be, Vincent," she told him, "and you are a handsome man. That can be blinding for even the most sensible of women. I hope you will consider that when you become a husband."

He seemed surprised by her sudden desire to steer him in the direction of his conscience, when clearly neither he, nor she, believed he possessed one.

"Indeed I shall," he replied nevertheless, "though I don't recommend getting your hopes up. We both know I will be a dismal failure at matrimony. I'm simply not cut out to be faithful."

She sighed over the fact that he had not changed, and likely never would. "Just as long as you are not too dismal a failure as a father."

His brow furrowed with displeasure. Or was it annoyance? She wasn't sure what to make of it.

"At least my mother will be close at hand to repair the damage when I live up to your meager expectations." With that, he stood and walked out.

Immediately after leaving Cassandra's bedside, Vincent entered his own bedchamber and saw his great-grandmother's necklace—the famous Pembroke Sapphire—sitting in an open velvet box on the bed. He stared at the dark blue stone for a moment, saw in his mind a headstone with Cassandra's name on it, then slammed the door so hard, the vase on the dressing table toppled to the floor and smashed to pieces.

Child or no child, he wished she had not come back.

Chapter 5

I can only presume that his fiancée is completely blinded by a hopeless infatuation. I suppose one can hardly blame her. I was blinded by it myself once.

—from the journal of
Cassandra Montrose,
Lady Colchester,
May 13, 1874

Vincent stepped over the broken vase on the floor in his room and walked to the rain-drenched window. He stood for a moment, looking out over the Italian Gardens, which had been torn apart by his father a month ago when he took it upon himself to move his beloved rosebushes to higher ground. He had dug everything up with his own bare hands, ripping the roots out of the ground and leaving nothing behind but a sea of mud surrounding the statue of Venus in the center of the square.

Aggravated by the sight of all that destruction, Vincent watched the raindrops pelting the puddles below, as merciless and relentless as the passing of time. It was a disastrous, depressing sight. Perhaps the Pembrokes were cursed after all.

Just then a commotion arose behind him. He turned, startled by the racket of someone bursting into his room without knocking—entering through the secret passageway behind the bookcases, which hadn't been used in years—and tripping over the corner of the rug.

It was his father, naturally.

"Good afternoon," Vincent said.

The duke righted himself.

Vincent took note of a rare phenomenon—that the duke's wild white hair had been combed that day. His valet was having a devil of a time with that particular task. But when he looked down at his father's feet, his relief vanished. Clearly, Jennings was facing a new challenge now. Footwear.

"May I inquire as to the whereabouts of your shoes?" he asked.

His father ignored the question and crossed the room. He dropped to his knees before Vincent, clasped his hands together as if in prayer and squeezed his eyes shut. "How can I ever thank you?"

Vincent regarded his father with growing

unease. "It would help if I knew what you wished to thank me for."

"For Letitia. She is the answer."

Vincent swallowed. "The answer to what question, exactly?"

"Not a question. She is the answer to the curse."

Vincent realized he had never in his life witnessed his father down on his knees, except in church, of course, and from a distance in the gardens occasionally, for he loved tending his own flowers.

More importantly, the duke had never looked up at him. It was always the other way around. Indeed, there were many memories of his own pleadings for mercy as a child, following some grand misbehavior. They had never worked. He'd learned at a very young age to hold his tongue and brace himself for his punishments. To never show weakness.

Vincent took hold of his father's arm and lifted him to his feet. "I don't understand," he said. "What do you mean?"

"Isn't that why you chose her?"

Vincent merely shook his head, confounded. "You were the one who chose her, Father, if you will recall. You brought her to Mother's birthday celebrations a month ago. You have given her your official approval according to the terms of your will."

The duke was not listening. "I dare say, if the first Duchess of Pembroke were alive today, they would be identical twins. The resemblance is astonishing. Surely this is evidence of a new beginning. And not to forget the birthmark on her hand," he said. "It is as clear as the nose on your face."

"What birthmark?"

He had never noticed anything about Letitia's hands. He wasn't even sure he'd ever seen them in the flesh, for she was usually wearing gloves.

Or maybe he had seen her hands. He had slipped a ring on her finger, hadn't he?

"She has the sun on the back of her left hand," his father said. His bushy eyebrows pulled together in disbelief, as if he could not understand how Vincent had missed such a thing.

"You mean a birthmark that *looks* like the sun?" Vincent asked.

"It is a sign. She is the one." He poked a finger three times into Vincent's chest and smirked knowingly, as if he'd just uncovered the fountain of youth. "Marry Letitia and you will not only secure your inheritance, you will hinder the curse, my dear boy. The rain will stop and the sun will come out."

Good God. He was truly living in a carnival of madness.

"You are the finest son a man could hope for," his father said, patting his cheek.

Now, there were words he had not heard before. These particular ones had always been reserved for Devon.

"Would you like to have my hunting boots?" the duke asked. "You know the ones. You've borrowed them before without asking, when you've gone out to bag some grouse with your friends early in the morning after a night at billiards. They're cozy and they keep the wet out." He nudged Vincent hard with his elbow. "But you know that, you rascal. You've worn them. Sneaky devil."

"I know the ones," Vincent said.

Abruptly, the duke frowned and looked down at his feet. "Where the devil are my shoes?" Then he turned and walked out into the corridor shouting at the top of his lungs, *"Jennings!"*

Cassandra looked up from the pages of her diary when a knock sounded at the door. "Come in."

An older gentleman, carrying a black leather satchel, entered the room. "Lady Colchester?"

"Yes."

He bowed slightly at the waist. "Good day, madam. I am Dr. Thomas. I understand you have not been well."

She set her diary and pen on the bedside table under the lamp and sat up.

"That is correct. It was good of you to see me."

Though it was not she who had requested it.

The doctor approached and set his bag on the upholstered bench at the foot of the bed. He was a tall, fair-haired man with an intelligent pair of eyes behind round spectacles. "May I examine you?"

"Yes, Doctor, though you needn't worry about the task of delivering bad news. I have already seen a doctor and know my prognosis."

"I see. Well, I shall have a look at you nonetheless, since Lord Vincent specifically requested it." He removed his stethoscope from his bag and came around the side of the bed. "If you could sit forward, I will observe your breathing."

She did as he asked, and he pressed the scope to her back. "Take a deep breath, please . . . Thank you. Again, if you will . . . And again." He moved it to a new spot. "One more time, if you please."

She inhaled deeply and let it out, then began to cough into her fist. He continued listening to her back.

"That is certainly quite a serious cough you have," he said, then shifted to her front and listened at her chest. "Breathe again, please . . . Thank you."

He asked her a number of questions—like how long she had been ill, how often she had fevers, whether or not she had any appetite, and was there blood when she coughed? He took her pulse, asked her to lie back and looked at her pupils. Then he pressed upon her abdomen, pushing firmly in various places while his gaze was fixed on the window.

After a thorough and lengthy examination, he returned to the foot of the bed and put his stethoscope back in his bag. "I am of the opinion, Lady Colchester, that the doctor who examined you previously was mistaken. You are definitely ill, but you will recover. You simply require rest and nourishment."

Feeling somewhat disoriented, she felt her eyebrows pull together in dismay. "I beg your pardon?"

"I said you will recover. You do not have consumption."

"I don't?"

"No, madam, you do not." He closed his bag and looked at her strangely. "Are you not relieved to hear it?"

It took her a moment to find her voice. "I am in shock."

"But surely you are pleased . . . " he prompted.

She smiled and let out a curt little laugh. "Yes, of course I am pleased. I am going to be all right!"

He smiled as well and nodded. "Yes, you are. So if there is nothing else . . . ?"

"No," she stammered. "Thank you."

He bowed again and left the room.

She lay there for the longest time, staring up at the ceiling as a tear trickled down her cheek. She was going to live, and would not have to say goodbye to June. She would be able to keep her!

Cassandra sat straight up as panic shot through her veins. Vincent had just agreed to raise June, and so had the duchess. What if they decided they did not wish to let her go? What if they insisted she be raised here at the palace, even though she was going to live?

Suddenly overwhelmed by a dozen-and-one uncertainties, she looked around the room at the gilt-framed portraits on the walls, the elegant wallpaper, and the fine mahogany furniture. Five minutes ago this was going to be June's home. She was going to be raised in one of the wealthiest aristocratic houses in England. A palace.

Could she deprive her daughter of all this, for the sake of her own emotions and desires as a mother? Wouldn't it be best for June to remain here with one of the most powerful families in England?

She lay back down again and tried to imagine giving her daughter up when she now knew she was going to live. Could she do it? Was it the right thing? Or would June be better off with her? The mother who loved her more than anyone else ever could?

* * *

"Look, Mother, now it is official." Lady Letitia held the Pembroke Sapphire out for all to see, then flashed her engagement ring in every direction.

Vincent stood back and marveled at the ridiculous notion that the brown blemish on his fiancée's hand held any resemblance whatsoever to the sun. It looked more like a peanut.

"Champagne everyone!" the duke said. "Come, come!"

A liveried footman brought a tray around the room, and everyone raised their glasses to Vincent's lovely future wife. Only then did he realize his mother had not been present for the announcement of his engagement. He looked around and saw her just arriving. She stopped outside the door and signaled to him with a hand.

He politely excused himself from Charlotte and Blake and made his way out into the hall. "What is it, Mother?"

She took him aside. "I am sorry to disturb your celebrations, Vincent, but I have some important news for you. Dr. Thomas has seen Lady Colchester. He has just informed me that she was diagnosed by a most incompetent physician. Dr. Thomas is of the opinion that she is not as ill as she was led to believe, and that she will recover fully. All she requires is rest and nourishment . . . Vincent, are you listening to me? Vincent?"

He realized with a start that he had been staring absently at the empty air between them. Focusing his attention more clearly on his mother, he said, "Yes, of course I am listening."

"Aren't you relieved?"

"Yes. That is good news."

But it was so much more than that. He was, quite frankly, disturbed by the measure of his relief.

"But we have already agreed," he said, struggling to keep his voice steady while turning his thoughts to more immediate practicalities, "to take Lady Colchester's daughter in and raise her as a Sinclair."

Devon approached him from behind. "It appears you are off the hook, Vincent. Shall I send for another bottle of champagne?"

Vincent strove to control his breathing. "This is none of your business, Devon."

"I only thought you might like to know," his brother said, "that the mother of your child is back on her feet, out of bed, fully dressed and headed for the nursery. Rebecca passed her in the corridor on the way here."

A look of panic flashed across their mother's face. "Oh dear. She is going to leave and take June. We will never see her again."

Devon spoke glibly. "Looks that way."

Vincent glanced toward his fiancée in the drawing room, proudly showing off her necklace and engagement ring. He did not wish to care one way or the other if Cassandra left, but he could not fight the tension building up inside his head. "Bloody hell."

"It is quite a sticky situation, isn't it?" Devon said, looking like he was enjoying this far too much.

"Why don't you just stay out of it?" Vincent gave his brother a look of warning, then turned and walked toward the stairs.

"What are you going to do?" his mother asked. "You can't just let her leave."

He stopped at the bottom of the staircase and rested a hand on the newel post. He could not look at either of them. "Why not? It's her child. She wants nothing from me."

"See, Mother?" Devon said. "He's pleased to be free again. He will not be required to care for anyone."

"She didn't want help from me before," he argued. "Why should she want it now, when all is well again?"

"But Vincent," his mother said, taking a few anxious steps forward, "what about June? She is a Sinclair. We must at least offer *something* to Lady Colchester."

He continued to stand at the bottom of the stairs with his back to them, saying nothing for the longest time, then he started off toward the nursery. "I will go and see what the lady will require."

Chapter 6

Last night I dreamed I shot him in the heart with a pistol, but then I was overcome with regret for my vengefulness. I ran to him, knelt down and shook him hard. He woke up and kissed me. I was terribly distraught when I opened my eyes.

—from the journal of
Cassandra Montrose,
Lady Colchester,
February 18, 1874

Vincent pushed through the door of the nursery with compelling force—not sure what to expect when he entered the room—and stopped abruptly just inside.

Cassandra's distressed gaze darted to him as she backed up against the far wall, clutching her baby protectively to her breast, as if he had come to do them murderous harm.

"You scared the life out of me," she said.

June began to wail.

Vincent stood inside the door, gazing intently at the two of them. "It was not my intention to startle you."

Cassandra cradled her daughter in her arms. She swayed back and forth, cooed softly and spoke in a soothing, melodic voice. "Everything's all right, my darling girl. I'm here."

June's cries subsided to mere complaints, then Cassandra met Vincent's gaze. "I assume you know that Dr. Thomas came to see me. You have heard his prognosis?"

"I have," he said. "You must be greatly relieved."

She chuckled somewhat bitterly. "Yes, I am. It's not every day one learns one has a second chance at life. But I doubt you would understand that kind of joy, or *any* deep feelings of a profound nature."

"Certainly not," he replied matter-of-factly. "I am far too shallow for that. I could not possibly comprehend it."

She regarded him with a hint of uncertainty, and studied him for a moment before shifting uneasily on her feet.

"I should like to inform you," she said, "that I will no longer be in need of your assistance." She glanced nervously at June, in her arms. It was the first time since her arrival that she appeared less than absolutely certain of what she wanted. "Let me add that I am grateful for what you and your mother were willing to do, and I thank you sincerely from the bottom of my heart."

It was more than clear to him that she was terrified he would not let her leave with her baby. Strangely intrigued by the first sign of a chink in her armor, he narrowed his gaze and took a step forward. He saw her delicate throat bob as she swallowed.

"How exactly do you mean to raise my daughter?" he asked, not inclined in the least to make this easy on her, for reasons he did not wish to explore.

She lifted her chin proudly. "I will return to my position at Madam Hilliard's, and I shall continue to rely on my landlady to care for June during my hours at the shop."

He strode even closer, wanting to test her, challenge her, subdue her. "And what will happen five years from now, Cassandra, when our daughter is ready to be schooled? Will she learn the letters of the alphabet, and eventually how to play the piano or speak French? Or will she be too busy washing out your landlady's dirty laundry?"

Cassandra began to move sideways along the wall as he drew closer. "I am not sure what the future will hold."

"No, clearly you have not given it a single thought."

"I will take good care of her," she assured him. "No one will do that better than I can."

He gestured toward her with a hand. "But you don't have the resources."

All at once her cheeks colored with anger and her eyes burned with resolve. "You don't know the first thing about 'resources' when it comes to dedicating your life to someone. What June will have from me is love. Beautiful, selfless, priceless love. Nothing is more important than that."

He scoffed. "And with your love, she will conquer the world, is that it?"

"Yes!"

Neither of them spoke for a moment, while Vincent was caught somewhere between resenting her for her idealistic notions about love, and respecting her for holding onto them, despite the fact that he knew she was fighting a losing battle—for love was simply not enough.

Her blue eyes flashed with determination. He hated to admit it, but she looked quite exquisite.

"Please," she said, "just let me go."

He strode forward and spoke in a gentler tone. "You are the mother of my child. I cannot let you leave Pembroke with nothing but the clothes on your back."

"I will manage."

"You are too proud, Cassandra, and you are a fool if you think I am going to allow you to simply walk out of here like this with June. How can I be certain you won't just disappear?"

"If you will recall," she said, "the brilliant disappearing act is yours, not mine. And why should it matter to you anyway if you never hear from me again? You don't care for us. You care for no one."

He glanced down at June, wrapped snugly in a soft white blanket, and felt a jolt inside his chest, as if he had been hit with something across the back.

"True," he replied nevertheless. "But I will not shirk my responsibilities."

She was quiet for a long moment. "If you wish to give me money," she said at last, "I will not be so proud as to refuse it. I will leave my address with the housekeeper, and you may send what you like. But I beg of you, Vincent, just let me leave with my daughter. There is no need for any connection between us in the future."

He frowned. This was all horribly, disturbingly, unpleasant. "Have you lost your mind, woman? I am a Pembroke, a member of one of the wealthiest, most powerful families in England. How can you say you do not want to be connected to me? Look around you."

She did as he asked, then her striking eyes settled upon his again. "I have looked around, Vincent, and I know what this world—your world—is like."

He shook his head. He could not understand this.

"I would like to go now," she said. "There is an evening train."

He was finding it increasingly difficult to accept how this was unfolding. "Are you certain you are well enough to leave?" he asked, hearing the desperate intonation in his voice and realizing that he was grasping at straws. He did not usually find himself on this side of the fence. He did not like it at all. "You seem to be forgetting that you are ill."

"I am feeling better now. My fever has broken, and the doctor's visit did wonders. In a few days I will be my old self again, I am certain of it."

His heart was pounding as she started for the door. Spontaneously, he stepped into her path and blocked her exit, bracing his arm across the open doorway. She smelled achingly familiar. It was not perfume or powder. It was just her.

"What is your hurry, Cassandra?" He leaned closer—almost close enough to touch his nose to her soft, smooth cheek—and spoke in a hushed tone. "Are you sure it has nothing to do with my presence in the house? Because it is quite clear you cannot stand the sight of me."

Her voice trembled slightly. "That is true, I cannot."

Something made him want to knock her off balance, which was cruel of him under the circumstances. An hour ago she had believed she was dying and would have to give up her child. Now she was on her own. But he could not stop himself. He wanted to lash out at her. He was angry with her—angry with her for coming back into his life and making him feel things he did not want to feel.

"So you do not have one single pleasant memory of me, or of that night?" he asked. "Because my recollection is that you quite enjoyed it at the time."

She practically ground out her reply. "Only because my head was in the clouds."

"Your head was in a great many places that evening, my dear, once our clothes were out of the way. Which was a complete delight for me, of course."

He was fully prepared for the fierce slap that struck his face in record time, for he was no stranger to the fury of passionate women. He accepted it without flinching, knowing he deserved it.

"How can you say such things when your fiancée is downstairs?" she demanded to know.

"It's not as if she cares anything for me. She cares only for herself."

Cassandra grimaced. "Then why in the world are you marrying her?"

He decided to lower his arm and clear her path. "Because if I don't marry someone," he said, "I will lose my inheritance. Did you not know that? Father wants us all cornered and wedded by Christmas, and Lady Letitia was the one he handpicked for Devon originally before he found Rebecca, whom you have met. He plucked Letitia like a bright red rose from the thorny bush of London society."

She shook her head, looking almost sickened. "I feel very sorry for her, and for all the people who must count you as a friend or acquaintance. But why are you telling me this? I don't care about your life."

"Leave then," he said, stepping back, clearing her way. "And take your illegitimate child with you."

He bowed to usher her out.

She crossed over the threshold, but something in her expression changed and she stopped in the narrow corridor. She looked down at the floor.

Vincent stood very still, his stomach in knots as he watched her.

She turned around and looked at him with sorrow. "Despite your great wealth and power, Vincent, I would not wish to ever be you, for you are someone who does not believe in love. You are a man who breaks women's hearts carelessly, without compassion or remorse. The world regards you as a rake, somehow appealing in your wildness, and I confess that I was enchanted by it once. I was seduced by what was so exciting and rebellious about you. But now I see more than that. I see that on the inside, you are heartless and unhappy and cruel."

He strode forward. "You speak of women's hearts as if they are always victims, but women can also be cruel. Perhaps I have no heart because mine was broken. Shattered to pieces. Crushed without compassion like gravel under one's shoe."

She seemed taken aback, and then, to his utter surprise, reached up and laid a hand on his cheek. "I am sorry to hear that, Vincent, and I hope that someday, for your own sake, you can forgive that woman, whoever she is, and learn for yourself that love is the only thing in the world that makes life truly worth living."

With that, she turned and walked out, and he was left standing there, his breath coming short, his heart beating so fast, one might almost think it was trembling.

Chapter 7

When I walked out of the palace, I had no idea what challenges lay in my future. I was terrified, yet strangely it was Vincent whom I pitied.

—from the journal of
Cassandra Montrose,
Lady Colchester,
May 13, 1874

For thirty minutes Vincent sat in the nursery alone, struggling to come to grips with his discontent. He should have been relieved, as Devon suggested. Cassandra was gone and he was off the hook, with no obligations to a child he had never wanted in the first place.

But then he thought of her. *June.* He remembered holding her in his arms and watching her tiny legs kick inside the blanket. She had weighed almost nothing in his arms. She was his own daughter.

And Cassandra . . .

God, Cassandra . . . She was so ridiculously idealistic about the power of love and the joy it could bring to a person's life. If anyone was naïve, it was she. She didn't have a clue about what went on in the real world. She was living in a dream.

Not that it mattered, he tried to tell himself. She was gone now. He had practically pushed her out the door.

But what else could he have done? She did not want him in her life, which incidentally still made no sense to him. He might be a disreputable rake, but this was Pembroke Palace—a house of dukes. His mother, the duchess, was one of the most beloved and respected women in England, and they were all astonishingly wealthy.

Surely her bitterness toward him could not be so very absolute. He was having a difficult time believing it, for at the last moment there had been something else in her eyes. A softness. A caring. She had laid her hand on his cheek.

He put his own hand where hers had been and closed his eyes, remembering how it felt. He could still feel the warmth. He could feel her tenderness—

A knock sounded at the door. He stood quickly and crossed the room to answer it, embarrassed to have been sitting in an empty nursery, touching his cheek.

It was his mother. He moved into the corridor and closed the door behind him.

"I thought you might still be here," she said. "Letitia is wondering what has become of you."

Hell, he had forgotten there was a gathering in his honor, occurring at this very moment downstairs to celebrate his engagement. "Forgive me. I lost track of time. I shall go down there straightaway and set her mind at ease."

They started down the corridor together.

"Has Lady Colchester left us?" he asked his mother, working hard to sound indifferent, while inside he was overcome by a piercing need to know.

"Yes," she replied. "The coach drove off twenty minutes ago. But do not worry, she has money."

His pride reared up. Or perhaps it was the inevitable bucking of his conscience, which he had been working so hard to restrain. "You gave her something? I was intending to—"

"Do not worry, Vincent. I took care of it."

He walked beside her in silence to the end of the corridor. "How much did you give her?"

"Enough to live on for about six months. But I will find a way to see her again before that time is up and give her more."

He was feeling more and more irritable with every passing second. "You won't have to do that, Mother. I will take care of it."

She merely nodded. "I know."

"I won't let them go hungry."

She smiled up at him. "You don't have to convince me, Vincent. There will be no need to speak of it in the future."

There would be no need, he thought, because his mother would simply take responsibility for the child herself. She did not believe he would do it.

His breathing quickened as he stopped in the corridor under a portrait of the first Duchess of Pembroke. He stared up at her perfect oval face, took note of her midnight black hair and creamy white skin. There was indeed an eerie resemblance to his fiancée.

"Do something for me, if you will," he said to his mother, who stopped abruptly ahead of him. "Inform Letitia that I had an important matter to attend to and had to leave the palace, but that I shall see her at dinner. And deliver my apologies, of course." He started off in the other direction, toward the servants' staircase.

"Where are you going?"

"I am going to the train station."

"What are you going to do, Vincent?"

"I don't know yet, but I suspect I'll have it figured out by the time I get there."

His heart was racing with an almost frightening impulsiveness as he started down the narrow stairs at a run to chase after the Pembroke coach.

* * *

Cassandra dug into her reticule for the money to pay for her train ticket back to London. She simply could not ignore the fact that she was still weak and had not yet regained her strength, and with all that had occurred that day, she was exhausted and completely overwhelmed.

"Are you all right, miss?" the station guard asked, his brow creasing with concern as he counted the shillings.

"I am fine, thank you," she answered, shifting June in her arms.

He did not appear to believe her, however, which was not surprising. As soon as the driver had pulled away from Pembroke Palace, she looked up at the nursery window and burst into tears. But why? Was it because she doubted her decision? Did she believe June would be better off at the palace? Or was it something else? Was it because of the intense emotions she'd wrestled with upon seeing Vincent again? He had made her so angry at times, frustrated and upset, yet she'd felt the strangest sense of loss when she walked out the palace door—perhaps because of those last few minutes with him, when he attempted in his own misguided way to explain his empty life.

The guard handed her the ticket. Keeping her gaze lowered, she thanked him and picked up her valise—which contained everything she owned in the world—and made her way to a bench at the back of the station.

Just then the main door opened, and who should step over the threshold on a violent gust of wind, top hat in hand, but Vincent, who attracted the attention of everyone waiting for the train. He looked like some dark, dangerous phantom with the fierce rainstorm behind him. His black hair was flying in the wind, his long, ebony overcoat flapping almost gracefully.

Her heart dropped into her stomach at the sight of him. He stood just inside the door, sweeping his disdainful gaze over everyone in the station until it came to rest upon her. She grew tense as he began striding purposefully toward her.

Only then did she realize she was squeezing the handle of her valise so tightly beside her that her knuckles were surely pasty white. Searching for calm, she looked down at June and adjusted the blanket around her face.

He stopped in front of them, almost toe-to-toe with Cassandra, which forced her to look up.

"I am pleased you are still here," he said.

"The train will depart in twenty minutes," she informed him.

He looked around again at the people who were waiting. Those who were still staring at him with curiosity and fascination quickly turned back to their books and newspapers.

Vincent took a seat beside her and spoke in a hushed tone. "I must speak with you."

Had he changed his mind about letting her leave with June? God help her, what would she do?

"What is there to talk about?" she whispered. "I thought we reached an understanding."

"We did, but I have been rethinking that understanding."

She swallowed uneasily. "But you said I could leave. You said you do not care."

"Perhaps I was . . . " He shifted with what appeared to be discomfort and looked around the station once more. "Perhaps I was too hasty."

God, oh God. He was going to try to take June away from her. Why else would he have come?

"Vincent, I am asking you. Please. She is all I have in the world. I love her. If you try to take her from me, I will not be able to bear it. I will have no choice but to fight you with any means possible to make sure that—"

His gaze shot to her face. "Calm yourself. I am not here for that."

She struggled to control the painful drumming of her heart. "Then why have you come?"

"I have a proposition for you," he said.

"A proposition? From *you*? I am not sure I want to know the particulars."

He stood. "Let us go outside to my coach where we can discuss it in private."

"I would rather not. I don't want to miss my train." And she was somewhat fearful of being alone with him, especially in that coach, where she had once lost her head.

"Five minutes is all I require."

When she continued to resist, he let out a breath in frustration. "Good God, woman. I am not going to ravish you, if that's what you are thinking." He leaned down and whispered in her ear—so close, the moist heat of his breath sent gooseflesh down the entire length of her body. "Besides, you know better than anyone that if I *were* planning something as exciting as that, I would require a great deal more than five minutes."

She raised an eyebrow. "I suppose I do know it. I can hardly deny your unfortunate prowess in that arena." He picked up her valise. She rose also, with June in her arms. "Five minutes, then."

She followed him outside, along the platform under the overhang, and was ushered into the familiar interior of his dry, luxurious coach, with its soft upholstered red seats and black velvet curtains.

She remembered every detail of this vehicle from a year ago, and all the passionate kissing and groping that had occurred inside. They'd both tumbled onto the seat on the left, and before the driver had a chance to say, "Walk on," her legs were wrapped around Vincent's hips, and he was sucking on her neck and sliding his hands up under her skirts.

Now, with a deflated sigh, Cassandra chose the seat on the opposite side. Trying not to wake June, she awkwardly maneuvered the baby on her lap.

Vincent climbed in behind her and pulled the door shut. He settled in directly across from her, his legs spread wide apart, fingers laced together in front of him.

"Well?" she asked, lifting an eyebrow. "What is it you wish to discuss?"

She glanced down at his long, lean body sprawled out before her in the dim shadows of the coach, and wished again that he were not so handsome, so perfectly formed of firm muscle and sinew and pure, unadulterated masculinity. He sat across from her like a dark and seductive king, and she hated him for it.

"I want to discuss a possible arrangement between us. I know that you have had some trouble providing for our daughter in the past and will no doubt have trouble in the future if you are forced to work. My mother has given you something that will ease your burden for the short term, but what if I offer you more? What if I offer you something that will last much longer?"

She regarded him skeptically. "I don't quite understand."

"What if I provided you with a home and an

income? You could live quietly with June in the country, and when she is older, when the time comes for her debut in society, my family would present her as a distant relative. A Sinclair. I would of course provide her with a substantial dowry, and as for you . . . " He paused a moment, as if he hadn't yet worked out all the details in his mind and was only now deciding upon certain things. "You could keep the house. I would put it in your name."

"And how, pray tell, would *you* benefit from that arrangement?" she asked. "I know you well enough to know that there must be something in it for you."

But then, all at once, the shock of understanding hit her full force, and her mouth snapped shut. She could not believe she had failed to predict this. She should have guessed it the very instant the word "proposition" flew out of his mouth.

"Good God," she said. "The answer is a firm no."

She stood up, bumped her head on the roof of the coach, but did not allow herself to wince as she reached for the door.

His hand came up at lightning speed and seized her arm in a tight grip. "Where are you going?"

"I am getting out of here."

"Why?"

"I was foolish and naïve a year ago," she said,

"but I have since learned my lesson. I do not wish to be that woman again. I must protect myself."

"What do you mean, protect yourself? I am offering you a chance to live in the manner to which you are accustomed, and to provide your daughter—*our* daughter—with all that she is entitled to."

"And to be your mistress!" she blurted out. "To be available at your whim when you grow tired of your wife in your bed, which will no doubt be less than twenty-four hours after you deliver your shabby vows of fidelity." She ripped her arm free and fought with the door latch.

"That is not what I am proposing," he argued, sounding quite convincingly offended as he grabbed hold of the door handle and held it shut.

"I don't believe you." She tried to pry his hand free of the handle, but he would not budge.

"For God's sake, Cassandra, sit back down. You're going to wake June."

She felt dizzy all of a sudden, backed into the seat, then sank into it.

"Are you all right?" he asked. "You do not look well."

"I am fine." She opened her reticule, withdrew a handkerchief and dabbed at the perspiration on her forehead.

Suddenly he was on the soft seat beside her, cupping her whole head in both his hands. "You're burning up. You shouldn't have left the palace today—that was foolish—and you certainly should not be traveling."

Closing her eyes, she leaned her head back against the high, upholstered seat. "It is all of this rain. It has me chilled to the bone."

"It is not the rain." He took June from her and laid her carefully on the seat beside him, then shrugged out of his long coat and covered Cassandra with it, tucking it in all around her. She felt the heat from his body still in the lining, and smelled the familiar musky scent of him around the wool collar. It made her want to weep.

"My five minutes is up," he told her as he felt her forehead again. "And you need to rest."

"I can rest on the train."

He frowned at her and shook his head. "I believe you are the most stubborn woman I have ever met."

"I am not stubborn."

"Yet you are still arguing with me."

She began to shiver, and pulled the coat higher under her chin. "Refusing to become a gentleman's mistress does not make a woman stubborn. It makes her sensible. I will not be the one to provide you with your frivolous sexual amusements outside of your marriage bed."

He frowned. "Did you not hear a word I said? I told you that is not what I am proposing."

"Then what are you proposing, exactly? What do you expect from me in return?"

"As I said, I am offering you a house and an income, with nothing asked of you except . . . " He paused, as if having a hard time getting the words out. "Except that you allow me to see June."

She could have fallen off the seat. "Are you quite serious? The rake without a heart wants to see his daughter? You actually care to know how she is faring?"

"I am rather astounded by it myself," he said in a contemptuous, detached voice as he looked toward the window. "But don't get excited. It doesn't mean I'm developing a conscience, nor does it mean I'm ever going to marry you, because I am not."

"So you've said before. I don't know why you feel the need to repeat it. I am quite aware that you are going to marry Lady Letitia, because evidently all that matters to you is your inheritance."

"Indeed, my father adores her, and according to the terms of his will, he has the power to approve or reject my bride. So there it is in a nutshell. He would certainly never accept *you*."

She felt the insult like a kick in the stomach.

"Besides," he continued, "what an incompatible pair we would make. You believe blindly in the divine power of love, while my jaded eyes are wide open in that area."

"I do not believe in it blindly. My eyes are quite wide open as far as *you* are concerned."

He returned his steely gaze to her face. "Ah, then you have learned a thing or two."

"Thanks to you."

He looked away and brought the subject back to where it began. "I am only putting forth this offer because I want to prevent my daughter from turning out like you. Forced to work in a hat shop, that is."

She ignored his spiteful attempt to belittle her, and considered what he was proposing. "I suppose it would not be such a bad thing, to have an income. I would not have to be away from June." Her voice became resigned. "I have struggled with that more than you can ever imagine."

"I can see that."

Did she detect a hint of sympathy? A trace of remorse? Was it possible?

Leaning closer, he tucked his heavy coat around her again before he crossed over to the other side, pulled out his pocket watch and checked the time. "The train will be here in ten minutes." He pulled a curtain aside with one finger and looked out the window.

"I confess," she said, studying his face as the gray light shone in on it, "that I am still finding it difficult to believe you are acting out of the goodness of your heart. That you only wish for our suffering to end."

"I simply do not want June to go hungry," he replied.

"But how can I trust you?" she asked. "This moment of generosity is very nice on your part, but we are talking about a lifetime of responsibility, and you have hardly been dependable in the past. You satisfy your urges and impulses, then you dash off when the initial excitement fades. How can I know that you won't one day change your mind and turn us out? Or try to claim some other form of compensation for your kindness when your charitable inclinations toward us are forgotten? I do not wish to feel indebted to you, Vincent, nor do I wish to be at your mercy or in your power. I cannot spend my days living in fear that June and I will one day be homeless again."

"June will never be homeless," he said. "And the only compensation I will require will be a right to see her when I wish it."

"But how can I *trust* you?" she asked again.

He looked at her carefully. "You won't have to trust me, nor shall I have to trust you. We will put it all in writing, and you can choose your own solicitor. I will pay his fee."

"A formal contract?"

"Yes."

"You would agree to that?"

"Yes, because it would protect my rights as well." His eyes clouded over with distrust. "You are not the only one with something at stake here, Cassandra. I certainly cannot have *you* changing your mind and running off in six months' time when you are feeling better, or if you are feeling reckless again and wish to take a lover."

"That will never happen."

He narrowed his dark eyes at her as if he knew the opposite were true, then shrugged scornfully. "Those will be my terms."

She considered it a moment. "What if I wish to marry someday? *Respectably*. What then?"

Not that she would ever desire such a thing. All she wanted was her independence, but there was the principle of the matter to consider.

"No. That would not be permissible."

She laughed. "I just said I did not wish to be in your power."

He merely shrugged again.

"What if I met a decent gentleman," she argued, "who would be a real father to June? You would still say no?"

"Yes. June will have no father figure but me. Unless I am dead, of course. Naturally, the contract will account for that possibility."

She answered in a rush of words. "So I am to live without hope of love, while you are completely free to marry whomever you choose?"

"I would hardly call my engagement the act of a free man."

She realized she was arguing now for the sake of arguing, because she had absolutely no desire to marry again.

"Then I would insist upon having terms as well," she informed him. "The first being that I would not be required to perform the typical duties one associates with a wife or mistress."

He chuckled. "You plan to put that in writing? The solicitors will enjoy wording that clause, no doubt, because they do love to be specific."

She ignored his flagrant mockery. "And I would require that the house be put in my name immediately, and not only that, my annuity will continue for my lifetime, because I do not intend to become penniless again when I am no longer needed for June's upbringing."

"Done. Anything else?"

She tried to think . . .

"You said June would someday be presented as a distant relative. Will she know that I am her mother and you are her father?"

He considered it a moment. "Leave me to work out the details of that." He leaned forward and pushed the curtain aside to peer out the window again. "Your train is here." Sitting back in his seat, he spread his hands wide. "So is that all? Do we have an agreement?"

She hesitated. "It will take some time to find a house for us. Where would we go for tonight?"

She had learned to be mindful about determining the existence and location of her bed on any given night. Especially in weather such as this.

"One option is for you to remain at the palace until we find a suitable residence."

"Is there another option?" she asked. "Because I would prefer not to find myself in the awkward position of explaining myself to your fiancée. Remember, I was in her shoes not so long ago, forced to endure the humiliation of an openly adulterous husband."

He leaned forward in that familiar, seductive manner, which exuded sexuality and burned with physical desire. It set her own senses burning as well.

"But I was under the impression," he softly said, "there would not *be* any adultery. You were going to put it in writing, remember? Unless you've changed your mind already, in which case I am game. Although in that case, the dower house—which is the other option for the evening—will need a new bed. The one that's there now . . . " He crinkled his nose and shook his head. "We would definitely need something better."

"I have not changed my mind," she informed him, "nor am I amused by your teasing, Vincent."

He leaned back again, while the image of sex,

dark and enticing, was still visible in his eyes. "I never tease. I just thought, since you were offering . . ."

"I was not offering!" She clamped her jaw together. "If we are going to do this, I must insist that you forget what happened between us a year ago and treat me with due respect. I am the mother of your child, and I want June to grow up in a proper, upright home. There can be none of this cavalier flirting."

Because, heaven help her, if he ever became that man again—the man he had been in the ballroom a year ago—she feared she might not have the will to resist.

"I was hardly flirting," he casually said.

"Everything you say and do—if it is not something completely hateful—comes across as a flirtation. It is in your nature, so you are going to have to curb that."

Somewhat perplexed, he tilted his head to the side. "I was not aware."

She strove to calm her frustration. This was not going to be easy. "If I agree to this, will I stay at the dower house tonight?" she asked, purposefully redirecting the conversation back to more practical matters.

"Yes."

The train whistle blew outside, and the station guard called out, "All aboard!"

"Have we reached an agreement, then?" he asked for the second time.

She hesitated—this time for no other reason than to make him wait—then at last she gave him her answer. "I believe we have."

He sat forward and held out his hand to shake on it.

She stared at that strong male hand and remembered how intoxicating it had been once, roaming over her body and overcoming her good sense by relaxing all her inhibitions . . .

Looking him straight in the eye, promising herself that she would be stronger this time, she accepted the deal.

"Excellent." He let go of her hand and lounged back against the seat, appearing vastly satisfied.

She was satisfied as well, for she would no longer need to worry about June's future. Her daughter would be provided for. They would live in a house in the country. June would not have to scrub floors or do the landlady's laundry. She would be educated and have a proper dowry one day.

Oh, sweet Lord in heaven! She reached down and scooped June up into her arms. If only Vincent knew how her heart was leaping with joy at this moment. Even *she* had not realized the weight of that burden upon her shoulders until now. She had not let herself think of those painful, unpleasant matters.

She looked across at him with surprise and a strange sense of wonder. He had been the cause of her downfall, but today he was her salvation.

Seeming unconcerned with her happiness, he opened the door of the coach and spoke to the driver. "To the dower house, Jenson."

He shut the door, and the coach lurched forward. They sat on opposite seats facing each other without conversing, rocking back and forth as they rolled away from the station.

Vincent looked up at the ceiling of the coach. She noted he appeared rather bemused.

A few minutes later he spoke with a hint of skepticism. "Surely not *everything* I say and do is a flirtation."

She pursed her lips to give it adequate thought, then answered him honestly. "For the most part, yes, it is."

"Hmm," he said lightly. "How does one go about curbing something like that?"

She shook her head at him, ignoring the question, and instead began to prepare herself for the great joy of starting a new life with her daughter.

Chapter 8

For a brief moment in the carriage, I wanted to hug him. I must be very careful in the future not to ever mistake my gratitude for some other kind of admiration or affection.

—from the journal of
Cassandra Montrose,
Lady Colchester,
May 13, 1874

The Pembroke Palace dower house was an elegant Georgian mansion built of brick, cloaked in ivy, and sitting proudly on a high hill-top overlooking the river.

It was built in 1760 for the aging dowager duchess, who found the main palace too daunting in her old age and wished for a comfortable dwelling of her own, where she could live out her days in quiet solitude, growing her own flowers. Hence, the house was surrounded by gardens, decorative birdbaths and fruit trees, and two enormous oaks flanking the front entrance.

To Cassandra, who so recently considered herself fortunate to have a bed and a blanket in a cold, damp boarding house on any given night, it was a vision of Paradise.

"I used to come here often as a boy," Vincent said as the coach pulled to a halt in front of the stone steps. "My great-grandmother lived here until she was seventy, and my father's sister lived here as well, until three years ago."

"It has been empty since then?" Cassandra asked.

"Yes, but not to worry. Before I left for the station to fetch you, I sent an efficient team of servants here to open the house, take up all the dust sheets, and prepare for your arrival."

She eyed him judiciously. "You were that certain I would accept your proposition?"

"Of course."

"What if I had said no?"

"You wouldn't have," he flatly stated.

He opened the door and stepped out into the rain, which in the past half hour had changed from a sharp, stinging downpour to a soft, fine mist. Still slightly feverish, Cassandra managed to rise from her seat with Vincent's heavy coat draped over her shoulders. Holding June in one arm, she reached for her bag with the other.

"Do not bother with that," he quickly admonished. "The footman will get it."

She realized a return to this life was going to take some getting used to. "I am going to have a footman?"

He held out his hand. "You will have everything."

Uncomfortably aware that she was expected to behave as a lady, yet was not wearing gloves or a hat, she slid her hand into his and allowed him to help her out of the coach. He escorted her up the stone steps to the front door, where she handed his overcoat back to him.

They entered the house and stepped onto a gleaming white floor that took Cassandra's breath away. She looked up. The walls were painted butter cream, and there were two curved staircases at the back of the entrance hall, each the perfect mirror image of the other. Both boasted ornately crafted cherry banisters and led to a second floor landing furnished with a display case of fine china and glassware. A large crystal chandelier sparkled overhead, hanging from a gold medallion in the ceiling.

It was like some kind of dream, and dressed as she was—in tattered, shabby clothes—she felt unworthy of such grandeur.

A woman came to greet them, followed by a

younger maid. They both curtsied. "Welcome, my lord."

The woman was of medium height, with brown hair and dimpled cheeks. She wore a plain, dark green serge gown.

"Good afternoon." Vincent turned. "Lady Colchester, this is the housekeeper, Mrs. Bixby."

Cassandra struggled to accustom herself to the fact that she was no longer poverty-stricken and alone. A new life was beginning. "It is a pleasure, Mrs. Bixby."

"The blue chamber has been prepared," the housekeeper said.

"Very good," Vincent replied. "The nursery as well?"

"Yes."

"Then I shall leave you to show Lady Colchester to her room."

Mrs. Bixby took Cassandra's coat and handed it over to the younger maid. The housekeeper then dismissed her with a quick nod before starting toward the stairs.

Before Cassandra followed her, however, she turned to Vincent and whispered, "Do they know?"

"Know what?"

She had a hard time clarifying her meaning. "Why I am here. That I am . . . that June is yours."

"No," he replied, glancing discreetly to ensure they would not be heard. "As far as the staff is concerned, you are simply a guest here with your daughter." He checked his pocket watch again. "I must go. I am expected at dinner."

He looked back at the housekeeper and appeared somewhat agitated. Cassandra sensed he did not want to leave without making sure everything was in order.

"I am fine now," she assured him. "This is beyond generous. Truly. Go to your dinner."

Yet he still hesitated. "I have informed the staff that you are not well and need to rest. See that you do."

"I will. Now go, Vincent. I am more than fine."

He bowed slightly at the waist, then turned and left.

Cassandra stood in the entrance hall, staring at the oak door as it swung shut behind him. She was overcome by a desire to dash out and shout after him, *"Thank you!"* but resisted the impulse, and went to join the housekeeper waiting for her at the bottom of the stairs.

Vincent stepped outside onto the wet steps and placed his hat back on his head. He stood for a moment, taking in the familiar view of the river at the bottom of the hill, while he struggled to collect his thoughts and comprehend his emotions.

Of his own free will, he had just taken on a tremendous responsibility for both Cassandra and her daughter—*his* daughter—and it disconcerted him. In the past few years his relationships with women had been fleeting and superficial, but this was altogether different. It was substantial. Important. Permanent. He had created a new life with one of his lovers—one he had carelessly discarded after one very memorable night—and that new life was now connecting him forever to his lover, as if by an invisible thread.

This sudden change in his life was astonishing. Perhaps equally astonishing was the fact that Cassandra had agreed to depend upon him for everything she and June would require—for the whole of their lives. She was placing her life—and her daughter's—in very incapable, untrustworthy hands.

All at once he became aware that he was philosophizing. He was analyzing his decisions, questioning his worth, when there was no point in doing so. It wouldn't affect anything.

Intent upon changing the direction of his thoughts, he glanced up at the sky. It was no longer raining, but sunshine was still a long way off. He could not see any trace of blue just yet, but at least the dark thunderclouds had given way to a bright, cloudy sky of brilliant white.

As he hurried down the steps to his coach, he

prepared some possible excuses for Letitia when he reached the palace, and a courteous apology to go along with them.

He wondered with a nagging sense of dread what she had been doing all afternoon.

"Do you see that?" the duke asked, standing at the window in the drawing room with a glass of champagne in his hand. He pointed at the sky. "I believe the clouds have parted. Heavens above, I think I see blue!"

"Has it stopped raining?" Adelaide asked as she looked out the window. "My word, I believe it has."

The duke turned and wagged a finger at Letitia, who was seated on the sofa. "It is just as I predicted. You, my dear, have brought the sunshine."

She blushed prettily. "You are too kind, Your Grace."

Vincent, who had just arrived from the dower house, stood in the doorway, soberly watching the scene.

His father noticed him and sloshed his champagne on the red carpet as he raised his glass. "Vincent, my boy. You have returned. Have you noticed that little patch of blue outside the window? It is all your doing, you know—bringing this peach of a woman to Pembroke. Wherever did you find her?"

Vincent leaned a shoulder against the doorjamb. "You invited her to Mother's birthday ball, remember?'

The duke stared blankly at him, then threw back his head of wild gray hair and laughed. "Oh, yes, the birthday party. She was Helen of Troy, was she not?"

Rebecca, Devon's wife, approached the duke. "Lady Letitia came dressed as a fairy princess with wings. Do you remember, Theodore? It was I who was Helen of Troy."

He gazed with fascination at Rebecca's striking green eyes and red hair. "Oh yes," he said breathlessly. "*Helen* . . . My God, but you are lovely."

Bored out of his skull, Vincent rolled his eyes, then felt a hand on his shoulder. His brother Devon was standing beside him.

"You had better keep an eye on your Helen of Troy," Vincent said with disinterest. "It appears Father is about to launch a thousand ships. Look at that. His sails are lifting as we speak."

Their mother hurried over and ushered the duke back toward the window. "Come, Theodore, I thought I saw the sun just now."

"The sun?" The duke followed Adelaide, who was all but dragging him by the wrist.

"Where were you this afternoon?" Devon asked in a quiet voice laced with accusation. "You do realize we have guests—who are here for *you*, I might add."

"I was taking care of the situation you so kindly informed me about this morning."

"It was my understanding that Mother had already taken care of your lover's financial needs and had waved goodbye at the door," Devon said. "But curiously, I just learned that a pack of servants, along with a child's nursemaid, were sent to the dower house."

Vincent was not in the mood to discuss this with his brother. It had been a long day, and he certainly did not wish to delve into his more personal motivations. He was still reeling from them himself. "She is not my lover," he said. "I am simply taking care of a few practicalities."

"How?"

"It is none of your business, Devon. I do not have to answer to you."

"It is my business when it involves your betrothal to the woman seated on the sofa," he replied. "As you are well aware, we are all to be married before Christmas if we are to save our inheritances—you, Blake, and Garrett, as well as myself, of course. We must trust and depend on each other, and I have some concerns regarding your sincerity toward Lady Letitia."

Vincent faced his brother squarely. "You have concerns about *my* sincerity? Now I believe I've heard everything."

They stared at each other in grim silence. "It has

been three years since MaryAnn's death," Devon said. "I have been punished for it long enough, don't you think?"

"Three years. Practically a lifetime." All of a sudden Vincent could not bear to be in such close proximity to his brother, who had betrayed him so callously and was now self-righteous enough to accuse *him* of brotherly negligence.

"If you will excuse me." He pushed away from the door and entered the drawing room. He approached his fiancée, who was sitting on the sofa looking exquisitely pretty with yellow combs in her glossy black hair. She wore a bright satin gown with an embroidered sunburst on the skirt and a dozen tiny white bows along the hem.

"Letitia," he said, bowing his head. "I must apologize for my absence this afternoon. I was making arrangements for our honeymoon. Will Rome suit you?"

She raised an arched eyebrow. "I suppose. It will give me time to forgive you for abandoning me today—which I did not appreciate."

Vincent wet his lips. He had no interest in placating a spoiled female who had some very misguided notions about how attentive he was going to be as a husband. But when he looked across the room at Devon, who was expecting him to let them all down brilliantly by jilting her within the week, he decided to at least make a token effort. He would get through this engagement to the wedding day.

Lowering himself slowly onto the sofa cushion beside her, he looked around the room at his family. His mother was keeping his father entertained by the fire with hopeful predictions about the weather. His sister Charlotte was adjusting the lace on Rebecca's gown at the neckline.

He turned on the cushion and smiled affably at his fiancée. "Again, I do apologize."

"Apology accepted." But then she let out a sharp little sigh of displeasure and began to deliver what sounded rather like a lecture. "I am not a fool, Vincent. I know why you are marrying me. It is only because I am beautiful, and because your father, for some preposterous reason, thinks I am the cure to this weather."

Vincent looked her in the eye. He decided not to dispute what was fact. "You are most certainly a beautiful woman, Letitia."

"And I have no illusions about our marriage being a love match."

His silence caused her to shoot a look at him. "I hope you know how lucky you are to be engaged to me."

"Of course," he calmly replied.

Somewhat appeased, she took a sip of champagne, then watched the duke for a few moments.

"I pity your mother, being married to him. He's a bit of a lunatic, isn't he?"

Vincent, too, looked across at his father, who was warming his bare feet by the fire. "He is simply growing eccentric in his old age."

"If he were *my* father, I believe I would have him carted off to an asylum."

Vincent leaned closer and spoke in a firm voice. "But he is *not* your father."

"Oh, of course, I know that," she blurted out, stumbling backward over her words. "And it is not my place to judge."

"No, it is not."

She wiggled her bottom on the sofa seat and smiled sweetly at him. "What a delightful couple we shall make, Vincent. I am very pleased by our engagement." She held out her hand to admire her ring. "I am quite certain that my diamond is larger than Rebecca's. Don't you think so? And *she* is the future duchess." She laughed. "Imagine that."

He wished he could go to the billiards room and knock some balls around.

"She must be jealous," Letitia rattled on. "She simply *must* be. And surely your brother is jealous, too, over the fact that you shall be married to me. I suspect that is another reason why you proposed to me." She smiled flippantly. "Because it is obvious to anyone with a brain in their head that you two despise each other." She looked at

Devon, who was now whispering something in Rebecca's ear.

A footman approached with a tray of champagne, and Vincent gratefully helped himself to a glass.

"You are not sentimental, are you?" his fiancée asked with a knowing look in her eye, as she watched him swallow the entire contents of the glass in one gulp.

He wiped the corner of his mouth and set the empty champagne flute on the end table. "No, I am not."

She nodded and smiled coolly. "Then I believe we shall be a good match, Vincent, because I am not sentimental either."

He looked toward the door and wondered how long he would have to continue sitting here.

Chapter 9

I am now positively certain that sexual desire in its extreme can cause a genuine case of temporary insanity, even in the most rational, sensible, morally upright individuals.

—from the journal of
Cassandra Montrose,
Lady Colchester,
May 20, 1874

For one full week Cassandra dwelled in the cozy seclusion of her bedchamber with nothing to do but rest and recover. Her new maid brought a steady stream of quail soup and buttered biscuits, which Cassandra devoured. It was positively glorious, every last bit of it, from the lazy naps in the afternoons to the boredom and monotony. Even her red, sniffly nose was a tiny piece of heaven when she could blow into an endless supply of clean, starched handkerchiefs, each one lovingly embroidered with tiny pink and purple flowers, and folded neatly in a stack on her bedside table.

The best part of all, however, was the pure, unadulterated euphoria over this second chance at life. She pondered her good fortune almost continuously in the charming blue bedchamber—lolling upon the overstuffed chintz chairs and floral coverlets, sitting dreamily by the window, watching the blackbirds swoop over the garden below. She passed the quiet hours eating and reading and spending some of the most magical moments singing to June, snuggling with her on the enormous bed.

Little June spent many hours with the nursemaid as well—the kind and capable Aggie Callahan. Mrs. Callahan's daughter. When Cassandra required rest, Miss Callahan was at hand, scooping June up into her arms and cooing gently as she carried her to the nursery for a nap.

As that first week drew to a close, Cassandra no longer felt like a cold, empty tomb inside. She was much stronger. When she looked at her reflection in the mirror, she rejoiced at the return of color to her cheeks, which were no longer gaunt, but soft and rosy. Even her hair appeared thicker and shinier.

On the seventh day she felt ready to take her happiness one step further. She would get dressed and venture outdoors.

She could hardly wait to explore the house and grounds. She didn't care that the sky was overcast or that the wind was howling past the windowpanes like a weeping ghost. All she wanted was to breathe the fresh air. She wanted to smell the damp, spring earth in all its mucky glory, tramp through the matted grasses, and walk down the steep hill to the river.

Donning her gown, she went to June's room, a small yellow nursery on the top floor with oval windows and a mahogany cradle, which had been sent down the same evening Aggie arrived from the palace a week ago.

Cassandra found Aggie sitting in a rocking chair in the corner, sewing a small bonnet. The nurse raised a finger to her lips to politely say *Hush*.

Nodding as she entered, Cassandra tiptoed to the cradle. June was sleeping soundly, a tiny bundle of sweetness and joy beneath a soft white baby quilt.

"I am feeling much better today," she whispered. "I am going outside to explore."

Aggie smiled and nodded so as not to wake June. Cassandra tiptoed back out into the corridor and quietly closed the door behind her.

A moment later she was swinging her cape over her shoulders and walking out the front door. She paused on the cement steps, looking down the hill at the deep, meandering river below, flowing steadily toward the west. She glanced up at the overcast sky. The wind was brisk. Her cape was hugging her legs. The clouds were rolling fast overhead, swirling and changing, and the leafless branches of the two big oak trees were like vibrant paint strokes against the sky.

Gathering her skirts in her fists, Cassandra descended the stairs and circled the brick house. She wandered through the gardens, marveled at the statues of naked cherubs, and knelt down to spend time pulling a few dead weeds out of the soil, which were left over from the previous autumn season.

Before long, she heard a horse whinny from the lane and rose to her feet. Feeling almost sick with fear that someone had come to accuse her of trespassing and might send her packing—for all of this seemed too good to be true—she crept to the front of the house and peered around the corner. She discovered immediately that it was not that particular horror. It was quite another one entirely. It was Vincent, looking far more gorgeous than any man had a right to be.

Dressed in a long black overcoat and top hat, he stepped confidently out of his coach like the great English lord that he was, and looked up at the front of the house.

Cassandra remained hidden around the side,

watching him. Under one arm he carried a black leather portfolio. In the other gloved hand he held an elegant walking stick with a shiny brass handle. The wind blew his dark hair around his clean white shirt collar as he started up the steps.

Perhaps she should reveal herself, she thought, suspecting he was here to present the formal contract for their arrangement, but for some reason she could not move her feet. She could do nothing but remain hidden around the corner, silently watching.

He went into the house. Less than a minute later he came out again and paused on the step. Looking to his right, he spotted her standing with one hand on the corner of the house. Their gazes locked. He made no move to approach, nor did he offer any form of greeting.

She found herself frozen in place, entranced by how frustratingly handsome he was. It was simply not fair that any man could be so spellbinding, especially a man as wicked and coldhearted as this one. A man she had sworn to hate because of those very characteristics.

Although she supposed she could not continue to judge him so excessively. After all, he had agreed to raise her daughter when she'd come to him a week ago, and was now her very generous benefactor. She could not deny there was some goodness in that. He was atoning for his sins on some level, perhaps. She flirted with the idea that he might even possess at least a fragment of a conscience, despite the fact that he was engaged to one woman and supporting another.

And doing God knew what else with how many more.

"Mrs. Bixby informed me you are feeling better," he said to her from the step.

"I am, thank you."

She realized that her hair had become windblown and a few locks were loose around her neck. She tried to tuck them back into place.

Vincent strode purposefully down the steps and approached. "I am here on business."

She glanced at the black leather case he held under his arm. "That is the contract, I presume? Shall we go inside and look it over?"

He shook his head. "That won't be necessary at the present time. Since we agreed you would have your own solicitor, I took the liberty of enclosing a list of every reputable firm in London. Choose whomever you like and send for him. The man you select can look over the contract with you and make any changes you require."

He held the case out.

"It is important," he added, "that you go over every detail carefully before you sign. I will do the same when I look at your changes . . . that is to say, if you have any, which I am certain you will."

Somewhat taken aback by this very clear and easy transaction, Cassandra accepted the case. "Thank you."

They stood in the garden, saying nothing for a few seconds, then he spoke with cool detachment. "You look much better."

"I am a hundred times so. I have been treated most kindly. I've been eating and sleeping, and today, for the first time, I felt strong enough to come outside and look at the gardens. They will be lovely when the sun appears and works its magic." She looked up at the white sky. "If it ever does appear."

But he had no interest in the sun. He cast his eyes downward at her cloak and shabby dress. "You are wearing the same clothes you had on a week ago, Cassandra. Have you nothing else?"

"No, I do not."

"Then I shall provide you with a new wardrobe."

"But you have done so much already."

"If you are to raise my daughter in a standard acceptable to me, you cannot go around looking like a milkmaid." There was a chilly edge to his voice, which she had become accustomed to, and which in no way resembled her memory of him from one year ago. "That is not what you are."

"And what am I, exactly?" she asked, curious all of a sudden about the contract, and worrying that she would lose all her personal freedom in this strange bargain she had accepted. "All I know is that I am a guest here with my daughter. But who am I in relation to you? What is my status? Will June know you are her father?"

His expression was stern. "She will know me as a friend, and if you live a quiet life in the country without calling too much attention to yourself, no one will ever guess our true connection."

She lifted one eyebrow. "It all sounds very cloak and dagger to me."

"Well, it would have been much easier on everyone," he said with a clear degree of censure, "if you had not shown up on my doorstep after seeking the advice from a quack doctor who would declare you on death's door when you were merely nursing a sore throat."

She was taken aback. "I see. You would have preferred never to know about June? Pardon me, but I find that hard to believe, when you have just handed me a contract to protect your rights as her father."

He did not flinch in the slightest. In fact, he barely reacted to her explicit retort. He merely stared at her while a raven squawked in the skeletal treetops above.

"Perhaps while I am here," he said, "I shall visit June."

She could not help but laugh in utter disbelief, while a wild gust of wind whipped at her skirts. This was quite unbelievable.

"Of course," she replied. "You are welcome to see your daughter, although she was sleeping when I last looked in on her."

"I can sit in the nursery and wait."

Cassandra regarded him as she led the way up the steps to the door. The idea of this man sitting in a nursery with a baby was rather strange and incongruous.

"I don't have much experience with men and their children," she said, "but I doubt my own father ever set foot in the nursery to see any of his children, let alone wait for them to wake from a nap. He certainly had no interest in me until I walked through the door with a baby in my womb and the mark of a harlot on my forehead."

Vincent lifted his chiseled chin as he followed her. "Similarly, my father had trouble remembering my name. He knew me only as 'that other one.'"

She glanced back at him. "Really? Is that true?"

"He only had eyes for his firstborn."

"Your older brother, Devon."

"Yes."

She hugged the leather case to her chest and sighed. "So we have something in common after all. And here we are, parents ourselves. Shall we go inside?"

He gestured with a hand. "After you."

She pushed through the door, where Mrs. Bixby was waiting to take their coats.

Vincent was notably quiet as they climbed the stairs, but when they reached the top, he clasped his hands behind his back and said, "So tell me, Cassandra, how am I doing? Am I curbing my wanton flirtatiousness, which you find so terribly offensive?"

She stopped and turned around. "Yes, I suppose so," she replied, surprised by the question. "Thank you for your effort. It is much appreciated."

He bowed slightly. "You're welcome, and I appreciate the thoughtful encouragement."

But then he grinned at her, and there it was—evidence of that charmingly dangerous rake he had been a year ago. The rake who whisked her out of a ballroom and all but ravished her in a carriage. It was the first time he had shown that lighter side of himself since she came here to Pembroke.

Her lips felt dry all of a sudden. She slowly wet them. "You do realize you just spoiled it."

"How?"

"With that smile, that mischievous look in your eye."

"What look?" But clearly he knew exactly what she was talking about.

"That look. The one you have now." She gestured toward him. "That wicked glimmer, that teasing air. You are like a hungry black cat who wants to cause trouble." She turned and started climbing the stairs again. "I do not like cats."

"You prefer dogs?"

"Yes."

They continued along the second floor corridor toward the back stairs, which led up to the third story of the house.

"I suppose I am beyond hope, then," he said, following her up the steps. "I will either have to promise never to smile in your presence, or you will have to accept me the way I am—as a rake and a scoundrel. Perhaps I should have put something about that in the contract."

She stopped, gripping the railing and looking down at him again, a few steps below. "That won't be necessary. I am a rock, you see, and therefore shall weather your boundless charisma. And no one is ever beyond hope. Look at me. One week ago I was handing my child over to a housekeeper on your doorstep."

He did look at her. His gaze swept from the top of her head down to her toes, then back up to her eyes again. He rose up another step so they were face-to-face, and blinked seductively. "But now you have your life back, and you are looking like your old self again—quite healthy and attractive, I might add. Except for the hideous dress."

She placed all five fingertips on the hard wall of his chest and pushed him back down to the step below. "Put that flattery away, if you please. I know what kind of man you are, and I thought we agreed there would be none of this. I won't stay if there is. I shall leave."

He squinted. "And go where?"

When she did not reply—for she did not want to think about the answer—he smirked, quite satisfied with his sinister self.

"I thought you said you were a rock," he said, "and could weather my—what did you call it?—'boundless charisma.'"

"I assure you, my resistance to your very erratic appeal is as firm as stone, but . . . " She paused, at a loss for words for a second. "That doesn't make your presumptuous manner proper or acceptable. Besides, I fell for your superficial charm once before, and look what happened to me."

His eyes narrowed shrewdly. "Indeed, you are in a terrible predicament now, with a child you never dreamed you could have, an annuity forthcoming, and a house soon to be deeded to you. And may I remind you that you are not married to the very balding and bumbling Mr. Clarence Hibbert?"

She frowned. "You remember that?"

He merely shrugged.

She had not thought he remembered anything from that night. She'd assumed he tossed her into a crowded pot with every other nameless, insignificant bed partner he'd had in the past year.

Another confident, sinister grin stole across his face, and her senses began to whirl, which made her realize with horror that she could not trust herself to be quite so impervious as a rock.

"Would it surprise you to know," he asked, "that I remember a number of *particular* things about that night?"

Her heart pounded. "What sorts of things?"

He smiled deviously, and she felt as if she were looking at sin personified.

"I remember that your lips tasted like honey, and when you were naked and sitting on top of me with your eyes closed, and your soft flesh damp with perspiration, you leaned forward and brushed your hair over my face, and I swear it felt like the silky wings of an angel lifting me off the bed. I thought I'd died and gone straight to heaven."

She felt touched by heaven herself at that moment, standing in the private stairwell, trapped by his intoxicating sexuality. He smelled like musk and leather, and the vivid reminder of sitting naked on top of him without inhibitions made her desires spin so fast, she feared that if she let go of the railing, she would topple over head first and go rolling straight down to the bottom.

"When I accepted your offer a week ago," she said in a decisively sober voice that belied how frantically she was struggling to wrestle her desires to the ground and stomp on them, "I told you that you were going to have to treat me with the respect I deserve. That there could be none of this kind of talk."

"I did make an effort," he explained.

"For about five minutes."

He wagged a finger at her. "In my defense, you did ask what I remembered about that night. I was only being honest."

She inhaled deeply, knowing she had no choice but to surrender to that argument. "I should not have asked."

"No, you shouldn't have," he said. "It certainly doesn't help *me* to remember it. Not when I am about to be shackled into the tight bonds of marriage."

Cassandra turned and started up the stairs again. "What an enchanting way to look at your future nuptials. I am very glad I am not your bride."

They reached the nursery and paused outside the door. "Tell me," she whispered, careful to keep her voice low, "does your fiancée know about this arrangement we have?"

He spoke calmly and without reservation, revealed no hint of guilt or discomfiture. "No."

"Are you going to tell her?"

"Of course not. It's completely unnecessary. I am sure she is well aware of the fact that I will have mistresses."

"I shall remind you again, sir, that I am not your mistress."

"I was not talking about you."

Good Lord, he might as well have tossed a glass of cold water in her face. She reminded herself, however, that she did not care if he had a dozen mistresses today, or a hundred of them ten years from now. All she cared about was that he had given her the chance to spend her life with her daughter, and that he was providing a home where they both could live. That was the only reason she was having anything to do with him. If not for that, she would be running very quickly in the other direction.

The nursery door creaked as she pushed it open, and they walked in to discover Aggie still sitting in the rocking chair, working on the baby bonnet. She rose to her feet and curtsied to Vincent, while Cassandra set the leather case on the table by the door.

"Good afternoon, Miss Callahan," he said.

Cassandra crossed to the cradle and looked

down at her darling girl, who was awake and alert, smiling and kicking her legs. "Look who's come to see you," she said, gathering her up into her arms. "Lord Vincent is here."

"I see she's awake," he said.

Cassandra turned to Aggie. "Perhaps you could come back in half an hour."

"Yes, ma'am."

As soon as Aggie was out the door, Vincent crossed the room to where she stood. "May I hold her?"

It was astounding how all the problems of the world could disappear when one held a baby. One's very own baby.

"Here you are," she said.

He looked down at June and turned to pace around the room. Cassandra simply watched them with a strange, unanticipated quietness.

"Hello there, little one," he said. "You're very happy today. Did you know the rain has stopped? Is that why you are smiling?"

June cooed and gurgled in his arms while Cassandra stood back, continuing to watch.

Vincent turned toward her. "Isn't it amazing how she looks at you? She's very bright, don't you think?"

Cassandra approached. "Yes. Just watch." She held out her finger, and June grasped it in a tight grip.

"What a strong girl you are," he said.

"Let's spread a blanket on the floor," Cassandra suggested, turning to reach for the quilt in the cradle. She flapped the folds out of it and let it float lightly onto the soft rug.

Vincent lowered June down and sat back on his haunches, Cassandra knelt on the other side of her, and together they watched their baby girl kick and move and giggle. They glanced across at each other often, and after a time, they both lay down on their sides, cheeks resting on hands, their daughter between them.

"Vincent," Cassandra said, thinking back to their earlier conversation about his marriage. "How can you be so sure that Letitia is aware of the possibility that you will have mistresses?"

His eyes lifted but he did not respond.

"As I said before," she continued, "maybe she thinks this is her fairy-tale wedding. Maybe she thinks she is the woman who has tamed your philandering spirit. And what if she believes in the sanctity of marriage, like I did?"

He shook his head. There seemed to be a warning in the gesture. "The circumstances of my marriage don't concern you, Cassandra. You are not responsible for my behavior as a husband, or for my wife's happiness. Or mine, for that matter."

"I understand that, but in a way, I will be a part of your marriage, because June is an extension of you, and I am not sure I can bear to be the cause of anyone's unhappiness, even though there is no longer anything improper going on between us, nor will there ever be."

He looked at her doubtfully. "You're sure about that?"

"Of course I am sure." Yet here they were alone in a room, lying on a blanket, doting over their daughter. "I am a woman from your past, nothing more."

"Indeed," he said with a casual sigh. "There are so very many women from my past. I can hardly keep all of you straight."

She rolled onto her back and cupped her forehead in both hands. "I think you should tell her."

"Why?"

"Because she should at least have the opportunity to choose her future for herself, knowing all the facts. At least if she knows about me, I will not feel like such a dirty little secret." She sat up and looked at him. "Although you must be sure to tell her that I am *not* your mistress, nor will I ever be."

He shook his head. "I do not want the world to know that June is illegitimate."

"But if Letitia is going to be your wife, there should not be any secrets between you."

"I would not trust her with that information."

"You would not trust her." He never failed to

astonish her. "How can you marry someone you do not trust?"

His eyebrows lifted. "A strange question coming from you, considering that your husband spent all your money on his mistress, then died in her arms and left you destitute. Did you trust *him* when you married him?"

She felt flustered all of a sudden. "Rightly or wrongly, I entered into that marriage in good faith."

"To your detriment, obviously. You made quite a colossal mistake there, if I may say so, believing in happily ever after. There is simply no such thing, Cassandra." He offered his forefinger to June, who grabbed hold of it and smiled. "That is why I have chosen the *perfect* wife," he added with cheer. "She does not share your romantic views about love and marriage."

Troubled not only by Vincent's patronizing tone, but by the cavalier nature of his values, Cassandra rose to her feet. "Then we shall agree to disagree."

He looked up at her. "Where are you going?"

"I am tired. If you will excuse me." She turned to go.

"Tired of what?" he asked, craning his neck to follow her with his gaze. "Our lively debate on the institution of marriage? Or are you tired of fighting your honest desire to drag me to your bed, tear off your gown, and beg me to make love to you?"

She stopped dead in her tracks, resenting him deeply for having no scruples. None whatsoever. "I have no such desire."

She could hear him sitting up on the blanket, but was determined not to turn around.

"Come now, Cassandra," he said in a seductive voice, and she began to wonder if he was Lucifer incarnate. "We both know there is still a spark of attraction between us. There always will be."

She strove to control her anger. When she spoke, she managed to convey some polite courtesy as she moved toward the door and picked up the case that contained the contract.

"I shall go now and fetch Miss Callahan," she said, purposefully ignoring what he had said. "There is no need for you to hurry out. Stay as long as you wish. June enjoys your company."

At last she glanced back at him. He was sitting up and leaning on one arm. "Then I shall bid you farewell until next time," he said.

She left the room and made her way back to her bedchamber, hugging the contract to her chest and wishing he had not openly acknowledged what had once existed between them. She supposed it was her fault as much as his. She had allowed him to lead her down that path when she asked him what he remembered about their wild night together.

She stopped in the corridor and laid a hand on her belly. That moment in the back stairwell had been excruciating.

She started walking again and decided it would perhaps be wise in the future to leave the house when Vincent visited June. She did not need to be present, hovering nearby and watching him play with her baby. She did not need to see June smiling up at her father and giggling happily. That simply would not do, not when he seemed determined to shock and humiliate her at every turn. He truly was a scoundrel.

Chapter 10

I found it very difficult to concentrate on anything today. I could not stop thinking about certain, specific details of that night. There are some moments I recall so vividly. My body remembers the sensations. I wish I could keep myself from remembering it.

—from the journal of
Cassandra Montrose,
Lady Colchester,
May 20, 1874

Vincent walked into the billiards room to find Blake asleep on the sofa with his boots on, still wearing the clothes he'd had on the night before. For a moment, he considered turning around and walking out so as not to wake his younger brother, but it occurred to him that he might end up in the drawing room going over flower arrangements with Letitia, so he decided to hit some billiard balls around instead.

Blake responded with pained annoyance to the noisy clack of the three balls as Vincent dropped them onto the tabletop. He rolled over with a scowl and a groan. "What the devil are you doing? And what time is it? Bloody hell."

"It's almost four in the afternoon," Vincent replied, circling around the lavishly carved oak table and placing the cue ball behind the balkline. He glanced briefly at Blake, who was rubbing his eyes with the heels of his hands and straining to sit up.

"Late night I presume?" Vincent said.

Blake tipped his head back against the sofa cushions. "I should know better."

"Should you? And when would you have learned? You've never been one to misbehave like the rest of us." Vincent went to fetch a cue stick from the rack on the wall.

"Was it really necessary to come in and do this just now?" Blake asked. "I was dreaming."

"Well, I hope it was a pleasant dream. I apologize for interrupting, but may I remind you, you do have a bed of your own in the south wing?"

"I couldn't make it that far this morning."

Vincent noted the empty brandy bottle and glass on the end table. "Rough night?"

"It was, in a word, intriguing."

"Care to tell me about it?"

His brother seemed to consider with great care whether to reveal where he had been. Then, at last, he began to explain.

"Promise me you will keep this between us for the time being, Vincent, because I am not yet ready to announce anything officially."

Vincent bent forward to take aim at the cue ball.

"I have met a woman," his brother said.

Vincent straightened before he took the shot. "You don't say."

Rubbing a hand down over his stubbled cheek, Blake paused. "I shouldn't even be speaking about it. I know so little about her."

Vincent, who was more than familiar with the nuisance of prying questions when he was in Blake's condition—which was often—was far too curious to let the subject go.

"Does she come from a good family?"

"Indeed she does. Her father is on the board of directors for the London Horticultural Society, which incidentally is the beneficiary in Father's will if we do not abide by his orders to marry. How could he argue?"

"That is an interesting coincidence, I must say." Vincent bent forward and took another shot. "Is she pretty?"

"Devastatingly so."

He moved around the table. "She wasn't the one who kept you up until dawn, I hope, because you know Father. He will require nothing less than a respectable young lady." He tapped his cue stick on the floor. "No illegitimate children allowed."

Blake laughed. "No, it was not she who kept me up all night, but I've struck up a friendship with her brother, and the chap likes to gamble."

Vincent pointed the cue stick at his brother. "Be careful, Blake. You never did have much luck at the tables."

Blake rose to his feet and fetched another stick from the rack. "Don't worry, I have a good head on my shoulders. Let's play to three hundred. Loser sits beside Father at dinner."

Vincent chuckled. "Deal."

Simultaneously they hit the two white balls up the table. Blake's ball came back closest to the balk cushion, and he chose the marked white ball to begin. He made his first strike, then they played in silence for a time, earning points at equal measure.

"Can I ask you something?" Vincent said, circling around the table, studying the lay of the balls. "Do you think you will be faithful when you marry?"

"I don't know. It depends on the wife, I suppose."

"Does it?" He took another shot.

"I believe so. Look at Devon. Can you imagine him being unfaithful to Rebecca? I certainly cannot."

Vincent straightened and took a deep breath to stem the resentment he still felt toward Devon, which was only aggravated by the idea of his marital bliss. "I suppose if one is fortunate enough to find a woman like that."

"I take it, you don't imagine yourself being faithful to Letitia?"

Vincent looked up from the table with a raised eyebrow.

"I didn't think so," Blake said.

Vincent hit his brother's ball, then potted the red, scoring an easy cannon. He circled around to the other side. "Do you think she'll mind? If she were the docile sort, I would have no concerns, but she seems rather . . . "

"Rather what, Vincent?"

He paused and ran his fingers along the cue stick. "While she claims she is not sentimental, she is most definitely spoiled. I am having visions of coming home to the surprise of razors or snakes in my bed if she does not feel she is getting what she wants." He took another shot and knocked the red ball off the side cushion.

Blake chuckled. "Maybe you shouldn't marry her, then."

"If I don't, Father will go into convulsions. We'd all end up without a bloody farthing to our names. That damn birthmark," he added.

"It doesn't look anything like the sun to me," Blake said. "I don't know how Father imagined that."

"He's mad as a cuckoo bird."

"Like a monkey in a drainpipe." Blake missed a difficult shot. "Bugger." He backed away from the table.

"I suppose I could simply *ask* Letitia."

"Ask her what?" Blake questioned. "If she'll mind if you sleep with other women?" He shook his head at the foolhardy notion and set the cue handle on the floor, gripping the stick with both hands. "Do that and you'll end up with worse than snakes in your bed. She'd stuff you down the drainpipe with father."

Vincent chuckled bitterly. "At least we would keep each other company." He took another shot and completely missed the ball.

"I am curious, Letitia," Vincent said, having decided to join her in the drawing after all, to clear the air, "did your parents marry for love?"

She looked up at him with those very ambitious brown eyes. "Heavens no. My father thinks my mother is as dense as a post, and most of the time I agree with him." She gave him a naughty little smirk, then turned her nose up at a vase of orchids, which was presented before them. "No, I do not like those," she said. "Their scent is revolting."

The maid quickly steered them away, and another maid approached with a vase of red roses mixed with some kind of white concoction.

Vincent smiled dutifully at the arrangement, which Letitia seemed to approve of, then they were left alone again while her preferences were being noted out in the hall.

"Though to be completely honest," she said as she bit into a chocolate biscuit, "I don't think my father even notices my mother's silliness anymore. He spends all his time in Yorkshire with his mistress. They have a cottage there."

Surprised by her candid confession of her father's infidelity, he sought to clarify her opinions on the subject. "So you are aware of your father's mistress."

She nodded. "Yes, of course."

"It doesn't bother you that he has . . . " He paused. "Other interests?"

She shook her head. "Why should it matter to me?" As soon as the chocolate biscuit was down her throat, she glanced abruptly at him. "Oh, I see. I know why you are asking me these questions. You want to know if I am fretting about your reputation with women."

He took a breath to comment, but she smiled with understanding and spoke openly before he had the chance.

"There is no need to worry," she said in a quiet, sensual voice. "I know exactly what to expect with you, Vincent, because I am fully aware that you have no scruples." She looked him over from head to foot and smiled alluringly. "Of course I must concede that you are incredibly handsome, which is very nice for me, as we will look marvelous together." She reached for another biscuit.

"I had no idea you were so liberally minded, Letitia."

"I am simply not foolish," she said. "I am an enlightened woman, and I know that you will have mistresses. I shall not protest, just as long as you are discreet about it."

He found himself thinking of Cassandra at that moment, and how very different these two women were. He felt oddly disappointed. "Then I shall only ask the same of you," he said to her, without antagonism, "if you ever decide to take a lover."

Which he was certain she would.

She reached for another chocolate biscuit. "Fair is fair, I suppose. And this shall be my last bite, I promise, because I do not want the buttons bursting on my wedding gown. That simply would not do, would it?"

"No, indeed."

She offered him a biscuit, but he found he had no appetite.

Three days later the solicitor Cassandra selected from Vincent's comprehensive list arrived at the dower house with a black leather folio in his arm, and spent two painstaking hours with her, going over every detail of the contract.

It was surprisingly fair, she discovered, almost too fair, for it focused mainly on her needs, liberties, and financial privileges. There was only one brief clause pertaining to Vincent's right to see June when he wished, without prior arrangement, and through that one her solicitor drew a big red X.

"I recommend that you require at least twenty-four hours notice," he said.

She understood it would mean that Vincent would never arrive unannounced and she'd never have to see him, since she could leave the house when he was expected.

She accepted the solicitor's recommendation, but rejected his further suggestion to restrict the visits to twice a week. It was not her wish to limit the frequency of Vincent's calls. She believed he should be permitted to see June every day if he wished it. And the contract had been so very generous.

The solicitor rewrote the clause to that effect. Vincent could come every day if he so desired. She could be at home or elsewhere. That would remain her prerogative.

The very next day, Cassandra received another unexpected visitor—Lady Charlotte, Vincent's younger sister, who arrived with a large trunk on the back of her coach. Cassandra had not met Charlotte during her brief stay at the palace, but knew who she was.

"I am pleased to see your health has improved," Charlotte said as she handed her heavy hooded cloak to Mrs. Bixby.

Cassandra admired Lady Charlotte's golden hair and striking blue eyes. She was an extraordinarily beautiful young woman, with little resemblance to Vincent and his dark features, but she looked very much like her mother.

"All I required was a few days rest," Cassandra said, adapting quickly to their assumed acquaintance. "And some especially delicious quail soup."

"Ah, yes," Charlotte agreed, smiling. "That recipe comes from the palace housekeeper, Mrs. Callahan, who is Aggie's mother. Vincent specifically recommended it, as it was always his favorite, ever since he was a boy."

Cassandra took note of the surprising fact that Vincent had personally overseen her recuperative menu that first week.

She led the way up the stairs to the drawing room on the second floor. As soon as the door closed behind them and they were alone, Lady Charlotte's shoulders rose and fell with what appeared to be a sigh of relief.

"Finally," she said. "I am here."

Cassandra wasn't sure what to say, or what to expect next.

Charlotte strode toward her and took hold of both her hands. "It is so nice to finally meet you," she said.

"And you as well," Cassandra replied, smiling.

Her guest pulled off her gloves and looked around the room. "I haven't been here since my aunt passed away. I forgot how charming it was."

"Yes. I am very grateful to be living here. Temporarily, that is."

Charlotte nodded. "I understand Vincent is going to find a house for you and June? Do you know where?"

Cassandra wondered how much Charlotte knew about their relationship and arrangement. Was the entire family aware of it? "I don't know yet," she replied. "We haven't really discussed that."

Charlotte moved to the sofa and sat down. "I apologize, I don't mean to pry. I only came to bring you some gowns. Vincent wasn't quite sure what to do in that regard, whether he should send a seamstress here or just arrange for you to have an account with one of the merchants in the village or in London. I told him I could help with that, so I thought we'd start with a few of my things—which you could borrow because he said we appear to be the same size—until we get it all sorted out. Personally, I think you and I should take a trip to London and visit Mrs. Leblanc." Her eyes lit up with excitement. "She's French, and specializes not only in gowns, but in the most exquisite undergarments."

Cassandra invited Charlotte to sit down. "You are very kind, Charlotte, but I don't think I'll need anything too fashionable, as I don't expect to be in London a great deal. June and I will be living a quiet life. I expect to be spending a lot of time gardening."

A great deal of time, in fact, if Vincent came to visit every day.

Charlotte sat back. "Yes, of course. I don't mean to be pushy."

"You're not."

"Oh, I probably am. I suppose I am looking for any excuse to escape the goings on at the palace. It has been very . . . "

Curious, Cassandra leaned forward. "Yes?"

Charlotte gave her a melancholy smile. "Forgive me. I came to bring you gowns, and I am waxing on about my own life."

A maid appeared then with a tray of tea and cookies.

Cassandra poured them each a cup, and they chatted about the delightful presentation of sweets and how perfectly hot the tea was.

"I must confess," Charlotte said, "I fell in love with little June the day you brought her to the palace, and I was delighted when I learned that Vincent intended to take care of both of you. He has not had anything to focus on in a very long time, and I've noticed a difference in him already."

"How so?"

Charlotte looked up at the ceiling and shrugged. "It is not easy to explain. I suppose it almost seems like a remedy of sorts. He's been more cheerful lately, if you can imagine that, even under the difficult circumstances of his engagement."

Cassandra set down her teacup. "Difficult?"

"Well, it is not exactly what one would call a love match, but it is certainly very beneficial for Lady Letitia."

"Isn't she the daughter of the Duke of Swinburne? One would think she could have any man she wanted."

"With her beauty and position, certainly yes, but her family is deeply in debt. All the children will have to marry money, and I suspect most will end up with Americans. But not Letitia. She would never have that. Nothing less than an English lord will do for her, and of course he must be the most handsome of men. Unfortunately, most of the eligible bachelors in England are as broke as her father. And not nearly as good looking." She raised the teacup to her lips.

"The men of Pembroke, on the other hand . . . " Cassandra grinned playfully at Charlotte, rather surprised at herself.

Charlotte laughed. "Most women share your opinions, I dare say. May I ask you a question, Cassandra?"

"Of course."

"It is rather personal."

"I don't mind." The truth was, she found Charlotte delightfully sincere.

Charlotte set down her teacup. "On the day you brought June to the palace, some of us wondered if Vincent might try to wiggle out of his engagement to Letitia and marry you instead. Obviously that did not happen, and I am wondering . . . did he suggest that to you at all?"

Cassandra swallowed uncomfortably. "Perhaps you should ask your brother that question."

"I already have. Everyone seems quite certain that Father will never accept anyone for Vincent except for Letitia, which is probably true. He has some very strict ideas about the kind of woman who is suitable as a Pembroke wife. The fact that you and Vincent have already had a child . . . "

She dropped her gaze. "Do forgive me. I didn't mean to imply . . . "

"There is nothing to forgive, Charlotte. I understand the ways of the world." Indeed, she was all too aware that she was a fallen woman. The son of a duke would require someone respectable.

"But I told Vincent that he shouldn't care about any of that," Charlotte said passionately. "I told him he shouldn't sacrifice his happiness because of Father's ridiculous, stubborn ideas. But then he told me that you would never accept him in a hundred years, regardless, but I find myself wondering if he is completely daft to think so."

Cassandra looked down at her tea. "Your brother is correct in that regard. I do not wish to marry him. But even if I did, he is already engaged to Lady Letitia, and a gentleman is not at liberty to break an engagement. That is up to the lady."

"I know that," Charlotte said, "but perhaps Letitia might release him if she knew about you and June." She dropped her gaze again and added under her breath, "I am sure she would be just as happy with Blake, or Garrett, for that matter."

Realizing that Charlotte was not fond of Lady Letitia, Cassandra moistened her lips and decided to trust her with this, at least: "There is no point in hoping that Letitia might release him, Charlotte. Even if your brother were free, my feelings would still be the same."

"Because of his reputation?"

"That is a large part of it, yes."

She inclined her head. "So you do not think he is capable of true love."

"No, I do not."

Charlotte leaned back and nodded. "I thought that might be the case, and I cannot blame you. I am sure—given what is printed about him in the newspapers and how unimaginably beastly he can be sometimes—that most women would share your opinion."

"But clearly you do not."

Charlotte sat very still, her blue eyes gleaming. "I realize that on the surface Vincent appears cold and unfeeling, and he has certainly lived the life of a shameless libertine over the past few years, but I have known him all my life and believe him to be the most loving, kindhearted, devoted of brothers. He was not always as cynical as he is today. Did you know that he was engaged once before, and that it was a true love match? At least on his side."

Cassandra nearly choked on her tea. "A true love match, you say?"

"Yes. Her name was MaryAnn. He had been in love with her since they were children, desperately so, but she died tragically."

"I did not know that," Cassandra replied, sitting very still, almost unable to move. "When did this happen?"

"Three years ago. It is part of the reason for his feud with Devon."

Cassandra inclined her head with curiosity. "I know that he resents his older brother. I assumed it was envy, because your father favored him."

"He certainly did favor him, but Vincent never blamed Devon for that when we were growing up. They were the best of friends, at least until MaryAnn fell in love with Devon."

Cassandra could not contain her curiosity. "How did it happen?"

"One week before she was to become Vincent's wife, she wrote a letter to Devon, and they had a secret tryst in the forest. They were returning to the palace together afterward when there was an accident." Charlotte looked down at her hands on her lap. "The horse they were riding slipped in the mud and threw them both, then fell upon MaryAnn, killing her instantly. Devon was injured as well, and returned to the palace with a broken leg to reveal what had occurred. Vincent went riding to the scene like a madman, not believing that MaryAnn was dead. He arrived there and discovered it was true. He found and read the letter in her pocket, and had to shoot Devon's horse. It was a terrible nightmare, every bit of it. Devon left for America the very next day, and Vincent has never been the same since then. It was a double betrayal, from both the woman he loved and his own brother."

"I cannot imagine . . . "

"And I cannot bear to remember it. I don't think Vincent can either."

They sat in silence while Cassandra remembered what he had said in the coach when they were discussing the contract—that it would protect his rights as well. *I certainly cannot have you changing your mind and running off in six months' time.*

She had not trusted him, that was obvious, but he had not trusted her either. And here they both were.

"I want to tell you another story," Charlotte said, "of when we were children—an image that has never left my mind or my heart since the day it occurred.

"Once, when we were playing in the woods, we found a fawn whose mother had died. We all wanted to leave her, because we were sure we would get into trouble if we did not, but Vincent carried that fawn back to the palace stables and demanded that he be allowed to keep her until she was fit to survive on her own. He fed her and cared for her, and when he took her back to the forest, he shooed her away, then dropped to his knees and wept. But then, after he wiped his tears away, he smiled and was content. He was twelve."

Charlotte glanced toward the window. "I was happy that day, too, and so very glad I was his sister. I always knew I would be able to depend on him for anything—as you are doing now. He will never abandon you and June. I can promise you that. And not because of the contract, or because it is his duty, but because he is caring and steadfast, despite what the gossips say. And most of all, despite what *he* says."

Cassandra looked pointedly at Charlotte. "Is that why you came here today? To tell me all these wonderful things about your brother?"

"Yes," she said matter-of-factly. "I simply wanted you to understand him and know the kind of man he truly is, despite appearances, so that you can perhaps . . . *forgive* certain things."

"What kinds of things?"

"Like why he never answered your letter or contacted you again after meeting you."

All at once Cassandra felt torn by conflicting emotions. She was shocked that Charlotte knew all these things, and wondered if Vincent confided in her about such intimate matters. She was fascinated as well by these arresting stories that seemed to contradict everything she knew and believed about him.

Beneath it all, she felt fearful. She had been ducking under a shield whenever Vincent walked into a room and sent her heart flip-flopping inside her chest. That shield seemed to protect her, but all these things Charlotte was telling her were hammering away at it.

"What do you know about that?" she asked, referring to the letter she'd sent Vincent, and his lack of response, working hard to remain clear-headed.

Charlotte began digging into her purse. "I don't suppose this is yours . . . "

She withdrew a mother-of-pearl hair comb and handed it to Cassandra.

"I was wearing this the night we first met," she said, running her fingers lightly over the graceful pink and white design. "I thought I'd lost it." She looked up. "Where did you get it?"

"In Vincent's room, in the drawer next to his bed. It was wrong of me to take it, but I wanted you to know that he had kept it."

"But how did you know it was mine? I was not the only woman he had been with."

"He told me about you. He probably doesn't even remember it now, for he was completely foxed. It was late one night, and I came upon him sitting at his desk, staring at your unopened letter and clutching your comb in his hand and rambling on about how you were going to be the end of him."

Cassandra did not know what to say.

"I put him to bed and told him to go and see

you, but of course he never did. I should have been more persistent."

Cassandra set the comb on the table. "What do you hope will come of this?" she asked. "Do you expect me to take one look at a hair ornament and forget everything that happened over the past year, and believe he is redeemable? Shall I put my heart into his hands?"

"That all sounds rather perfect, actually."

Cassandra shook her head. "You forget there is another woman in this scenario—a woman who believes she is about to become his wife."

"But she doesn't love him."

"How is everyone so sure of her feelings? What if she is simply reserved?"

Charlotte laughed. "No. Letitia is not reserved."

"I presume you are not fond of her."

"I regret to say I am not."

Cassandra sat for a moment, trying to imagine giving her heart to Vincent, freely and without inhibitions.

She sighed, then put her hand on the comb and slid it across the table, back to Charlotte. "I am afraid there is too much water under the bridge when it comes to your brother and me. We have a contractual agreement now, and it provides me with everything I could ever want. June will be taken care of, and so will I. I will have my freedom as a woman. Why would I want to complicate or jeopardize that?"

"But—"

Cassandra stood up and walked to the window. "I am sorry, Charlotte. I do not wish to become involved with him—or any other man, for that matter. I do not wish for emotional upheaval. I've had quite enough to last me a lifetime. I do not need the insanity of lust to make me foolish again, nor do I want to steal a man away from a woman who does want him, whatever her reasons." She turned to face Charlotte. "Besides, what if your brother is not redeemable? What if the damage has been done and cannot be undone? He is no longer that boy who carried the fawn home to the palace stables. Because of what happened with his former fiancée, he is a different person now, a grown man who drinks and gambles and breaks women's hearts. He has changed."

Charlotte did not say anything for a long time. She simply sat on the sofa, gazing at Cassandra with what appeared to be compassion. "I think you might be wrong about that," she softly said. "I cannot give up my opinion that he is still that person."

"How can you be sure?"

"Do you not see, Cassandra? My brother has brought another fawn home to care for, and that fawn, my dear, is you."

Chapter 11

Sometimes I wonder if I really know him at all. Or myself, for that matter.

—from the journal of
Cassandra Montrose,
Lady Colchester,
June 1, 1874

After her most unsettling conversation with Lady Charlotte, the following week was surprisingly tranquil for Cassandra. Warm, cloudy days came and went without a single drop of rain. Sparrows chirped in the treetops against the bright sky, and spring-scented breezes wafted over the damp earth in the gardens.

She spent hours outdoors with her hands in the soft dirt, cleaning away the dead leaves from the previous summer and making room for new growth, while June slept in the pram nearby.

For seven full days Vincent did not make any

arrangements to visit, which made it possible for Cassandra to forget about her conversation with Charlotte and go on as if nothing had changed regarding her association with him. And in all practical matters nothing had.

At the end of that tranquil week, however, he made appointments to visit June on three consecutive days, at 3:00, 4:00, and 5:00 P.M., respectively.

Cassandra decided that she would go for long walks across the estate on each of those days. That is exactly what she did. She did not return until he was gone.

On the following day, however, a palace footman knocked on the door and delivered a note from her benefactor himself, requesting an appointment for the next morning to discuss a contractual matter. Cassandra felt she had no choice but to agree, and sent the footman back to the palace with her reply.

The next day, she waited at the drawing room window, wearing a peach-colored day dress from the collection of gowns Charlotte had brought, watching for his coach and hoping that nothing of a personal or intimate nature would be discussed. She hoped Vincent did not know that Charlotte had come to speak with her. She did not wish to discuss any of the things his sister had confided nor engage in a conversation about the painful troubles of his past. Having worked diligently to push all that from her mind, she did not want to ever cross over the wall that stood between them—the wall that separated light conversation from intimate matters of the heart.

The drawing room door opened and a maid walked in with a vase of fresh tulips, which she set on the table in the center of the room.

Cassandra stopped pacing. "Thank you," she said. "Those are my favorite flowers. They always lift my spirits."

The maid simply nodded without looking up. Cassandra watched her for a few seconds.

"We haven't met," she said, moving closer. "What is your name?"

"Iris, ma'am. I come to the dower house only when I'm needed to clean the grates."

"I see," Cassandra replied with a smile. "*Iris*—that is another beautiful flower." She felt a chill suddenly and rubbed her hands over her arms.

"Shall I light a fire for you, ma'am?"

"Yes, please, Iris. That would be lovely."

A short time after the fire was lit, Vincent's shiny black coach rolled up the lane, precisely on time at 10:00 A.M. sharp. Cassandra went to the window. He stepped out with what appeared to be a ball of fur in his arms.

"What in the world has he brought?" she asked, but when she turned around, she was alone again. Iris had left.

A few minutes later there was a knock on the drawing room door, and Vincent was shown in by the housekeeper.

"I have something for you," he said. Bending down, he set a black and white puppy on the floor.

All Cassandra's anxieties vanished instantly and her heart melted into a puddle of sweet nonsense. She covered her face with both hands and carefully approached the little dog, who plopped down at Vincent's feet and sniffed the floor.

"Oh, good gracious," she cooed, kneeling down to let the puppy sniff her fingers. "What is your name?"

"She has no name yet," Vincent said. "I thought I would leave that to you."

Cassandra patted the puppy's soft, fluffy head, then scooped her up into her arms with a smile. "She's so tiny. What kind is she?"

"She is a rare breed from Cuba called a Havana silk dog. I got her from the Earl of Osborne, who went traveling abroad last year and brought back a number of them to breed. She has a gentle disposition and is bred for children. She doesn't shed."

"You don't say." Cassandra scratched under her floppy ears and turned to cross the room. "And you brought her as a gift?"

He followed her to the piano. "Yes, for both you and June. Every little girl should have a dog, don't you think?"

Cassandra smiled. "Absolutely—and especially one as adorable as this little bundle. Truly, Vincent, it was so kind of you." Joy bubbled up inside of her and a cry of laughter broke from her lips as the puppy began to lick her chin.

"She likes you," Vincent said.

"That's good news, because I certainly adore her."

"You shall accept her, then?"

"Definitely." Entranced and smiling, Cassandra set the puppy on the floor and watched her sniff around the piano legs.

A moment later she met Vincent's gaze for the first time since he'd walked in, and realized with surprise that she had been completely distracted by the little dog and had forgotten to be cool and collected.

"There is something you wanted to discuss?" she prompted, willing herself to focus on matters of business, rather than the length of his eyelashes and the manner in which his thick black hair fell in waves over his shirt collar.

He clasped his hands behind his back. "My fiancée has set a date for our wedding in two months' time, so I must begin looking at suitable properties for you and June. It would be appropriate, I believe, to have you settled comfortably before then."

"And to be gone from the estate, so as not to raise suspicions," she added for him.

He made no reply.

Taking a deep breath, she gestured with a hand for him to take a seat on the sofa. She sat in the chair by the fireplace.

"Is there anywhere in particular you would like to live?" he asked, crossing one long leg over the other. "As you know, we agreed you would be convenient to London."

"That will be fine," she replied, "and I have no preferences, nor do I require much. The most important thing is that we have our privacy. I do not wish to move about in society."

He nodded. "That will not be a problem. Will something similar to this suit you?" He looked about the room.

"Oh, nothing so extravagant. A small country cottage will be much more appropriate, and will require fewer servants. But I would like to have gardens."

"I will keep that in mind when I view the properties. I have arranged to see a few places tomorrow."

"So soon?"

Just then she spotted blood dripping down the back of his hand from under his sleeve. "Good heavens, Vincent, you've cut yourself!"

They both stood up. She crossed to him, while he pulled a handkerchief from his pocket and wiped at the blood on his knuckles, turning briefly to make sure he had not stained the sofa.

"Do not worry about that," she said. "What happened? The dog didn't bite you, did she?"

"No, no. I do apologize. This is from this morning. The bandage must have come loose."

She reached for the lapels of his jacket and helped him shrug out of it, then slid it down over his arms. "What in the world were you doing this morning? Polishing your swords while blindfolded?"

The sleeve of the white shirt he wore beneath the green brocade waistcoat was bloodstained, but baggy enough for her to roll it up to his elbow and look at the wound. There was a bloody bandage wrapped clumsily around his wrist and forearm, which had become unraveled.

Momentarily stalled, her eyes lifted.

Silence loomed between them as he met her intense, questioning gaze, then he frowned and shook his head.

"Good God, woman, it's nothing like that," he explained. "I have no death wish. Quite the opposite, in fact, for I was defending myself—deflecting a china figurine that was launched at my head."

She exhaled a tight breath of relief, followed instantly by disapproval. "I see. It must have been a very exciting morning indeed."

Crossing to the bellpull, she called for a maid, who appeared within the minute. "Bring us water and something to use as a bandage," Cassandra instructed. "Lord Vincent is bleeding."

The maid gasped and fled from the room.

"That one doesn't like the sight of blood," he casually said.

Cassandra glanced at the puppy, who was busy chewing on the corner of the fringed carpet.

She took Vincent by the arm and led him to the polished table in the center of the room, then pulled a Chippendale chair up for him.

"Sit down here," she instructed as she went to fetch a second chair.

She took a seat before him and began to unravel the blood-soaked bandage. Neither of them spoke as she focused on the task. All the while, she was glad he could not read her thoughts, for she was thinking of little else but the way the broad bands of muscle lined his strong arm, and how masculine his big veins were, visible to the eye, so unlike her own. And his hands—those large, manly hands. She remembered how they had moved so lightly and teasingly over her skin a year ago.

The maid returned with a bowl of warm water and a handy box of bandages, which had likely just been torn from someone's petticoat in the kitchen. "Shall we send for the doctor, ma'am?"

Cassandra swept her wayward musings from her mind and examined the wound. It was a deep gash indeed.

Vincent addressed the maid himself. "Thank you, but that will not be necessary. I believe we have everything well in hand. Lady Colchester should be able to tie a better knot than I did."

"You tended to your own wound without assistance?" she asked, looking up.

"It was early. I didn't want to wake anyone."

Cassandra glanced at the maid. "Thank you, that will be all."

The young woman left the room, and Cassandra set about washing the wound and rewrapping his arm.

When the task was complete, she leaned back in her chair. "There. That should suffice."

He examined her handiwork, nodded his approval, then began to roll his bloody sleeve down again. He rose from the chair, scooped the puppy up in his good arm and rubbed the top of her fluffy head as he strolled around the drawing room.

"Did she find out about me?" Cassandra asked. "Is that why she was angry?"

Vincent paused and looked at her, bewildered. "Who? Letitia?"

"Who else would I be talking about?" Cassandra replied. "Unless it was some other woman who used a knickknack to brain you. I suppose I didn't think of that."

"It wasn't a woman," he said. "It was my father, and may I inform you, that so-called 'knickknack' was a weapon of the highest order—a very heavy statuette with a sharp point like a spear."

"Your father?" She stood and returned the chairs back in their proper places. "Why would he do that? Did *he* find out about me?"

Vincent chuckled. "The whole world doesn't always revolve around your scandalous life, Cassandra Montrose. People have problems of their own, you know."

She swallowed over her embarrassment. "Of course. I just assumed . . . "

He said nothing more. He merely strolled around the room with the puppy in his arms, scratching behind her ears.

"What happened?" Cassandra asked, unable to curb her curiosity. "Why did he do it?"

"It was a simple misunderstanding," Vincent explained. "We encountered each other in the gallery at dawn, and he thought I was a ghost."

"A ghost?"

"Yes, he believed I was a monk of the old abbey coming to murder him while the rest of the household was asleep."

"What old abbey?"

He faced her. "Have you not heard the history of the palace and the stories of our ancestry?"

"No, I regret to say I have not."

"It's built on the ruins of an ancient abbey where a prior was murdered by two of his own canons, who discovered he had a secret mistress."

Well, there, she thought. It appeared mistresses ran in the family. "How dreadful."

"Yes, disgraceful business, my family's history, and I know exactly what you're thinking." He looked at her shrewdly. "You're thinking we have far too many mistresses in our past."

She frowned at him. "What happened afterward? How did the abbey become Pembroke Palace?"

"After the prior's death, his mistress bore his child—a son—and then you can refer to the English history books for this portion of the story. King Henry dissolved the monasteries, including this one, but the prior's illegitimate son nevertheless grew up to become a trusted friend of the king. He later became the first Duke of Pembroke, and built this palace as homage to his dead father and mother. The truth was only discovered after his death, when he revealed everything in his will."

"I had no idea."

"No? I've always thought it was one of the things that gave our family a certain air of excitement and mystery. The locals and servants continue to tell stories of how the palace is haunted, which is probably what has my father behaving so strangely in his old age. He is sixty-nine now, and has become very aware of his mortality."

"Hence the self-protective measure with the china figurine."

"It was a blue sheep—a tawdry affair which my grandmother adored. It was the shepherd's hook that cut me when he hurled it."

Cassandra couldn't help herself. She put a hand to her mouth to stifle a laugh. "You're lucky he didn't put your eye out."

"It amuses you, does it?"

"Forgive me. It's all just so . . . bizarre."

"You've found the perfect word to describe the comings and goings at the palace these days. Sometime I'll tell you the rest of our trials and tribulations, but not today. I must be going."

He handed the puppy to her, and she escorted him downstairs to the door. The butler brought his hat and coat.

"Have you thought of what you will name her?" he asked, patting the puppy in her arms.

Cassandra considered it a moment. "I think she looks like a Molly."

"Indeed she does. Well, good day, Molly." He leaned down and lifted her floppy ear to whisper into it. "If you can help it, try not to wet on the Persian carpets after I go."

Cassandra laughed. "I promise I shall have her trained in no time."

He touched the brim of his hat and turned to leave, but paused briefly. "You look very nice today, by the way. That color suits you."

"Thank you."

She followed him out onto the front step, realizing it had been a visit entirely free of both his customary animosity and his frivolous flirting—with the exception of that one compliment just now, but she was quite certain he was merely being polite.

Imagine that. Vincent Sinclair, saying something courteous.

He walked down the steps to his coach.

"I am hoping for sunshine tomorrow!" she called out, just before he stepped inside.

He stopped and turned, then, to her surprise, came leaping back up the stairs, taking two at a time to the top to reach her. "Would you like to come with me to see the properties?" he asked, slightly out of breath. "It will be a few hours by coach. I expect to be back at the palace by nightfall."

She could not mask her surprise. "You would not prefer to choose it on your own?"

"It will be your house. You should take part in the selection."

She could not deny that she would greatly enjoy choosing her new home. And yet . . .

"I am not sure it would be wise."

"Why not? Are you afraid of being alone with me?"

She shifted the puppy in her arms. "No."

"Then what causes you to hesitate?"

"Well, I . . ." She couldn't seem to come up with an answer.

"For God's sake, Cassandra, just say the word yes and I will pick you up at eight."

She looked away toward the horizon. Molly squirmed and licked her chin.

"All right," she replied at last, admitting to herself with more than a little chagrin that she wanted very much to accompany him, even if they spoke not one single word to each other all day. "I shall join you. I would like to see the properties you are considering, and it will do me good to get away."

"And me as well." He ran back down the steps to his waiting coach, opened the door, but called out one last thing. "Do not fret if the puppy cries tonight. She will be lonely for her mother. You might want to keep her close to you. Will you do that for me?"

"I shall." Cassandra kissed the top of Molly's soft head.

"Then I will see you in the morning." With that, he climbed into his coach and drove off.

Cassandra looked down at Molly and scratched behind her soft fluffy ears. "Did you hear that? The gentleman is worried you will be lonely tonight. He wants me to take good care of you."

As she turned to go inside, she remembered Charlotte's tale about the fawn, and could not deny that her heart softened just a little.

Chapter 12

I pray that he will never touch me. I live in constant fear of what will happen if he does.

—from the journal of
Cassandra Montrose,
Lady Colchester,
June 5, 1874

The next day splashed onto the horizon like a wave upon rocks, splattering the morning sky with a dazzling pink sunrise. The thick cover of clouds that hung heavy over England for weeks had moved on, clearing the way at last for the sun's radiant heat and the brilliance of a bright blue sky. There was hope now for the disastrous flooded fields and the muddy palace roads.

By the time Vincent arrived at the dower house to pick Cassandra up in the coach, she was ready and waiting at the door, wearing a blue and white striped traveling gown of light muslin. It belonged to Charlotte and was the perfect dress for springtime weather.

Vincent complimented her on her appearance and assisted her into the comfortable vehicle, and together they drove off, crossing over the estate border, speaking very little to each other as they headed east in the direction of London.

The journey was long, but for Cassandra it was not the least bit tedious. How could it be, when the sunshine outside the window was shining in on her lap, warming her legs and brightening her mood? She did not mind the rocking and jostling over the uneven, rutted roads either, for her mind was occupied by the glorious view of the English countryside beyond the glass, and her private thoughts of June.

She imagined her new life with her daughter in a new home, surrounded by flowers and grass and birds chirping in the treetops. There would be so much for a little girl to discover, with her puppy as a playmate. It would be a good life—a proper, respectable one, as long as she could keep her wits about her where her benefactor was concerned.

Cassandra glanced across at Vincent and took in his overall appearance. He was immaculately dressed in black trousers and a three-quarter-length coat, a dark crimson brocade waistcoat and necktie, and a silk top hat.

He met her gaze and nodded coolly, then looked

out the window again. For the rest of the journey, his lack of attention and the silence between them helped free her of any doubts she had entertained about spending this long, intensive day alone with him. His ignoring her was a blessing. It kept the wall between them solidly in place, which was what she wanted.

Eventually they turned off the main road to view a property near Newbury, which was available for purchase. They pulled to a stop in front of it.

The minute Cassandra stepped out of the coach, however, and took one look at it—a thatched cottage close to the road and adjacent to a churchyard cemetery—she knew it was not at all to her liking.

Vincent stood beside her in the sunshine just outside the coach, holding her gloved hand at shoulder height, staring at the front of the cottage. "I don't like it," he said.

She let out a breath. "That's a relief. Neither do I. But you have the key. Should we take a look inside just the same?"

"I don't see why we should waste our time, unless you think you might change your mind."

She considered the possibility for a moment, then shook her head. "No, I don't think so, not when we have other places to see. Perhaps we will like them better."

"We shall hope."

With that he handed her back up into the coach and they set off again.

"A place near a lake would be nice," he commented as they rumbled past the small stone church.

"Yes. I could teach June to swim."

"And I could teach her to fish."

She lifted an eyebrow. "Do you really believe that is a proper accomplishment for a young lady?"

He gazed across at her with resolve. "It will be for *my* daughter."

Amused by his unusual paternal ideas, she chuckled to herself.

They passed the church and drove for miles down a narrow, winding lane, across green hills dotted with white sheep, through sections of wooded farmland until they came to the next property.

It was a large farmhouse built of gray stone, with small windows and a heavy slate roof that sank like a hammock under its own weight. The barn was snug to the house, and Cassandra was sure she would be able to smell the pigs from her bedroom window.

"I don't even think we need to get out," Vincent said as he opened the door and looked at the craggy, weather-beaten house.

"I quite agree. Would it be acceptable to move on?"

He tapped the roof with his walking stick. "Next property please, Jenson."

The coach lurched forward again, and they were soon rolling along the open, English countryside.

"How many other properties are there to consider today?" Cassandra asked, feeling somewhat discouraged as she folded her gloved hands on her lap.

"I regret to say only one."

"And if it is not suitable?"

His voice was reassuring. "Then we shall head home and try again another day. There is no need to rush into anything. There will be other properties."

Relieved, she settled back in the seat and retreated into her private thoughts again, thinking of Molly and June and how lovely the dower house was compared to the properties they had just seen. She did not want to be difficult to please, but perhaps they might need to consider a different price range.

A short time later they came to a stone carriage house and wrought-iron gate, which required them to stop so the driver could step down and push the gate open.

"This looks more promising," Vincent said,

leaning forward to admire the wooded acreage as they crossed onto the property.

They traveled up a long, shady, tree-lined drive to an exquisite manor house built of brick and surrounded by overgrown rose gardens, not yet in bloom. A wide lawn stretched down to a private lake with a boathouse and dock—just as they had spoken about on the way there. The coach pulled to a halt in front of a flagstone walkway, which led up to the house.

"This is Langley Hall," Vincent informed her, as if sensing her interest in the origins of the house. "It was built in 1792 by a French military officer."

"You left it for last intentionally, didn't you?"

He smiled, and it filled her with excitement, which was very much in contrast to the proper, respectable rapport they had been maintaining all day.

"I cannot tell a lie," he answered.

She was forced to wrestle with the disarming effect of his masculine appeal, while he assisted her out of the coach and up the steps to the front door, nestled under a high, arched portico. The door was open for them, and they entered without knocking.

"There is no one here," he told her. "The house has been empty for a year, and the solicitor in charge of it is at the pub down the road, awaiting our arrival."

"Is he that confident we will want to purchase it?"

He shrugged casually, and she looked away from his darkly handsome features, which were all the more striking now that they were on their feet, wandering together through an empty mansion, just the two of them.

Their footsteps echoed off the high ceiling as they circled the main hall and looked up. "It's very spacious," Cassandra said. "Certainly bigger than I require."

"It is about the same size as the dower house."

"It has a similar charm."

They toured all the rooms—the cozy parlors, kitchen, bedrooms, dining room, and servants' quarters, concluding their tour in the library. Wainscoted in panels of oak, it boasted a floor-to-ceiling bookcase filled with volumes of books, which the previous owner had left behind.

"What do you think?" Vincent asked, randomly choosing a book and pulling it out from the collection. He blew a cloud of dust from it before he let it fall open upon his hand and flipped through the pages.

Cassandra took in a deep breath and let it out. "I think it is perfect, though it is more than I ever dreamed, and I shall feel very indebted to you."

His dark eyes lifted, revealing an animal gaze

of tempting sensuality. "We can't have that, now, can we?"

His deep voice seemed to touch her from clear across the room, causing a tingling sensation to settle in the pit of her stomach.

"How far is it from London?" she asked, quickly turning away from him to prevent any further sparks of excitement, and to keep the conversation from heading into dangerous territory.

"About two hours by coach."

"You would be agreeable to that?"

"Undeniably so." She could feel the heavy intensity of his gaze following her around the room. "I am already salivating over the idea of escaping to a quiet country setting on those days when I can no longer endure the dismal London fog and the mind-numbing society balls. Let us not even mention the monotony of my club."

"I always thought a gentleman's club was his prized haven."

"Perhaps for some gentlemen it is, and perhaps it will be for me as well, once I am married." He slammed the book shut with a poof of dust and slid it back into place on the shelf.

"Do you really think your marriage will be that bad?"

"I have no doubt."

She continued to stroll around the room, tilting her head to the side to read the titles of all the books. "Then why did you ever propose to her, Vincent?"

"You've asked me that question before," he replied, moving along the bookshelves, running his fingertip across the spines, "and my answer is still the same. I had to marry someone to satisfy Father and keep my inheritance. Besides, she is the perfect woman for me. She is beautiful and does not fancy herself in love with me. What more can a heartless rake such as myself ask for?"

She glanced at him briefly with reproach, but felt a strange touch of understanding emerge between them—as if they were both accepting these roles they had fallen into and were now expected to play. She was the fallen lady determined to behave properly; he was the wicked rake who expected to be reprimanded for his shocking behavior.

But then he began to elaborate.

"I suppose, if you must know, there is something more to the story."

"There is?"

"Yes—a reason why I must handle this betrothal with a certain degree of care."

"What is the reason?"

After a moment's hesitation, he turned away from her and began to pace about the room. "I have already told you how my father has been behaving oddly lately—becoming aware of his mortality, throwing dangerous knickknacks at people . . . Well, that is because he is going mad and believes the palace is under a curse."

"A curse."

He nodded broodingly at her. "He believes Pembroke will be swept away by a flood if all four of his sons do not marry according to his plan."

Straightaway, she lost any lingering interest in the books. "Why did you not tell me this before?"

"It is a family secret. Although Letitia has discovered some of it and understands that Father believes she is the cure to this putrid English weather—with the exception of today, of course."

"How?"

"She has a birthmark on her left hand which he thinks looks like the sun, and she happens to hold an uncanny resemblance to the first Duchess of Pembroke."

"I see."

"The point is," he said, "the very day she arrived, the rain stopped and the sun came out, and it has been fine weather ever since. I never thought I would say it after the wettest spring this century, but I wish the sky would bloody well open up and pour buckets."

She took in a breath. "So that is why he has his heart set on her, and why you do not feel you can disappoint him."

For the first time, she saw a trace of disquiet in his eyes, as if he *did* care what his future held.

"There have been moments I've been tempted to pick up a loaded pistol and blow my bloody brains out."

"Oh, Vincent . . . " She took a step toward him.

As quick as a flash, he held up a hand and gave her a firm look. *Stay back,* it warned. "If it weren't for the fact that all three of my brothers are depending on me to do my part—and betraying a brother is not an option—I assure you I would be choosing my own future, with or without my inheritance." His eyes turned cold. "I would *not* be getting married."

She watched him for a moment and understood his implicit message—that he did not want her to pry too deeply into his emotions. So, instead, she turned and feigned interest in the book titles again.

"Do you think all marriages are hopeless?" she asked after a short time, speaking lightly in generalities.

"Most of them among our set, yes," he replied. "We do not marry for love. You know that. We marry for duty and position—or in my case, a loyalty to my brothers."

She faced him. "But weren't you going to marry for love once yourself?"

She had not intended to venture into intimate

matters of the heart, but suddenly it was too late. The words were out.

It was at that moment, however, she realized how desperately she wanted to hear him speak about it.

His expression darkened. He moved to the desk and sat on top of it, leaning forward on the heels of his hands. "It appears that when Charlotte delivered the gowns to you last week, she delivered also a juicy account of my tragic past."

"Do not blame her," Cassandra said. "I pried."

"*Did* you?" She could see he found that hard to swallow.

"She told me about MaryAnn," she explained, bringing the conversation back around to the original point. "I was sorry to hear of it."

"I appreciate your condolences."

"Is that why you wanted a written contract with me?" she asked. "Because you were betrayed once before? You believe you cannot trust me?"

He lifted his strong chin and breathed in deeply through his nose. "I did not make that conscious connection, though I suppose I have learned to be careful in whom I choose to trust, especially when the person in question is a woman."

She took a few steps closer. "I hope you know that I am not like other women, Vincent, and that you can trust me. Contrary to what you must think of me after that night we spent together a year ago, I am not a careless or wanton woman." She paused. "I am very loyal and I feel things deeply. That woman who slept with you so casually in that hotel room . . . that was not really me."

He squinted at her, studying her eyes with interest.

She struggled to explain herself better.

"Just so you know," she said, "I intend to live a respectable life with our daughter. There shall be nothing casual or careless about it. I shall never take a lover and I am deeply devoted to this new life you are giving to the both of us. I assure you that I will not run off at the first whiff of excitement. There will never be anything like that, I promise you."

"Yet you warned me not long ago," he said, "that you might someday wish to marry. Believe me, I've known far too many women who start off with grand ideals, then get bored with their lot and take a lover behind their husband's back. I know because I am usually playing the part of the lover."

She squeezed her reticule in front of her. "First of all, you are not my husband, so there is no issue of me being unfaithful to you. And second . . . " She spoke with passion. "Do not compare me to those women who betray their husbands. I told you I am not like that, and if I *was* your wife or even your fiancée, I would never even consider being unfaithful to you. I am one of those rare people who believes in the sanctity of marriage. And love."

He hopped down from the desk and strode slowly toward her, tilting his head curiously to the side. "But what if you were not my wife or my fiancée, but merely my mistress? Would I be able to trust you to be faithful to me then?"

She was growing uncomfortable with the direction the conversation was taking. "A mistress is generally considered to be a temporary alliance. There is no binding vow of fidelity."

"But what if," he said, strolling even closer, "your lover was not free to marry you. Do you not believe you could have true fidelity of the heart, without the marriage contract? It is only a piece of paper, after all, usually entered into for the sake of duty."

"You of all people are suggesting it is possible to have lifelong fidelity of the heart? That sounds a lot like love to me, Vincent, and may I remind you that *you* are the one who is suspicious and mistrusting of love. Not me. And you are the one who wanted a legal binding contract between us."

He stopped before her, only inches away. "Keep in mind that when I suggested a legal contract, we were not entering into an affair of the heart. You even went so far as to say you hated me, hence I required the contract."

"I do not hate you," she told him in a calmer, gentler voice.

"I am glad to hear it. I don't hate you either."

She tried to moisten her lips, but her mouth had gone dry. "Just for the sake of argument," she said, "if it *had* been an affair of the heart, and I had told you I loved you, would you still have wanted the contract? Would you have trusted me to be faithful and steadfast?"

He considered it, his stare bold and assessing.

"No," he said finally. "I still would have wanted it."

She squared her shoulders, wondering suddenly why she was so eager to debate the subject of fidelity with him, when she was already well aware of his opinions on the matter.

She supposed Charlotte's account of his past and her unremitting belief in his character had cast a shadow of doubt over her own assessment of his values and principles.

Vincent was still standing very close, looking down at her face. "Do you think you would ever change your mind?" he quietly asked.

"About what?"

His gaze was riveted on her eyes, then it moved down the length of her body. "About becoming my mistress. We are, after all, bound to each other forever by a legal contract, and also through a child we have created together. Why not seek some pleasure out of the partnership? And I guarantee there *would* be pleasure, Cassandra—a tremendous amount of it, in fact. You know that as well as I do."

Suddenly, her breathing was out of control and her heart was in a frenzy. She backed away from him. "You promised you would not require that of me. You agreed to it in writing and signed your name with witnesses."

"I am not *requiring* it," he said. "I am merely offering my services to you, if you should decide at any time that you would enjoy them."

"Your services?"

"Yes, I would satisfy all your desires. You could call on me, day or night, to relieve the heated tensions of your womanly urges. And I know you have them, Cassandra, even when you are trying very hard to convince yourself you do not. This business of *never* taking a lover . . . " He shook his head at the notion. "You would be miserable."

She felt a swirling jumble of both anger and excitement deep inside. One minute she was beginning to believe what Charlotte had said—that he was a caring and constant man, merely caught in a difficult predicament because of his father. But then he said something like this, and all she could see was the wild, sexual rake. "You promised, Vincent."

"Yes, I did, but on the day I agreed to your very proper and unimaginative contractual terms, I was not feeling particularly adventurous. I had just brought a fiancée home and learned I had sired an illegitimate child. Hence I crushed the memory of how dazzling you were to me that night a year ago—so dazzling, in fact, that I could not even control my orgasm."

"*Which* orgasm?" she angrily asked. "There were quite a few, if I recall."

He ran the back of a finger along her cheek. "Yes, there were a number of very remarkable ones that I would not mind repeating."

Her chest was heaving from the effect of his touch. Her legs felt heavy and warm, and she knew if she did not soon regain control of herself, she might very well end up in his arms.

She hated that she was so weak when it came to her desires. She simply could not conquer them.

"I would be carrying another child of yours within the space of a week," she argued, trying to focus on the more practical and dangerous implications of such an arrangement.

"Yes, you probably would." He thought about it for a moment, then ran the tip of his finger across the soft line of her jaw. "But what would it matter? We are legally bound to each other for life. Remember? You could fill this entire house with children if you wanted to. You could give

June brothers and sisters to play with, and I could enjoy a lifetime filled with phenomenal orgasms."

Good God! She laughed out loud with shock. "I believe you've gone mad!"

His voice was humorless. "Maybe it runs in the family."

He cupped her head in his hand and pulled her to him. His mouth covered hers in a hard, deep, demanding kiss that made her go weak at the knees.

Cassandra let out a tiny whimper of surprise. God help her, the taste of his lips lit her on fire. He deepened the kiss, devoured her with his mouth, and she reveled in the delicious sensation of his tongue mingling hotly with hers. His lips were soft and full and wet. He tasted better than wine. He was so much of a man and knew just how to fire her passions.

Suddenly all she wanted was to feel that wild insanity again, to drop to her knees right here and pull this man down to the floor—to feel the weight of his body, heavy upon hers. She wanted to slide her hands up under his clothes and wrap her legs around his hips.

Moaning with hunger, he backed her up against the bookshelves. His hands roamed over her body as he kissed and tongued her neck. He was aggressive and strong, his body thrusting. And her pulse was pounding with desire, even when she knew it was wrong. It was *so* very wrong. It was not what she wanted.

"No, Vincent," she said breathlessly, struggling to bring her desires under control. "We have to stop . . . "

She could not let herself surrender to this. She could not let him do this to her!

He took her face in both his hands and looked into her eyes. "Not yet," he ground out, then pressed his lips to hers again and kissed her with stormy impatience.

His hand slid down over her hip and gathered her skirts in a fist. She could feel them lifting . . .

Her body was exploding with white-hot, sizzling excitement, but she forced herself to push him back with all her might. She wiped her mouth with the back of her hand.

"What is wrong with you?" she demanded. "We had an agreement!"

His eyes burned with desire and frustration. Clearly he was not pleased to have had his passions so quickly curtailed. "You of all people should know I cannot be trusted."

"Yes, I certainly do know it. I am even more clear on the point now!"

Taking a step closer, he sneered devilishly at her. "You can't deny that you want this, Cassandra. I felt it in your body just now. You remember how amazing it was that night, and you want it again. Admit it."

She backed away from him along the bookcases, impelled by a torrential flood of fury. "You're going to have to learn to enjoy your orgasms with your *wife*, Lord Vincent, because I will not become your mistress."

"Why not? What stops you? You've already given up your position in society and do not plan to reclaim it. Your identity and the circumstances of your life will be a secret. You can be free to do what you wish and simply enjoy yourself."

"So you believe that makes it all well and good? As long as no one knows about my adulterous life, it will not be unseemly? It will not really exist?" She pointed at her heart. "*I* would know, Vincent, and I would have to live with my dishonor, not to mention the fact that I would be sharing you with another woman. I've already done that once before in my own marriage, and I assure you I did not enjoy it."

He said nothing. He simply stood there in the center of the room, staring at her with concern.

She was unable to stop her tirade. "On top of that," she continued, "I would not only be sharing you with your wife, but all your other transient lovers as well. You seem to forget that I know what kind of man you are. You enjoy women too much, and that is not the life I want. It would break my heart." She turned her back on him. "I cannot believe I am even discussing this with you."

She walked out of the library and left the house through the back door, which led to a path across the lawn, down to the lake. She forged it at a brisk pace, her skirts whipping between her legs with every rapid, agitated stride.

How could she have imagined this would be possible? God help her, it was as if this man had been dropped into her life intentionally, for the purpose of testing her resolve to be sensible.

He was no gentle foe. He had the power to make her forget everything she believed was right. She had just let him arouse her passions, for pity's sake! The kiss had been absolutely intoxicating.

The path came to an end, and she stopped on the wide lawn, acutely aware of her surroundings all of a sudden—the sheer beauty of the house and garden and the lake at the bottom of the hill. She looked up at the blue sky, breathed in the scent of spring lilacs, heard a mockingbird singing somewhere in the distance.

Was this beautiful house and property all part of the larger temptation that was Vincent and everything he offered? Was it part of the test? Could she be bought?

"Cassandra!"

She jumped when she heard him call her name.

Turning, she saw him walk with purpose down the gravel path toward her, hat in hand. When he reached the end of the path and stepped onto the grass, he was out of breath. She braced herself for whatever depravity was about to come pouring out of his mouth next.

"I apologize for what just happened," he said, knocking her completely off balance yet again with words she had not expected. "I did make a promise to you. I gave you my word that I would not ask you for anything more than a chance to spend time with June. I should not have said those things in the library. I shouldn't have kissed you. I am a devil and a rake. I know I am, but the strange thing is—it has never bothered me before now." He paused, turning his hat over in his hands and looking down at it. "I am beginning to wonder if you were placed into my life for some clear purpose, to give me a chance to behave honorably for once—as honorably as a man can behave with a former lover who has born him an illegitimate child."

She had no idea what to say. All she could do was stand there in the hot, bright sunshine, looking down at the ground, realizing that his thoughts about being tested mirrored her own.

"I know I do not deserve it," he said, "but can you forgive me?"

She looked up hesitantly. "I don't know, Vincent. You say and do the most wicked things sometimes."

For a long moment he was quiet, and then, when he spoke, his voice was resigned. "I shall offer no excuses, because even when I recognize how you value your honor, I still let you bring out the devil in me. I am learning that lust is a very powerful thing."

"But you are no stranger to it."

"You are wrong there, Cassandra. I am a stranger to what exists between us. It is the reason I did not read your letter a year ago, and why I avoided you—so that I would not run the risk of falling in love with you."

She was speechless.

He wiped the back of his hand across the sparkling perspiration on his forehead and squinted down at the lake. "All I know is that there was an extraordinary spark between us from the beginning. Don't you remember how it was that night?"

"Of course I do," she confessed. "It made me insane—not just that night, but in the weeks following, when you would not see me."

"I was a cad."

"Yes, you were."

He sighed. "I must ask you again, Cassandra, can you forgive me? You are the mother of my child. I cannot bear for you to think me hopeless. I do not want to *be* hopeless."

The breeze blew gently at the ribbons on her hat. She could not believe he had just said all these things to her. She'd convinced herself she had imagined the gentler side of him from that night a year ago, and that he did not care what anyone thought of him. She was wrong. It appeared he did care for something.

"A lot has happened since that night," she said. "Our lives have changed and fate has placed us in a difficult predicament. You are engaged to another woman, you do not wish to let your brothers down, and I quite frankly do not wish to allow myself to believe that I could ever trust you. I would prefer to remain on guard."

"Cassandra . . . "

"We have each made our mistakes and now must live with the consequences. As for myself, I would like to do so without any further transgressions."

"I should resent you," he said.

"Why?"

"Because you make me want to be a better man, when it is so much easier not to care one way or another."

They started walking slowly down to the lake, glancing tentatively at each other while taking in the beauty of the surrounding vista.

After a time, Cassandra slipped her arm through his and gave him a tiny, cautious smile. "Perhaps there can be some hope for this arrangement," she said, feeling her animosity toward him begin to soften. "But please, do not say those wicked things to me again, Vincent. Or do not kiss me again, because I cannot bear it. Truly, I cannot. If you do, I will have to make sure we do not see each other—because you are right. The spark is still there and I find you difficult to resist . . . There, are you happy now? I have confessed it."

"I wouldn't call it happy," he replied as he placed his hand upon hers to lead the way down to the water. "But I have learned not to hope for happiness. It is inevitable that one will end up disappointed."

Chapter 13

I sometimes wonder what is more powerful—the burning intensity of lust, or a quieter affection that blooms slowly over time. I certainly know which of the two is more meaningful, but meaning is not always what guides us through life. Sometimes we are victims of our impulses.

—from the journal of
Cassandra Montrose,
Lady Colchester,
June 23, 1874

Three days later Vincent made good on his commitment to Cassandra and June with the purchase of Langley Hall and all the surrounding acreage. The deal would be closed the day after his wedding, when he'd receive five thousand pounds from his father just for saying "I do."

Over the next two weeks, he traveled to and

from London to take care of various details regarding the purchase of the house—such as the acquisition of furniture and the hiring of servants. His mother, his fiancée, and the Duchess of Swinburne also traveled to London to make purchases for the wedding, which gave him the freedom to visit his daughter as often as he pleased.

More often than not he found June in the pram in the gardens, sleeping soundly beneath an organza cover, while Cassandra pulled weeds from the earth or planted new seeds. Sometimes he found his daughter lying on her belly on a quilt under the oak tree, while Cassandra sat beside her with an open book in her hands.

Through it all, he was perhaps most pleased to discover that she chose not to disappear when his coach pulled up in front of the house at the prearranged time. Rather, she would take June into her arms and greet him on the steps—always eager to place her into his outstretched hands.

Over those busy few weeks, he also discovered that he could be an affectionate, doting father, and even a gentleman, too—and that it was not quite as difficult as he'd imagined it would be. He was surprisingly capable of resisting his attraction to Cassandra, and when he contemplated the reasons why, he understood that it was more than a mere matter of being in breach of their contract. The truth of the matter was—he did not want to lose what was becoming a comfortable friendship.

So they spent many hours together in a congenial, companionable manner, strolling down to the river or through the Pembroke forests with the puppy, the core focus of their conversations always one safe thing—little June.

After two weeks of perfectly respectable contractual visits—during which neither Cassandra nor Vincent so much as mentioned their passionate kiss at Langley Hall—Cassandra managed to convince herself that everything was going to work out. She even began to accept the fact that she enjoyed Vincent's company. She allowed herself to look forward to his visits, because despite their turbulent past, he was the one person in the world who understood and shared her infatuation with her baby. He, too, was enamored and delighted with every little gurgle and burp, every cry, every dazzling, delightful smile.

As for the kiss, she forced herself to forget about it. She put it out of her mind completely, pretended it never happened.

And so, on those slow, lazy days of early summer when the air was humid and heavy with the fragrance of lilacs and roses, she and Vincent took great pleasure in watching June sleep on the blanket, which they spread out on the grass in a shady grove of sycamores beyond the garden farthest from the house. That particular spot soon became their customary destination at the same time each afternoon when June was ready for her nap.

"Tell me about your marriage," Vincent said one warm afternoon, while June slept and Molly bounced about nearby, chasing butterflies. "How did you meet your husband?"

Cassandra stretched out on her back in the sun, shaded her eyes with a hand and crossed her legs at the ankles. "It was all arranged by my parents, and I was simply presented to him at a dinner party. He was looking for someone young who could provide him with children. It all happened very quickly, and I was rather swept away. He was twelve years older than I, and I imagined him to be very dashing and charming. I truly believed I was in love."

"Only believed?"

"It wasn't long after we were married that I discovered he was in love with another woman—a woman he had known when he was a young man but had not been free to marry because she was already someone else's wife. They had not seen each other for many years, and it was shortly after he married me that they met again and became involved with each other. She was a widow by then and was free to enjoy my husband's attentions. I am quite certain their affair would still be going on today if he were still alive."

She paused a moment, watching a blackbird soar high above in the clear blue sky. "It was devastating and humiliating to me, because when I married him, I truly wanted it to be perfect. I wanted a happy, successful marriage, but I understand now that he only ever wanted her. She was the great love of his life."

Vincent sat up and rested his arm on a knee. "Sometimes I wonder if there are people in the world who are simply meant to be together, people who are connected to each other somehow. Even if they go away and are forgotten for years and years, they are never really gone, and if they reappear, which in all likelihood they will—"

"The connection is still there," Cassandra finished for him, "as strong as ever, as if not a day has passed."

She was surprised to hear him speak this way.

He plucked a blade of grass and wrapped it around his finger. "And what does one do if that person is forbidden?" He gazed directly at her. "As this woman was with your husband?"

"Perhaps that is what makes it so intense," Cassandra answered. "That person becomes the forbidden fruit." She sat back. "It might also have the allure of unfinished business. Perhaps in some cases all it requires is fulfillment, and then it can become like every other infatuation that eventually burns itself out."

"Maybe so." He tossed the blade away. "Or maybe it is more than that. Maybe some connections never burn out."

Cassandra could feel her guard lowering. She sat up and waved a moth away from June's face, adjusted the blanket, which covered her legs, then lay back down again.

Vincent's voice was low. "You are a very principled person, Cassandra," he said, "refusing to be my mistress when there is 'unfinished business' between us."

She sat up again. "I believe the only thing that was unfinished between us was the sex. You left without saying goodbye, and I, for one, was still amorous. *At the time*."

"As was I." He spoke more pointedly. "Do you think it is possible to separate sexual desire from friendship between a man and a woman?"

She gazed into his dark eyes. "I believe it is worth a try," she said, more than a little surprised by this calm and honest communication between them, "because I am discovering that I would not wish to give up the friendship that has been growing between us."

Friendship. It was a difficult concept to fathom where he was concerned.

She leaned up on an elbow. "I don't want to

spoil it, Vincent. It has been very pleasant these past few weeks."

"Yes," he agreed, with a melancholy smile. "It has."

"Was MaryAnn the great love of *your* life?" Cassandra asked the following day, as they pushed the pram through the quiet, shady woods, where there was not even the slightest hint of a breeze.

Vincent removed his hat and carried it in his hands, looking down at it as he spoke. "I believed so at the time. I was ready to be a husband, after all, and never imagined I would not love her devotedly until the day I died. But knowing what I know now, I recognize that I was a pathetic, lovesick fool. Not only that, it was completely one-sided. We did not share a true bond, because she had never revealed her heart to me. She kept things secret and revealed them only to Devon. And because she died so suddenly, I didn't get the chance to ask her why . . . to try to understand."

"Did your brother love her?"

Vincent paused. "I don't know."

"Have you ever asked him?"

He looked down at the soft ground as he walked. "On the day she died, I asked him whether or not they had been . . . " He seemed to be searching for the right word. " . . . if they had been lovers. He confessed that they were on that day. I was too angry to ask for details and I suppose I didn't really want to hear them. Now, we do not make a habit of discussing it. We don't discuss much of anything. He knows I still have the letter she wrote to him, which I found in her pocket. I suppose it will always be a reminder of how he betrayed me that day."

She looked up at him. "Will you ever forgive him?"

He stopped on the path. "Do you think I should?"

June began to cry in the pram, and they both bent forward to see what was wrong. Cassandra picked her up and bounced her gently up and down until she stopped fussing. "There, there, now."

Vincent adjusted his daughter's baby bonnet and touched her tiny nose with the tip of his finger.

"He is still your brother," Cassandra said, not forgetting their conversation. "And you and I both know that everyone makes mistakes."

Vincent glanced meaningfully at her. "Spoken with great perspective, I dare say."

Cassandra placed June back in the pram.

"I have grown rather weary of my bitterness lately," he admitted. "I suppose I have you and June to thank for that. You have given me something to focus on other than my feud with my brother and my ever present sense of impending doom around my future marriage." He made a face.

Cassandra chuckled softly.

Turning toward a bridle path that veered away from the one they were standing on, Vincent pointed. "Just over there is where MaryAnn died."

Cassandra studied his face in the dappled sunlight shining down on them through the leaves. "Have you ever gone back there?"

"Not since that day."

She turned the pram around and nodded. "Shall we go home?"

"Yes."

"Are you hungry?"

"Famished."

"Then I will send for a light lunch. We can enjoy it in the garden."

Two days later Cassandra was in the nursery with June and Molly, waiting for Vincent to arrive, noting with some impatience that he was late. So late, in fact, that she had to put June down for her nap in her cradle and give up the idea that they would take her for her usual walk.

As soon as June was asleep, the puppy followed Cassandra downstairs to the drawing room, where she rang for tea, paced around the room restlessly, then finally sat down and picked up a book. She could not concentrate on what she was reading, however, for she was on edge, looking up whenever she heard a noise outside, her heart skipping a beat when she thought a carriage was rolling up the drive.

Was he not coming today? she wondered anxiously. He had said nothing yesterday about canceling his visit.

She slammed the book shut and cupped her forehead in her palm. Oh, Lord. Her stomach was turning somersaults. Was this getting out of hand? She supposed it was and that it was pointless to deny it any longer. She was becoming infatuated with him—*infatuated*—despite all her efforts to defend herself against such feelings toward a man who was engaged to another woman. And how ironic that it had not been her lust that knocked the shield from her grip, when that was what she'd feared most of all in the beginning.

It had been their friendship—the very thing she'd pushed for in order to avoid a more dangerous kind of intimacy.

Now it appeared she was coming to care for him on a much deeper level. When she thought of Vincent, she pictured him holding June with affection, being a considerate, loving father, the complete opposite of her own. She remembered their comfortable conversations and how well he understood all her thoughts and opinions.

Those were the moments when her heart felt

most happy. Even now she was imagining his warm and wonderful smile, the smile he gave to her when he first said hello each day.

He had been so good to her, a gentleman through and through over these past few weeks. She had never believed it could be possible.

Just then, from the open window, she heard the familiar sound of his horse trotting up the drive. Her heart began to hammer inside her chest. Molly barked and ran to the door, while Cassandra tipped her head back on the chair and sighed with both happiness and defeat.

A short time later Vincent walked into the drawing room. He looked handsome and powerful and completely mesmerizing. Molly wagged her tail, and Cassandra's heart flipped over again, just from the mere sight of him.

Feeling greatly distressed, she stood.

"I am so sorry," he said, out of breath. "Is June asleep now?"

"Yes. I took her to the nursery some time ago."

His shoulders rose and fell with a sigh of disappointment. "I tried to get here, but Father had an episode." He bent down and patted little Molly, who was desperate for his attention.

"What kind of episode?"

"We finally received word from my youngest brother, Garrett, who remains in the Mediterranean. He refuses to come home."

The maid entered with a tray of tea. Cassandra went to pour. "What does this mean for you and your brothers? Your Father wants all of you married by Christmas, does he not?" She walked toward him and handed him a cup and saucer.

"Yes, and he is adamant that Garrett be forced to return. He wants Blake to go and fetch him, and drag him back by the ear."

She poured a cup for herself as well. "Is Blake prepared to do that?"

"We don't know yet," he replied. "He didn't come home last night, which was what sent Father over the edge. The doctor had to physically restrain him."

"Oh, Vincent, I am so sorry. Is there anything I can do?"

He moved to the sofa and sat down. "You are doing it now, just by being here. It is nice to have a place to escape to at times like this."

She sat down beside him and set her teacup and saucer on the table. "Sometimes it feels like our friendship is exactly that—a secret, parallel life no one in the world knows about except for us. It is as if this house exists in the clouds or something. Does that sound foolish?"

"It sounds exactly right."

Before she realized what she was doing, she placed a hand on his knee. "You may come here whenever you wish, Vincent. I know the contract requires that you give me a day's notice, but in circumstances such as this . . . "

She worried suddenly that she was making a mistake, relinquishing her control over this arrangement, giving in to her emotions and, worse, revealing them to him. She hastily withdrew her hand from his knee and cleared her throat.

He gazed at her, then spoke in a cool tone. "It would not be wise to start bending the rules."

All at once she was angry with herself for letting down her guard. She could not forget that he was still the notorious Vincent Sinclair, a man who did not seek true intimacies with women. She could not let herself imagine he was changing overnight, becoming the man she secretly wished he had been a year ago, when she surrendered to the magic.

And God, oh God. He could see straight through her and knew every thought and feeling she was having. He could see that she cared for him. She was going to frighten him off. He might disappear again, simply leave Pembroke without saying goodbye, dash back to London and return to his life as a rake. She'd said it herself—this place was in the clouds. It was not real. Or was it?

He finished his tea, then set it on the table. "I am afraid I cannot stay. I am needed at the palace."

She wanted to sink through the floor. She should not have reached out to him. She wished she could take it back.

"I would tell you to give your mother my best," she said, trying to keep her tone light, "but I don't suppose that would be proper."

He stood, but hesitated before heading for the door. "If you don't mind," he continued, "since I missed my visit with June this afternoon, may I return this evening? I realize I have not given you the proper notice . . . "

"That would be fine." In fact, she was relieved.

She rose to see him out, hoping the duke would be feeling better by then. She also hoped she would not lose whatever was left of her prudence and her ability to protect her heart—because clearly, her heart was not listening to her head.

"Do you mind if I stay a little longer?" Vincent asked that evening, after setting June into her cradle for the night. "I am not quite ready to go back yet."

They had been sitting in the nursery with Molly and June for a full hour after dark, while Cassandra worked on an embroidery cushion she intended to give to Miss Callahan as a birthday present.

"You can stay as long as you wish."

It was not lost on Vincent that Cassandra had been quiet all evening. She had seemed melancholy. Remote. Now she was yawning. She rose from her chair to go to bed.

She turned to leave, but paused at the nursery door for a moment, her troubled gaze fixed upon him as he moved to the rocking chair and sat down. He looked at her across the room and admired not just her physical beauty—which always arrested him on the spot, no matter how well he managed to conceal it—but the gentle quality of her spirit, even now, when she seemed so very unsure of what was happening between them. He felt a great need to reassure her.

"This is working out quite fine, Cassandra," he said. "We are going to muscle through."

Her sad smile reached him across the dimly lit room, and he felt almost drugged by the effect of it.

"Yes, I believe we are." Yet there had been something so very distant in her nature tonight. It worried him. "Good night, Vincent."

"Good night."

She closed the door with a quiet click and left him sitting alone by candlelight in the cozy little nursery.

For at least twenty minutes after June fell asleep, he rocked in the creaky chair, his head tipped back so he could look out at the stars through the high oval window. The sky was clear. He could even hear the faint noise of crickets and frogs outside in the grass.

He should go back to the palace, he supposed,

do his duty and ask after his fiancée. She would be playing cards with her mother in the drawing room, no doubt. It would be fitting for him to put in an appearance, even if he simply poured himself a brandy and read the paper by the fire.

Rising to his feet, he stretched his arms over his head, then went to look at June one last time, peaceful in her cradle. He reached in and gently rubbed the top of her tiny head. Her hair was soft as silk.

"Sleep well," he whispered, with a strange aching sensation in his chest.

A short time later he was trotting up to the palace on his horse. He stopped to look up at the brightly lit drawing room window above. Letitia passed in front of it, unaware of his presence below. She stood for a moment with her back to him, chattering on about something to someone, then walked away.

Devon came to look out the window next and looked down at him with a cool stare, as if he knew where he had been all night and greatly disapproved.

Contempt shuddered through Vincent as he imagined going up there and sitting down with the rest of them. They would ask where he had been. Devon might even call him into the study to have a reproachful word with him about his activities and remind him of his duty to the family. His brother would warn him not to become distracted and tell him to spend more time at the palace.

Devon had already fulfilled his duty by marrying Rebecca, entering into that marriage when he had not loved her in the beginning. He would therefore offer no sympathy to anyone not willing to do the same, for they were all depending on each other in order to safeguard their inheritances.

Vincent watched him raise a brandy glass to his lips and turn from the window when his wife slipped her arm through his and drew him away.

Outside, alone in the dark, Vincent remained seated on a restless horse that could not, for some reason, keep still.

He felt restless himself. He did not want to be here. He wanted to be at the dower house, in those small, cozy rooms, sitting by a fire.

He turned and gazed back in that direction. It would be wrong to return. Cassandra would most certainly be angry with him. It could spoil everything. He should not do it.

But he wanted so badly just to kick in his heels and urge his horse to a gallop—to speed across the moonlit hills and feel the wind in his hair, to leap over this particular hurdle in his life.

He looked up at the full moon and watched the wispy clouds float in front of it, thin and transparent, incapable of dimming its illumination.

He breathed deeply, seeking the calmness and

dispassion he required to get through his betrothal to Letitia, his usual detachment, but all he felt was an ache of longing deep inside his chest. It was so relentless and severe, it almost made him double over in pain.

In the end he did what he knew he should not do. He kicked in his heels and galloped off.

Cassandra lay in bed exhausted, yet unable to sleep because of all the thoughts darting around inside her brain.

She looked out the window at the full moon overhead and thought wistfully about the many hours she had spent with Vincent over the past few weeks, strolling leisurely to the river, spoiling June with their immeasurable affections, and speaking openly about so many things.

She had not expected it to be so pleasant. Not with him—the man whose heart she had believed was made of stone. This strange arrangement of theirs had been going on for quite some time now without a single hitch.

Though perhaps "without a hitch" was not the most accurate turn of phrase. True, there had been no arguments or disagreements since that day at Langley Hall, no improper flirtations or advances. But beneath all the courtesy and manners, she had been fighting against a new kind of desire that simply would not die.

It was, in a word, admiration.

Every time Vincent stepped out of his coach, dressed in his elegant black coat and top hat, smiling up at her with those dark, mesmerizing eyes, she melted. When he held her daughter in his arms, gently and with affection, she fell to pieces like a lovesick pup that did not know the meaning of restraint.

But she *did* know the meaning of it, and she understood the consequences of giving in to temptation. She had already paid a handsome price for her impulsive transgressions in the past.

She also knew that even if she did give in to her desires, she could never endure the heartache of sharing him with another woman. She was simply not built that way. If she loved someone, it would have to be all or nothing. She'd need to give of herself completely, and would require the same in return. She could not settle for less, and was still not sure Vincent was capable of such a devoted love, for he was broken inside.

Or was she wrong about that? she wondered as she stared out the window at the darkness beyond. She had been wrong about so many other things, and he'd done nothing but surprise her with his integrity over the past few weeks. Perhaps he wasn't completely broken. And what if what existed between them was real? What if it could be—if nurtured—the truest kind of love that existed in the world? What if they were meant to be together, against all odds, no matter what?

If so, could she sacrifice her principles to be with him?

A light knock sounded at her door, and she sat up in bed. "Come in."

The maid, Iris, entered the room. "Begging your pardon, ma'am, but you wanted a fire lit?"

Cassandra's brows drew together in confusion. "I didn't ask for one."

"Pardon me, I thought you did." She looked around. "If you don't mind my saying, there is a wee bit of a chill in here."

Cassandra felt a shiver, and smiled at Iris. "Indeed you are right, there is. Since I am awake, a fire would be lovely, thank you." She fluffed the pillows behind her and leaned back against the headboard. "I am having some trouble sleeping."

The maid moved to the hearth and knelt down, then set about her work. "I could bring you some brandy, if that might help."

"I doubt anything will help at this point," Cassandra said. "I have far too many conflicting thoughts dashing around inside my brain. It is an exploding battlefield in my head tonight."

The maid laughed quietly. "I know what that is like, milady." She swept the ash out from under the grate. "I don't suppose it has anything to do with that handsome young lord who comes to visit every day. He would keep me awake, too, I dare say."

Cassandra couldn't help but give in to a melancholy smile. "I suppose it doesn't take a genius to see that we are . . . " How could she put it? "That we are friends."

Keeping her back to Cassandra, Iris laid out the kindling. "No, milady, it doesn't, and if you don't mind my saying, I understand how difficult it must be for you. I was in your shoes once myself, a very long time ago."

Cassandra tilted her head to the side. "May I be so bold as to ask the particulars?"

"I loved a man I could not be with," the maid replied without hesitation. "There were circumstances keeping us apart, which seemed impossible at the time. We had a child together."

Cassandra's heart beat uneasily inside her chest. "I see."

Iris lit a match and sat back on her heels. Still, she did not turn around. "But then my love died, and I had to raise my son without him."

"I am so sorry," Cassandra said.

"It was a very long time ago." She brushed off her apron and rose to her feet, facing Cassandra at last. "The good news is our son went on to accomplish great things."

"Where is he now?"

"He is passed on."

Cassandra cleared her throat. "My deepest condolences, Iris."

"Thank you. That is very kind."

"Do you have any regrets about your . . . association with that man?" Cassandra asked.

Iris shook her head. "Not about loving him, and if I could do it all over again, I would. I wouldn't change a thing, except for the fact that I wasted so much time fighting it. Life is so very short." She picked up her bucket and made for the door. "Maybe you should reconsider that glass of brandy. It might help you sleep. I just refilled the decanter in the drawing room."

"Thank you, Iris."

The maid left, and Cassandra lay for a long time staring up at the ceiling. Iris was right. A glass of brandy might ease the burden of her thoughts, and after hearing what her maid had chosen to disclose, she had even more to think about.

She slid out from under the covers and touched her feet to the cool floor, then padded across the room to fetch her wrapper.

A moment later she was in the drawing room lighting the lamp and tipping the crystal decanter over a glass. She raised it to her lips and sipped, squeezing her eyes shut as the drink blazed a searing path down her throat. She took another sip and strolled to the window.

It was a beautiful night, brightly lit under a full

moon and a star-speckled sky. She looked up and imagined herself at Langley Hall, far away from here, miles from Pembroke Palace.

It would be less complicated then, she told herself, when she and June were not so convenient for daily visits from Vincent. It was less likely he would come so often, once the weather turned and snow blocked the roads.

Just the thought of it made her feel lonely inside. She would miss him. She could not deny it.

Oh, Iris was right, she admitted to herself at last. Life was short. And love was a rare and precious gift.

She raised the glass to her lips and swallowed another mouthful of brandy. When she looked out the window again, however, a nervous fluttering arose in her belly, for she spotted a man. He was sitting under the tree on the bank of the river at the bottom of the hill. The moonlight was reflecting off the water, and he was silhouetted against the sparkling ripples. His horse was tethered to the tree, its long neck bowed down to the grass.

It was Vincent—that much she knew, even though it was impossible to identify anyone from such a distance in the darkness.

What was he doing there? She had heard him leave almost two hours ago. Had he been sitting there all this time, or had he left and returned?

She set her glass down on the table. If she

knew what was good for her, she would go back to bed this instant and forget she ever saw him. She would try to remember her principles and convictions.

But that would require her to guzzle the entire contents of what remained in the brandy decanter, enough to knock her out until dawn, because the fact of the matter was—she cared for him. She cared for him a great deal. And somehow she knew that he needed her.

She watched him rise to his feet, pat his horse on the neck and wander along the river's edge.

Cassandra picked up her glass and finished what was left in it. Iris's words kept repeating themselves over and over in her mind. *Life is so very short.*

She could not fool herself. She wanted to go down there. Her heart was telling her it was the right thing to do.

Perhaps it would be all right if she did. She could ask him why he was here. She could behave as she always did, with restraint and in a manner consistent with their newfound friendship. It was such a beautiful night, and she had come to trust Vincent not to behave dishonorably.

But could she trust herself?

That, perhaps, was the burning question of the moment, for she could almost feel the slow and reluctant surrendering of her heart.

It left her terrified.

Chapter 14

I believe I am doomed. Yet somehow, inexplicably, I am bursting with joy.

—from the journal of
Cassandra Montrose,
Lady Colchester,
June 25, 1874

Ten minutes later Cassandra found herself standing on the riverbank in silence, filled with self-doubt and apprehension, while she faced Vincent squarely. A warm breeze fluttered her white wrapper around her ankles, and her hair blew loose around her shoulders.

"I thought you were a ghost," he said, "when I saw you floating down the hill."

"I was hardly floating. I was wincing over all the thorns that were pricking my feet."

Amused, he looked down at her toes, which

were peeking out from under her white nightdress. "Really?"

"Yes," she replied. "I am in great pain presently, but doing my best to keep a stiff upper lip."

He laughed. "Cassandra, my dear, let me help." He moved toward her and offered his hand. "Sit down. I shall take a look."

Slipping her hand into his, she lowered herself to the grass and stretched her legs out in front of her.

He knelt down and took her bare foot in his hand. "No thorns visible. Where does it hurt?" He ran both his thumbs along her arch.

"Everywhere."

He proceeded to massage her foot, rubbing his thumbs in small, slow circles, which was most decidedly outside the bounds of propriety and exactly what she feared would happen when she debated coming down here, but she could not bring herself to tell him to stop. It felt far too wonderful, as all the tension she'd endured in bed drained from her mind and body.

"I didn't mean to disturb you," he said. "Did the puppy bark?"

"No, I simply couldn't sleep. I was already up when I saw you down here."

He nodded and turned his attention to the other foot. His hands were warm, his fingers skillful, as he stroked and probed in all the right places. She breathed deeply the fresh, spring fragrance of the night.

"Does this feel good?" he asked a moment later, lifting his gaze.

Her head was swimming in the pleasure of it, even though she knew it was terribly wicked and very, very dangerous.

She blinked rather drunkenly at him. "Yes, but I wish it did not."

He continued to stroke her foot, and went so far as to slide a hand up the back of her leg and massage the muscle of her calf before he hesitated, stared fixedly at her for a moment, then drew his hands away and sat back on his heel.

Folding his wrists over a knee, he said, "I wish the same thing, so I shall stop. I have been doing very well behaving myself over the past few weeks, wouldn't you agree? I would hate to spoil it now."

They gazed at each other in the moonlight before he moved to sit beside her, leaning back on one arm and lifting a knee.

"What a night," he said, looking up at the stars.

"It is perfect, isn't it?"

"Not *quite* perfect, Cassandra."

Keeping her eyes on the sky, she slowly exhaled. "Only seconds ago you said you were going to behave yourself."

"I will if you want me to."

She looked at him. "Sometimes I don't know what I want." She turned her eyes to the stars again. "Tonight you said that we would be able to muscle through this, yet here we are only a few hours later, sitting alone in the moonlight when we should not be together like this. I should be inside sleeping, and you should be at the palace with your fiancée."

"I am aware of that," he said, "and I promise I will not offend you by asking for more. No matter how soft and delicate your foot was in my hands just now, and no matter badly I want to touch you everywhere else. And I do, Cassandra. I cannot lie about it."

And she could not deny that his words filled her with pleasure and joy.

"I should not have come out here," she said. "I knew it would make things more difficult, but I could not help myself. How is it you have such power to crush my resolve to be good? I am drawn to you like steel to a magnet."

"I worry that I am eventually going to spoil what has become very comfortable between us."

"Comfortable in some ways, excruciating in others."

He leaned closer. "How is it excruciating for you? Tell me. I need to hear you say it. Perhaps it will be enough to satisfy me."

She shook her head. "I don't want to say it. I want to deny it, hide it away and bury it."

"Burying it will not make it go away."

"Perhaps it will in time," she argued.

He sat back farther and sighed. "I don't want it to."

All of sudden her eyes were filling with tears, and she could not believe she was in danger of losing this battle she had been fighting for so long. "I don't want it to end either."

A gentle nighttime breeze blew her hair across her face.

"You are so beautiful," he whispered, inching closer on the grass and nuzzling her ear. The feel of his hot breath against her skin sent her spiraling into a very dangerous place.

"Please," he whispered, "let me kiss you. Just once."

Closing her eyes, she rubbed her nose against his cheeks and lips, even while a part of her was still fighting to resist. She should not let him kiss her. She should put a stop to this now by returning to the house. But she knew she was not going to do that. She had traveled too far down this tempting path.

"Perhaps just one kiss," she replied, touching her lips tentatively to his.

His hands cupped her face and he tilted his head to the side. Suddenly there was nothing tentative about it. He was devouring her with his open mouth, caressing her with his soft, skillful tongue. Her body melted against his as passion pounded from her heart to the very edges of her existence.

The next thing she knew, he was easing her down onto the cool grass and settling his heavy body upon hers. Nothing could stop the desire burning through her veins and her need to touch him. She slid her hands into his jacket and ran them over his waistcoat, glorying in the firm muscles of his torso.

It had been more than a year since she dashed out of a London ballroom with him, was kissed senseless in the carriage as they drove across town, and lost her mind to ecstasy. She felt the same way now—wild and reckless and oblivious to her morals and values. All she wanted was to tear off his clothes, feel the heat of his body and his breath in her ear as he whispered her name.

"I'm sorry, Cassandra," he said, dropping hot kisses across her cheeks, her eyelids, her forehead. "I tried, but I cannot keep my hands off you. This madness I feel for you knows no bounds."

"I feel it, too." She could barely breathe enough to speak. "It doesn't matter how much I try to resist, or how much I once hated you, I am powerless."

"You don't hate me now, do you?"

"No. I suppose I haven't hated you for quite

some time. All I want now is to feel your hands on me."

He kissed her again and pressed his body tight against hers until they were both writhing with need on the riverbank.

"I must have you," he said.

She threw her head back on the grass, giving him leave to press more kisses down her neck. "This is wrong. I should tell you to stop. I should run back to the house. I should send you home. Why can't I do any of those things?"

"Should, should, should." He lifted his head. "Stop saying that word. What about what you *want*?"

"It doesn't matter what I want, nor what *you* want. There is duty and honor and decency to consider. You are betrothed to another woman."

"But it was my father who chose her, not me, and he is mad." He lowered his mouth to her neck again, and she quivered at the sensation of his lips and tongue, probing hotly across her collarbone. "There must be a way we can be together," he said.

"God help me," she said, arching her back and looking up at the stars, "I cannot resist you."

"Then don't fight it," he said.

He pushed her wrapper aside and reached down to lift her nightgown to her waist. He shifted his body and mounted her.

"Vincent . . . " Barely able to breathe, she parted her legs for him, pointing her knees toward the sky.

"Don't say no." He fumbled with the fastenings on his trousers. "Say yes for me," he whispered, kissing her neck again. His knees in the grass provided the thrust for his hips. "We must be together, Cassandra."

"Yes." The instant the word breezed past her lips, he was sliding into her with hot, slick ease, slowly and torturously. Her body shuddered with pleasure.

"God in heaven," he groaned.

She arched her back in response, grabbing hold of his firm buttocks and pulling him in deeper. "You feel so good."

"I can't live without this," he said. "I cannot keep up the pretense of friendship . . . "

She pushed forward with her hips against every furious thrust of his. "Nor can I."

He wrapped his arms around her waist, pulled her tight against him, held her bottom in his hands and lifted her clear up off the ground. He drove into her with insistent, pounding force, grunted and groaned into the night, while her own pleasures mounted to impossible heights.

The magnificence of her climax astounded her. It could not be matched.

"I can't hold back any longer," he said.

"Please, Vincent, do what you must to prevent another child."

With one last thrust, he shuddered, then withdrew. He quickly pulled back onto his hands and knees, wrapped his hand around his shaft and spilled his seed onto the grass.

Cassandra inched backward out of the way. He toppled over onto his back beside her and lay there in silence for a long time.

"I am spent," he finally said. "I don't think I'll ever be able to move again. You'll need an ox and harness to get me up."

For Cassandra, however, playful smiles or laughter would not come. All she could do was stare up at the stars in dismay. "I cannot believe we just did that."

He turned his head toward her. "I must have you this way, Cassandra. As my lover."

"But you were not free to have me this way tonight. You are engaged to another woman."

"To a woman who does not love me and accepts openly that I will have mistresses. She will also have lovers of her own. It is not a love match, and we both know it."

"It seems unfathomable to me."

"Why? Can you not comprehend that a man and woman of our social class might marry for property or position? It is the norm, Cassandra."

She did not answer for a while. "Perhaps you

are right," she said at last. "Perhaps I am too romantic. Perhaps I have always been."

He rolled onto his side to face her. "What is the point in fighting this? We desire each other, that is obvious. You have already borne me a child. You are not an innocent. I shall ask you again. Be my mistress."

Her body was still weak and languorous from their lovemaking, and she had to struggle to keep a clear head. "Romance and idealism aside, what of my principles? How can I, in good conscience, say yes to that?"

He seemed to be searching for more arguments to convince her. "Most of the married men I know have mistresses, and you've heard me declare that I shall be no different once I am wed. But *you* are the one I want."

"And do you always get what you want?" she asked heatedly.

He frowned. "The answer to that is a very definitive no."

She lay there for a long time, finding it hard to believe she was even having this conversation. Was it because of what Iris had said?

"What if I were to try to find a way to marry you?" he asked. "If there was something that could be done. If I said to hell with my father's will."

Her heart began to pound. It was an enormous

concession for him just to say those words. She could not ignore that.

"Then that would be different," she replied.

He covered his eyes with a hand. "But my brothers . . . "

She wished she could be selfish, just once, but alas she could not. "You cannot betray them for me. You would only resent me one day. I know you would."

For a long time they lay there saying nothing, just looking up at the sky.

"If I were to agree to be your mistress," she carefully asked, "how long would it last? Until the excitement wears off? What if it wore off for one of us and not the other? What then?"

He turned his head toward her. "Then we would return to the terms of the contract. You would always have what you need to raise June, no matter what happens."

"I don't know if I can love someone that way, Vincent. I am not sure I can enter into something knowing it will be temporary, no matter how pleasurable it is at any given moment."

He rolled onto his back again and, almost physically, she felt him retreat into his callousness. The change was like night and day.

"Sometimes I wonder if it is just the label of mistress that offends you," he said, "because you seem to enjoy the rest of it."

Her temper flared. "And you seem to enjoy punishing me and pushing me away with your cruel mask of indifference whenever you feel I am not giving you exactly what you want. Try to keep your bitterness toward MaryAnn and your brother separate from me, please. I am not her, and I have never betrayed you. At least not yet."

He looked at her in shock.

"And it is not just the label of mistress that offends me," she continued. "It is the whole idea of it. You forget that I was part of an adulterous triangle once. My husband's mistress spoiled any chance I had for happiness in my own marriage. If it were not for her, we might have had a chance."

"Well, perhaps you need to separate your bitterness toward your husband from what exists between us," he countered.

She folded her hands over her stomach and looked up at the sky again.

A moment later, after their tempers had cooled somewhat, he spoke without hostility in the darkness. "Isn't it clear to you that we cannot be just friends, Cassandra? There is something more between us, and we must see it through. Somehow we must find a way to be together."

She sighed. "Perhaps we can simply guzzle each other like wine and toss the glass away before you are married."

He rolled onto her again and touched her face.

"I would never toss you away. The contract will protect you against that."

"That is not what I am talking about, Vincent, and you know it."

He was hard again. She could feel him against her thigh.

"I suppose I do."

She closed her eyes, and despite all her fears and self-recriminations, her body was responding to the heat of his touch.

"Take the pleasure, Cassandra," he whispered in her ear, seducing her with his lips and his potent sexuality. "Let me give you this at least. Agree to be my mistress."

She began to slowly spread her legs. "I thought you said it would take an ox to move you."

"It was no lie. I merely underestimated my resilience."

Her head was telling her one thing—that she could not survive this; that she would end up with a broken heart, shattered into a thousand unrecognizable pieces—while her body was demanding something else entirely.

In the end it was her body that won out. She could no longer fight this.

She cupped his buttocks in her hands again, and with a firm thrust, pushed her hips upward to pull him inside. He filled her completely, and passion surged to her core.

From that moment on, all that mattered was the wicked bliss of his body slowly driving in and out of hers, filling her with sweet, slow agony.

She lay her head back in the cool grass and allowed passion to overtake her.

Chapter 15

My thoughts keep drifting back to those words he spoke on the riverbank: "What if I were to find a way to marry you?"

I confess I cannot help myself. I am imagining myself as his wife. I suppose while I am at it, I might as well imagine myself as Queen of England, too.

—from the journal of
Cassandra Montrose,
Lady Colchester,
June 26, 1874

Vincent was in the library the next morning, lounging in a chair and staring up at the ceiling in a blurry haze of sexual arousal, when the door burst open and startled him out of his mood. He lifted his head off the back of the chair to discover Letitia sweeping into the room like a dust mop, slamming the door shut behind her with a resounding crash.

"You, sir, are a cad."

He relaxed and tipped his head back again. "But my dear, you and I both know that is yesterday's news."

"I thought we agreed you would be discreet," she accused him.

The comment roused his attention. He sat up and looked at her. "What exactly are you referring to?"

"I am referring to your tawdry mistress and bastard child in the dower house!" she shouted, then instantly calmed her voice: "Vincent, my love. We are not even married yet."

He had the distinct impression she was advising him that such activities would be quite acceptable after the wedding day, but not before.

He rose to his feet. "Wherever did you hear that?"

"I was out this morning with my maid," she explained, "and we drove past your house of sin and debauchery. I said, quite innocently, 'What a charming house. Who lives there?' My maid was able to answer the question." She glared at him. *"Servants hear things you know."*

"Ah, yes, I suppose they do." He would have to remedy that. They would begin anew when they reached Langley Hall.

"Well?" she said. "Do you have anything to say to me?"

He paused a moment, while her simmering anger rose again to a rapid boil. "I confess all. I am guilty as charged. My lover is living not five miles from here in the Pembroke Palace dower house."

Vincent watched her carefully, not unmindful of the risk he was taking. She could easily decide she would prefer not to marry him after all. And where would that leave him? Free of her, to be sure, which would hardly leave him broken hearted. Quite to the contrary, he might even be inclined to hold a party where there would be dancing. But he would be without an acceptable bride to protect his inheritance.

Suddenly, he found himself imagining the possibility of wedding Cassandra instead, as he'd suggested to her last night on the riverbank, and he realized that if he did marry her, he would not only be forsaking his brothers, but would be marrying a beautiful woman for love.

Love . . .

Love?

Oh God.

Letitia strolled closer. "Who is she?"

"Someone I met a year ago," he replied, feeling both disturbed and shaken. What the devil had happened to him over the past few weeks? Had he become that lovesick young fool again? Had he forgotten the promises he made to himself—to never be that weak again? Bloody hell, he might as well throw himself into the path of an oncoming train. It would be much quicker than this alternative.

"That is all you are going to tell me?" Letitia prompted, tearing him away from his thoughts.

He labored to recover his customary boredom, both inside and out. "She is a widowed lady of rank. We shared a night of perfect ecstasy one year ago before she disappeared from my life."

Letitia seemed eager to understand the circumstances. "If she was a lady of rank and carrying your child, why did you not marry her?"

"She did not reappear until after you and I announced our betrothal."

She moved slowly around the room. "Let me be sure I understand this. She arrived too late, after your father had become attached to *me*."

"Yes."

She took a deep breath, seeming satisfied with his answer and somewhat more at ease in her position. "Are you not worried that I will be hurt and scandalized by your behavior, and will not wish to marry you?"

"It was my understanding, Letitia, based on our recent conversations, that you knew I would have mistresses and that it was acceptable to you.

And that you, in turn, would only ask for the same freedom when the time came that you wished to take a lover."

She glared at him from across the room. "That was before I knew about the woman in the dower house. We are not yet married, Vincent. I do not wish to be jilted or, heaven forbid, left at the altar."

He understood that it was a matter of pride with her. He supposed it was preferable to tears and pleading.

"Do not concern yourself," he said, striving to retreat back into his armor—to become the man she had accepted to be her husband. The rakish, unsentimental young lord who was never going to be faithful to anyone. "The duke wants you to be the next bride of Pembroke, and that is what you shall be."

"But do *you* want me?" she asked. "I need to know that I am desired not by my future father-in-law, but by my betrothed."

It was still a matter of pride, he knew—this need to be desired. She was accustomed to always being regarded as the most beautiful woman in the room, wherever she went. She did not like this competition.

Sauntering toward him with a seductive glimmer in her eye, she swayed her slender hips as she drew near, then slid her palms up his chest to the tops of his shoulders. "Why don't you take me now," she whispered in a low, husky voice of sensual allure, "right here on the sofa? I am feeling rather amorous, darling, and I see no reason why we should wait for the wedding night. No one will know if we consummate our vows a few weeks early."

She rose up on her toes and pressed her mouth to his. Her lips were soft and moist. She smelled of expensive French perfume. It was exactly the kind of advance he had always favored—clear and to the point. Physical. Devoid of sentiment. And she was without question a beautiful woman.

Vincent slid his hands around her waist and deepened the kiss. He waited almost frantically for the sexual arousal to begin. He expected it to materialize at any moment, for this was exactly what Vincent Sinclair—heartless, dissolute rake—should want. Sex with two different women in the space of twelve hours.

But something very deep inside him was not working. This particular woman's body, though attractive, did not appeal to him. He didn't like the way she kissed. Her lips were too tight, and her perfume was too strong. It was almost nauseating. He felt no desire for her. None whatsoever.

He quickly took hold of her hands and pried them off his neck. "I do not wish to spoil the wedding night," he explained in a rush, to put some distance between them. He did not want to touch her. He did not even want to be in the same room with her.

"That cannot be true," she said, resolve still burning in her eyes. "I've heard the gossip—that you are always ready and willing to please a lady, and that you never fail to live up to your reputation as a master fornicator." She spoke the words with malice as she slid her hands up his chest again. "Surely I am beautiful enough for you. You could enjoy me freely, Vincent, because a child a few weeks early would hardly raise an eyebrow. You could do anything you wanted with me. I would offer no resistance."

He backed away from her, feeling sickened by the idea of bedding her, even on their wedding night, when it had never been an issue before, despite his lack of feeling for her. He could barely comprehend what he was feeling. "As I said, I do not wish to spoil things."

"I see." She glared at him with loathing. "You have your little harlot to keep you satisfied between the sheets. I suppose I should thank her for sparing me that odious wifely duty in the future." She turned to leave but stopped in the open doorway. "Be aware, Vincent, that I know how these things play out. Like you, my father was a philandering dog, so I understand that you are obliged to provide for that woman because of your bastard child. I also know you will tire of her in due course and move on to other mistresses. But do not forget that you are engaged to me. I will always be your wife, till death do us part. There will be no moving on where I am concerned. In that regard, I must remind you that Pembroke Palace is my domain, as the future Lady Vincent. Not hers."

His stride was fluid as he moved across the room and poured himself a drink. He kept his back to her as he spoke. "Permanent accommodations for her have already been arranged. She will be gone from here the day after our wedding."

Part of him wished it was sooner. He felt unsettled, confused.

He waited for his fiancée to depart from the room, but she remained in the doorway, saying nothing for the longest time. The muscles in his neck and shoulders felt as rigid as steel. He tipped his head back and took a drink.

"I must know, Vincent," she said at last. "Are you in love with this woman?"

The rest of his body went stiff with tension as well. There was a knot in his gut the size of a brick.

Turning his head to the side, he spoke over his shoulder in a low voice. "No. You of all people should know I am not capable of that."

"Ah," she replied, her confidence returning. In

fact, he was almost blinded by the illumination of her pride and vanity. "That's a relief, I must say. Because for a moment I thought you might be fool enough to forsake your family and inheritance, all for a tawdry one night tumble." With that she walked out.

Vincent poured himself another drink and slowly sank into a chair.

Cassandra set June into her cradle for a nap, stayed for a moment until she was settled, then left the nursery. She'd spent most of the day with her daughter, outside in the sunshine pushing the pram, but was in a dazed stupor the entire time, distracted by thoughts of Vincent and what they had done on the riverbank the night before.

She'd relived in her mind many of the erotic details—the words he whispered in her ear, how his hands felt on her hot, bare skin, and how terribly wicked it had all been.

By the end of it, she had become his mistress.

It was almost impossible to comprehend, considering how persistently she'd fought to protect her principles and her heart. She had been dead set against anything like this from the beginning, yet here she was, having just fallen head first into temptation. She had lived recklessly and would now have to live with the consequences. Again.

She went downstairs, informed Miss Callahan that June was sleeping soundly, then retired to the drawing room for a cup of tea. Vincent was due to arrive at any moment for a visit. He had arranged his weekly schedule days ago.

Would he wish to take his pleasures with his newly acquired mistress? she wondered uncomfortably, feeling rather warm under her dress all of a sudden. Or would he simply go straight to the nursery?

She had just poured herself a cup of tea when she heard a carriage pull up in front of the house. She glanced at the clock. It was half past four. He was exactly on time. She did not rise from her seat, but simply waited.

A few minutes later he was announced and shown into the drawing room. Her heart pounded feverishly at the sight of him, so tall and dark and commanding. She was pleased he had not asked to be taken to the nursery directly, but of course he would wish to see her.

She rose to her feet as the maid showed him in. "Lord Vincent, welcome," Cassandra said. "Would you like a cup of tea?"

The maid curtsied, backed out and closed the door behind her.

He gave the maid a few seconds to reach the stairs, then turned around and locked the door. Slowly, without warmth, he sauntered across the room, appraising Cassandra with a sexual eye. "I didn't come for tea."

"What exactly *did* you come for?" she asked with burning anticipation, aware of a dark and dangerous intensity about him as he backed her up against her chair.

"I came to see what you are wearing." He reached her, slid one arm around her waist and pulled her close.

"Now that you've seen it, do you wish to pay me a compliment about the color?"

"No, I wish to see you unbuttoning it."

Even while her conscience was telling her to be sensible, she was wildly aroused by the dangerous ferocity of his passion, which seemed especially intense today. There was something very different about him. "You are most presumptuous, my lord."

"It is one of my best qualities, don't you think?"

"I think you are the very devil."

His gaze darkened. "Perhaps that is what you like most about me."

She studied him for an intense moment. "Are you drunk?"

He looked down at her lips. "Yes, I believe I am."

It should have mattered to her that he had come

here in such a state, but for some reason it did not. Though she was curious as to why he had been drinking in the afternoon.

With seductive insolence, he pulled her tight against him and pressed his mouth to hers. The kiss was rough and deep and tasted of brandy.

He took her by the elbow and led her quickly across the carpet, around the tea cart to the sofa. "Tell me your conscience has not gotten the better of you today," he said, "and convinced you to resist this."

Her hip bumped into the arm of the sofa, then he eased her down gracefully onto her back. "I regret to say it has not."

Standing over her, he ripped off his jacket while he kept his eyes trained upon hers. Then he lowered his body. He was heavy and warm, and his movements were fluid.

"Tell me, Cassandra, what would you like today? What tricks and pleasures? I have not forgotten the promise I made to you at Langley Hall—that I would fulfill all your desires."

There it was, that rakish seduction, the dangerous, sexual charm. It was what had lured her to that hotel room a year ago—the promise of forbidden pleasures. She could not deny it still had a strange power over her, for she wanted all of that wickedness, and more.

Yet at the same time, she did not want that rakish, predatory lover she barely knew. She wanted the man she had come to know over the past few weeks—the man who held his infant daughter in his arms with fatherly affection, the man who could talk to her for hours and hours on a blanket in the grass, laid out under the trees. That man for some reason was out of reach. She could feel it in the way he touched her.

He kissed low along her neckline, then gathered her skirts in a fist, tugging them slowly up her leg. His gaze traveled down the length of her body. He did not look her in the eye.

"Is everything all right?" she found herself asking, mindful of the fact that she was interrupting things.

Still he did not meet her gaze. "Let us not talk."

He ran his tongue over the top of her breast, gave her an open-mouthed kiss along her collarbone, and she quivered with desire. "You came only for this?"

"Yes."

He continued to lay intoxicating kisses down the side of her neck, then began to undress her with impressive efficiency. When at last—after a minimal amount of foreplay—he entered her, she felt the intensity of his need and realized it was she who was fulfilling all of *his* desires today. For some reason he had retreated from her, and he needed to possess her in this way.

One week ago she would have reacted very differently. She would have rejected him in no uncertain terms and sent him on his way. But today she did not wish to deny him. She wanted only to give of herself, to reach into the very heart of him, wherever he was, and bring him back.

He rose up on both arms and made love to her in the afternoon light, all the while looking down at where they were joined, watching himself move in and out of her.

She watched his face.

When his climax loomed, she held him close and did not let him withdraw. He poured into her with a force she felt in the depths of her womb.

Only then did he finally look at her, deep into her eyes. He pushed a lock of hair back from her temple. "I'm sorry," he said. "I didn't mean to be rough."

"You weren't," she replied, speaking the absolute truth, for he had not been rough at all. Not in the slightest.

With tenderness, he kissed her lips, slowly, languidly.

Afterward, when he could not kiss anymore, he fell asleep in her arms, pressed close to her body on the sofa.

She was not sure what had just happened between them. It was as if he had come here feeling angry, determined to conquer her, or conquer something.

She had a feeling, however, that whatever it was, it had conquered him instead.

Chapter 16

I cannot even try to pretend that I am his mistress for the sake of pleasure. Now I know my heart has become engaged. I am his, body and soul, and I am terrified.

—from the journal of
Cassandra Montrose,
Lady Colchester,
July 8, 1874

It was dark by the time Vincent arrived back at the palace, leaving just enough time to wash and change for dinner. His thoughts in turmoil, he delivered his horse to a groom at the stables and strode to the palace door. He had not felt anything like this in a very long time, and could barely manage to get a handle on it. It was somewhat similar to the powerlessness and grief he had felt after the loss of Mary-

Ann. It was like a death. But the death of what? Himself?

He was breathing hard as his boots crunched over the gravel in the stable courtyard. He was still astonished by the fact that for a brief time today he had been able to forget about his duty to his brothers and the so-called curse upon the palace. He had forgotten everything unpleasant in his life. After waking up in Cassandra's arms on the sofa in the dower house drawing room, he had made love to her again, and she melted for him and gave up all that remained of her internal resistance. She welcomed him into her soft, quivering body with eager relish, and by the end of it, had become the assertive lover he remembered so well from that perfect, magical night a year ago.

Although nothing else about it had been the same. Which perhaps was why he felt such discomfort now. He had gone there today with the objective to have sex with her—simple, uncomplicated sex, nothing more. He had gone there to prove that was all he really wanted. But he had felt things beyond the physical. There had even been a moment when he felt like weeping. It was as if he had flown outside of himself.

Still deeply disconcerted by this change he did not welcome—because the entire world seemed to be positioned between them—he walked through the palace doors and encountered his mother, who was already dressed for dinner in her best pearls and a formal gown of pale blue silk. "I saw you coming up the drive," she said. "I was watching for you."

Vincent handed his coat and hat to the butler. "Were you worried I would miss dinner?"

Her shoulders rose and fell with a sigh.

At the sight of her distress, he quickly pushed aside his own personal introspections. "What is wrong?" he asked.

She started toward the stairs. "May I walk with you?"

"Of course." They crossed the great hall together.

His mother slipped her arm through his. She spoke quietly. "You have heard, I suppose, that Blake is nowhere to be found. Back in the days when you were children, all I had to do was go searching in the secret passages and I would almost always find the lot of you, howling like ghosts and frightening your sister."

"But he is not howling in the tunnels this evening?" Vincent hoped a touch of humor might ease his mother's anxieties, but she seemed unaffected. "He is not in London?"

"No. At least, he is not at the house in Mayfair, but he never leaves the palace without telling me where he is going and when he expects to return. He is the most responsible son in the world, and

I am worried. This is not like him, not at all. And your father is in a tizzy."

They reached the second floor and made their way down the corridor toward Vincent's rooms. "I am sure Blake is fine, Mother. He is out searching for a bride, no doubt, and has fallen hopelessly in love, which is why he is distracted and has forgotten to send word."

"That is what Devon said. He told me Blake had mentioned a woman who caught his eye."

"There, you see?"

She did not seem convinced. "Then why is it I am still so worried? Surely you and Devon are right, and I am just reacting to all the recent upheavals in our lives."

He remembered, however, his brother's most uncharacteristic behavior not long ago, when he fell asleep in the billiards room after a night that did not release him from its clutches until dawn. That was certainly not indicative of a proper courtship.

"Is there anything you wish me to do?" he asked. "I can go to London and hunt the rascal down. I know all the usual places where a man can lose sight of himself."

She shook her head. "No, that won't be necessary. I am sure I am simply being overprotective. Besides, you have a wedding to prepare for. Let us give him a few more days."

They reached Vincent's rooms, but his mother was not yet ready to let go of his arm. "In that regard, there is something else that is weighing heavily on my mind, Vincent. I suppose it is a mother's duty in life to worry about her children."

"And what, pray tell, is that?" He realized too late that he had just been short with her, for he had a feeling he knew what she wanted to discuss, and he was not inclined to talk about it. Not with anyone.

"You have been spending a great deal of time at the dower house," she said carefully, "and I wonder how long you plan to keep Lady Colchester there."

"Has Letitia said something to you about it?"

"No, I didn't think she knew, and those of us who do know have been making every effort to keep it from her, and to keep it from your father as well."

He looked both ways up and down the corridor. "Perhaps we should discuss this in private." He opened the door to his room, and she followed him inside. "You might as well know the truth, Mother. I have asked Cassandra to be my mistress, she has agreed, more or less, and I have no intention of giving her up. Unfortunately my fiancée is no longer in the dark about Cassandra's presence in the dower house, and she is not pleased about it. But she has not indicated that she wishes to break the engagement."

"I see." His mother moved around the room, her eyes trained on him. "Vincent, I will not waste your time or mine by asking if you love Lady Letitia. It is more than obvious to me that you do not, and thank God for that."

He appreciated his mother's candidness. There was no point in everyone going around pretending not to see what was as obvious as the floor under their feet.

"I also know," she continued, "that you have never proposed to Lady Colchester."

"That is correct."

She strode toward him. "But is it possible you might be happier with her?"

Happier. It had been ages since he'd entertained the notion that happiness was attainable through romantic love. In fact, he had come to believe the opposite. Yet here he was, rolling around like a confused fool in his own emotions, examining his inner self, and resisting—*denying*—the love he felt for Cassandra.

Yes, it was love. As much as he did not welcome it, he was not completely ignorant of his heart.

"If you thought you could be happier with her," his mother cautiously continued, "perhaps it is worth exploring the possibility that Lady Letitia might release you."

Vincent turned away from his mother and sat down in a chair. He closed his eyes, pinched the bridge of his nose. "Bloody hell."

"What is it, Vincent?"

He looked up and felt his eyes burning. "I do love her. Enough to die for her."

His mother's lips curled into a warm and joyful smile. "I am so pleased to hear it. So *very* pleased."

But he bowed his head forward and shook it. "But I am not pleased to admit it. I did not want this. I still do not."

"What *do* you want?"

"To fulfill my duty to my brothers and secure my inheritance," he replied. "I did not want my life to change, and I knew it would remain exactly the same if I married Letitia. She is a female version of me. She is bitter and cynical. Hard-hearted. In that way, we are perfect for each other."

"But that is not the real you," his mother told him.

"It has become the real me."

She was quiet for a moment. "No, I refuse to believe that. If you were truly as hard-hearted as you think, you would have allowed Cassandra to leave that day with June, when she learned she would recover from her illness. You would not have gone after her at the train station. You would have let me be the one to provide her with a means of support. You would have washed your hands of her and of your daughter, and never seen either of them again."

He frowned at what was unthinkable to him. "I could never have done that."

She did not need to say anything more. She was right, and he knew it. There *was* something left of his heart.

"But what about Father?" he asked. "You know what he is like. He wants Letitia to be my bride, he is obsessed, and he will never accept Cassandra. She is my mistress and has already borne me an illegitimate child. I cannot let my brothers down, not even Devon. I will never do that. And even if there was a way to change Father's mind, I am not even sure she would accept me as a husband. She does not trust me to be faithful. How could she, when I have made my opinions on marriage abundantly clear? I have told her time and time again that I do not believe in fidelity and that I will always have mistresses."

"But would you have mistresses if *she* were your wife?"

As he stared at his mother, he felt himself plummeting like a bird from high in the sky.

"No. There would never be anyone but her."

And with that absolute realization, he sat back in the chair, tipped his head to look up at the ceiling, and finally surrendered to the tough, uphill battle that lay ahead of him.

It was past midnight when Vincent stripped off his clothes and slipped into Cassandra's bed beside her. It was all he had wanted to do since he admitted the truth to himself and finally gave way to his feelings. The desire had been unbearable. Over dinner he had decided that he would not marry Letitia. He would demand that she release him, and in return he'd offer some sort of compensation. He would deal also with his father, but did not yet know how. It would require a great deal of careful planning. He could not afford any missteps.

Naked and ready for him, Cassandra sighed and wiggled erotically at his touch. "I thought you would never get here."

"I freed myself from the palace clutches as soon as I could. You smell like heaven." He kissed her mouth as he rolled onto her, settling upon her sweltering body, easing himself between her luscious pink thighs.

"Make love to me now," she pleaded.

Rising up on both arms, he looked down at her beautiful face in the firelight and her golden hair splayed out on the pillow, then gently slid himself into her engaging, heated depths.

"Oh yes," she sighed, her eyes falling closed.

A cool nighttime breeze blew in through the open window, carrying with it the fresh scents of lilacs and daffodils. Vincent made love to her slowly, achingly, and together they enjoyed the shared sensations of surrender and repletion, until their blood was fired to such intensity they could hold back no longer.

Cassandra quaked and shuddered with pleasure and cried out into the darkness. Vincent increased the tempo of his thrusts. Seconds later he throbbed wildly inside of her and drained every last drop of his desire into her womb.

"You did not stop me today," he said in a voice husky with exhaustion as he lowered himself down, "from coming inside you."

"I could not bear to deprive you of the pleasure that was mine, without constraints. And I suppose I have learned to live with the idea of consequences. They have not been so terrible thus far."

He could feel his hot breath trapped in the pillow as he spoke. "They shall be happy consequences indeed if you ever carry another child of mine, Cassandra, and I hope you will one day."

He also hoped she would be wearing his wedding ring.

"At this rate, it may happen sooner than either of us could expect."

God willing.

He rolled off her, and she snuggled into his embrace, resting her head on his shoulder and running a finger over his chest.

"I must confess to you," he softly said, "that I would dearly love for June to know me as her father."

Cassandra looked up at him. "Perhaps we can tell her the truth one day when she is old enough to understand and keep it secret."

He took in a deep breath. "Or perhaps there will be another way."

"What do you mean?"

He shook his head, for he was not yet free to propose, and he would not do it improperly. Not like this. He would first do what he must to make everything right. For her.

"I don't know. Perhaps I am dreaming." He turned his head on the pillow and touched her cheek with the tip of his finger. "What I do know, my darling, is that my heart is yours. Completely. Do you know that? Do you understand I do not ever want to be with anyone but you? That you satisfy me in every way a man can be satisfied?"

Her eyes filled with tears. "You satisfy me, too, Vincent. I have never felt so happy, even though I am also afraid."

He touched his lips to hers and kissed her in the quiet lamplight, then they lay beside each other for a long time until Cassandra's hand became limp upon his chest and her breathing grew slow and steady. She was asleep.

Vincent, however, was unable to rest, for his life had been spinning out of control for too long now. He did not want to wait for June to be old enough to understand that he was her father. He wanted her to know it now. He wanted the world to know. Surely it was possible. It was not as if it hadn't been done before. He recalled specifically the second marriage of the fifth Duke of Devonshire, who had lived in a ménage à trois with his wife and mistress for twenty-five years, then finally married the mistress after his wife passed away. She had borne him two children who were raised by the wife, and they were accepted in society. The son went on to become a baronet. The daughter married the brother of a viscount.

But Vincent did not want Letitia for a wife, nor did he wish to enter into a ménage à trois where she would be raising Cassandra's children. God forbid.

Of course, Devonshire was a duke. He could do as he pleased. In Vincent's case, his father would have to accept Cassandra, and in addition he would have to convince the world to turn a blind eye to her previous status as a mistress, which could not be kept secret because Letitia knew of it. Therein lay the problem.

Feeling restless, Vincent slipped out of bed and

picked up his discarded clothing. He dressed quietly in the darkness, then stood over Cassandra for a few minutes more.

The sheets were tangled around her long shapely legs, her moist lips were parted, her tousled hair spread out on the pillow like shimmering waves of silk. He let his gaze travel up the enticing length of her body, paused a moment to admire her sweet bottom, then his eyes came to rest on her face.

He had a vivid memory of that moment at the palace when he'd burst into the nursery to find her standing over the cradle with June in her arms, fearing that he would not let her leave with her daughter. How he had resented her that day for her optimistic ideas about love. It had forced him to examine more closely his own dark and cynical beliefs.

But how beautiful she'd looked—her blue eyes flashing with determination to survive and love her child on her own terms.

Cassandra had always been proud. She had never been weak, not even while asking for his help, pleading with him to raise her daughter—which could not have been easy when he'd been so heartless and cruel, and when she had despised him, and justifiably so.

He knew she no longer despised him, and he now understood that love between them was inevitable and worth fighting for. So there was at least some progress to celebrate. A great deal of it, in fact, if one remembered the man he had been not so long ago.

But it was not enough. He wanted more than just Cassandra's passions. He wanted her love—the kind of love only she could give. He wanted security, commitment, promises—and not the sort of promises written out by a solicitor.

God! He could not believe he was even thinking these things! In the past month he had been turned upside down on his ear. He wanted his daughter to know who he was, and he wanted Cassandra's heart, promised to him forever—happily, willingly, respectably, without guilt, for the rest of their days. He wanted no other woman but her. He supposed it was all he had ever wanted as a younger man—to be a devoted husband and to marry for love. That was the real Vincent Sinclair, as his mother had so wisely pointed out to him earlier in the day.

The sheer white curtain at the open window billowed inward on a breeze, and seconds later he felt its coolness pass over his skin. Glancing one last time at Cassandra on the bed, he debated whether he should slip back in and sleep all night beside her . . .

He decided against it, however, for he could not bear this sense of limbo any longer, with his future dictated by a father who was going mad, and a narcissistic fiancée who cared for no one but herself.

The time had come to do what he'd been avoiding since the moment he learned he had a child. He would have to ask for help—from the brother who had once betrayed him.

Chapter 17

Sometimes when he touches me, I feel as though all my sins have been forgiven. But other times, when I am alone, I wonder if I am dreaming all of this and will wake up one morning to find myself back in that cold boardinghouse, alone and bereft.

—from the journal of
Cassandra Montrose,
Lady Colchester,
July 8, 1874

Vincent arrived back at the palace at two in the morning. By then the cool spring breezes had disappeared and the night air was deathly still. Thunder was rumbling softly in the distance. Would there be rain? he wondered uneasily, looking up at the cloudy black sky as he led his horse into the stables. If so, he hoped the timing would not coincide with Letitia's departure from the palace. Such an ill-timed rainstorm would surely send his father somersaulting over the edge of sanity.

A short time later he was walking through the palace, checking to see if anyone was still up in the drawing room. The room was empty, the fire in the grate nothing but a pile of ash and the lamps all put out.

He went to the billiards room next, then the library and the study, but all the rooms were dark.

Too impatient to wait until morning, he went to his brother's bedchamber, paused briefly outside the door to contemplate how he was going to explain himself to Devon, then simply knocked. Receiving no answer, he knocked a second time, and heard some anxious whispering and the sounds of the bed creaking.

The door opened a crack, and he met his brother's intense, disapproving gaze. "Vincent. Has something happened?"

He took in a deep breath, realizing only then how strange this must seem, for he had not knocked on his brother's door in years, and certainly not at two in the morning. They hated each other.

"Nothing to be concerned about," he replied, detesting every minute of this. "I apologize for the interruption, but—"

He stopped suddenly. This was madness. It was

the middle of the night. This was the brother who had once stolen the woman he loved. He could not possibly confide in him. He pushed his hair back off his forehead.

"I shouldn't have knocked," he said. "Forgive me." He turned to go, but Devon came out into the corridor.

"Wait."

Vincent stopped and turned. His brother was wrapped in nothing but a sheet.

"Let me put something on," he said. "Meet me in the library in five minutes."

Vincent hesitated briefly, then nodded and left.

Devon was still tucking a wrinkled, full-sleeved shirt into his trousers when he walked into the library a short time later.

"I apologize," Vincent said again, holding out a glass of brandy to his brother, who was more or less his mirror image. Their height was the same, and Devon possessed a similar broadness about the shoulders, and sported a dark, wavy mane of hair as well. "It didn't occur to me that you are still on your honeymoon. I've been rather preoccupied."

Devon accepted the glass. "If my wife has anything to say about it, I may still be on this honeymoon fifty years from now, so it's just as well you did not wait."

Vincent could not deny that he resented his brother's good fortune, especially now, when he was so very far from his own.

"You are a lucky man."

Devon eyed him curiously. "And may I presume that is why you knocked on my door just now—because you are not presently feeling so lucky?"

All the weight of the world seemed to descend upon his shoulders at that instant, and he sank into a chair, raking his fingers through his hair. "I am feeling that damn family curse like a noose around my neck." He frowned. "I know things have been unpleasant between us lately, Devon, but I don't know where else to turn."

Thunder rumbled ominously, far off in the distance, and Vincent realized just how long it had been since he'd had a conversation with his brother that did not involve a verbal attack of some kind.

To his credit, for once Devon did not offer his customary brilliant, all-knowing wisdom or disparaging advice. He merely sipped his brandy and asked, "What can I do?"

Vincent looked up. "I presume you know the situation."

"That Lady Colchester is in the dower house with your child? Yes, I am aware."

"And did you know that Letitia is also aware of her presence there?"

Devon nodded. "From what I understand, your very accommodating fiancée has agreed to turn a blind eye to Lady Colchester and all your future mistresses."

Vincent took a drink. "There will never be any other mistresses." For a long moment he sat in silence, then at last looked up. "May I be so bold as to ask . . . would Rebecca ever agree so openly to turn a blind eye to that sort of thing?"

Devon laughed out loud. "The woman would have my balls in a bucket if I was unfaithful to her. Not that it would ever happen. I would never be so inclined, and even if I were, I don't believe I would have a shred of energy left over for another woman. Rebecca is . . . how shall I put it? She is somewhat *demanding* in that regard. And she believes in the natural fidelity of true love."

Vincent looked down at his brandy. "Every man should be so fortunate, to have such a wife."

"Or such a mistress?"

Vincent slouched back in the chair and spoke with conviction. "That is my problem, you see. It is my mistress I want as my wife."

Devon studied him. "But does she want you as a husband?"

"I don't know yet," Vincent replied, taking another drink. "But if I were free to woo her—honorably—I think I might be able to convince her that I am worthy."

He had convinced her of a great many things since the day she arrived here, despising the very ground he walked on. He had just come from her bed, after all.

"Do you love her?" Devon pointedly asked.

"Yes," he replied without hesitation, "and I do not think I could bear the loss of her."

Finishing his drink, Devon set down his glass and strolled to the window. He clasped his hands behind his back and looked out at the dark sky, which was flashing like distant cannon fire on the horizon.

"It can be difficult sometimes," Devon said, "or even painful, when one person loves more passionately than the other."

Vincent understood that his brother was referring not only to Cassandra, but to the woman who haunted both their pasts—the girl Vincent had loved his entire life, since he was a boy, and had intended to marry.

Perhaps it was time he accepted the fact that she had never loved him the way he loved her, he thought now. She had loved another. And that other man—Devon—had not loved her the way she had loved him. The scales had been all askew in that horrible, tragic love triangle.

"I am aware of that," Vincent said. "But this is different. There is no shortage of passion on either side. But Cassandra has been to hell and back because of me. I must step in and make an honest woman out of her."

Devon turned to face him. His eyes held a hint of amusement. "You wish to be her knight in shining armor, then?"

"As you were, with your own bride," Vincent reminded him. "You cannot deny you rode to Rebecca's rescue—literally, I believe—the first time you met her. And that particular good deed has not ended badly."

"Not badly at all." Devon sat back upon the windowsill. "Now that I recall, I knocked Letitia over onto her backside when I was galloping past her in Rebecca's direction. Figuratively, of course."

"Ah yes. She slapped your face in this very room."

"It was well worth the sting, I assure you."

Vincent gulped down the last of his brandy. "I would give anything to know the freedom of that sting, Devon. I just don't know how to get there. There is Father to consider, and you and Blake and Garrett. I do not wish to let you down."

Another flash of light lit the clouds on the horizon and flickered almost gracefully into darkness.

"I could talk to Father on your behalf," Devon said, "but I have tried before to convince him to free all of you, and he would not budge. He is like a mule when it comes to this ridiculous curse."

"Sometimes I think the only way one could ever succeed in changing his mind would be to convince him that Letitia is part of the curse, not the cure to it."

Devon narrowed his gaze. "You may have an idea there, Vincent. We could fight fire with fire."

"Or in this case, madness with madness."

"Yes, but how?"

Vincent turned his eyes to the window. "It looks like there is a storm coming. Father believes in signs. Perhaps there is a way to use this weather to our advantage."

Just then a few hard raindrops pelted the glass like flying pebbles, and a sudden, heavy downpour followed. It hissed and roared like an angry beast. Vincent joined Devon at the window, and they watched the trees bend and blow in the wind. The panes rattled in front of their faces.

"Would you look at that," Devon said. "Just what we were hoping for. Sometimes I wonder if there are in fact cosmic forces at work here. Honestly, what are the odds?"

Vincent raised an eyebrow at him. "Please, not you, too."

Devon smirked. "Do not worry, Vin. I am a man who lives according to facts, not sorcery." He raised his chin to gesture at the window. "And what is going on out there is nothing more than a theatrical display of our nation's standard springtime weather."

The both sipped their brandy for a few moments.

"But there is another type of display," Devon said warily, "that might cause problems for you, even if you are fortunate enough to win Father over and escape your betrothal to Letitia."

"What is that?"

"The scandal, Vincent. Surely you've considered it. It would be no small matter to restore Lady Colchester's reputation. Not only has she given birth to your child illegitimately, but Mother tells me she was disowned by her family and spent the past year living in almost complete poverty, working in a hat shop."

Vincent swallowed over the bitter taste in his mouth—which was quite a common occurrence lately, every time he imagined Cassandra's suffering. "That is all true," he said. "And I have no illusions. I know a scandal will be unavoidable, and sadly, even though he is the duke, Father doesn't have the presence of mind or the cleverness to squash it. It is too late to keep it secret. Not only does her family and brother-in-law know of it, for they were the ones to toss her out into the street, but Letitia knows, too."

"And we can hardly trust her to keep her mouth shut."

"Hardly." Vincent took a drink.

"Do you have any kind of plan that might at least diminish the gossip?" Devon asked.

"Only this: we will do what any sensible army would do in the face of such a foe. We will retreat from the battlefield, or in our case, go abroad or hide away in the country for a while. A long while. I have already purchased the perfect house, and to be honest, Devon, the scandal doesn't frighten me. Society can go to the devil for all I care."

"But what about Cassandra?" Devon said. "Perhaps it will matter to her. She might think herself unworthy and may not wish to sully our family name. She might be unhappy."

"I will make her happy."

"I have no doubt you will do your best, and perhaps love will be enough for the two of you. But what of June? Surely you would not wish to see her ostracized all her life. You have her future to think about as well."

Vincent sank into a chair and exhaled a deep breath. "Perhaps in time it will blow over. It's not as if no man has ever married his mistress before. It's been done. Hell, the Prince of Wales was in court just a few years ago for adultery. It won't stop him from being king."

"No, it won't." Devon finished his brandy and set it on a table. "Maybe there is hope. One day, I will be duke, and when that day comes, you have my word I will embrace both you and Lady Colchester, and with the Pembroke dukedom behind us, we shall not retreat. Your daughter and all your future children will have a great and powerful family behind them. You won't have to weather this alone."

Vincent rose to his feet and looked out at the storm, realizing how remarkable this moment was, as he stood without hostility beside his brother.

He turned to Devon. "I owe you my thanks."

"I haven't done anything yet."

"Nevertheless, your understanding means a great deal to me."

Devon met his gaze. "There is no need to thank me, Vincent. We both know I owe this to you."

Lighting flashed again, followed almost instantly by a deafening thunderclap that shook the foundations of the palace. They both looked outside.

"Good God," Devon said. "That was something."

"The entire household will be awake now."

But something caught Vincent's eye in the distance. "What is that?"

There was another flash of light—a small, flickering glow of pale yellow, close to the ground.

"Is it fire?" Devon asked.

Vincent cupped his hands to the glass to reduce

the reflections obscuring his view. "I believe it is. Lightning must have struck something."

Horror reeled in the pit of his stomach.

"Where?"

He knew exactly where.

Whirling around, he took off at a run, aware of Devon following close at his heels as he headed for the dower house.

Chapter 18

How clearly I remember my hostility toward my husband's mistress. I used to pray that she would leave him and that he would return to me for solace. I cannot pretend that I do not worry that Lady Letitia might one day feel that way about me.

—from the journal of
Cassandra Montrose,
Lady Colchester,
July 8, 1874

By the time Vincent reached the dower house, his horse was lathered and he was drenched in cold rain and sticky mud. The oak tree in front of the house was ablaze like a giant torch, illuminating the black smoke roiling over the rooftop. The front window of the second floor was broken, and the room inside was aglow.

He tossed a leg over the saddle and hit the ground at a run. He dashed up the steps and through the front door, where he met Aggie Callahan in the hall with June in her arms. His heart squeezed with relief at the sight of his daughter safe from harm.

"Take her outside," he said, "and down to the river to wait. My brother Lord Hawthorne is on his way in the coach and will arrive at any moment. He will see to your safety. Now quickly, where is Cassandra?"

Miss Callahan's eyes were wild with fear. "She went back upstairs to wake the other servants. I told her I would go, but she insisted!"

No more than a second later he was at the top of the staircase, swinging around the banister and running down the smoke-filled corridor toward the back stairs. "Cassandra!" He saw smoke rolling out from under a closed door—her bedchamber—but ignored it and continued on his way to the servant's quarters. "Cassandra!"

"We're here!"

The sound of her voice fired his determination, and he took three steps at a time to the third floor. He found her with Molly in her arms, escorting three women from their beds in their nightclothes.

"This way, hurry!" he said, addressing Mrs.

Bixby, the cook, and the maid. He waited for Cassandra, who was bringing up the rear, and took the puppy from her. "Are you all right?"

"Yes," she replied as she hurried down the stairs in front of him. "The tree outside was struck by lightning," she explained. "It came through my window. I ran out and shut the door behind me. The room must be an inferno by now."

"I believe it is, which is why we must get everyone out quickly. Is there anyone else?"

"No, this is all of us." She stopped suddenly. "Except for the maid who comes sometimes to clean the fireplaces."

"What maid?"

"Her name is Iris, but she isn't here, so she must be at the palace."

He looked at her uncertainly for a moment. "Aggie and June are safe outside," he said, "and Devon is on his way with the coach."

On the second floor, they paused to look at the smoke filling the corridor. Vincent felt the heat blast on his cheeks, making his eyes and nostrils burn. He held the puppy close. "Hurry now!"

They started off again to the main staircase and descended as a group. Cassandra held a fist to her mouth to stifle her coughing and wheezing.

"Everyone outside," he shouted, "and go straight down to the river!"

They all ran out of the house just as the Pembroke coach arrived, followed by two wagons, each carrying close to a dozen tenant farmers, buckets in hand. Everyone spilled out of the wagon beds and ran down to the river, forming a line from the bottom of the hill to the house. Sparks flew from the rooftop up to the black, smoky sky.

Devon stepped out of the coach and waved to Miss Callahan, who still held June in her arms. The young nurse ran toward him, while Vincent handed the puppy over to Mrs. Bixby.

He turned to instruct Cassandra to hurry to the coach, but before he had a chance, a loud crack exploded overhead and sparks flew everywhere like fireworks. He looked up.

An enormous burning branch from the oak tree had snapped and was plummeting to the ground.

"Make way!" he shouted, stepping forward desperately, but his warning did more harm than good, for Cassandra stopped to look up.

The branch came down on top of her. She was crushed to the ground.

He charged forward, dropping to his knees at her side. "Cassandra!"

She was not moving. Her scalp was bloody. His gut churned with dread.

Then Devon was beside him, shouting, "Grab hold!" He took one end of the heavy branch—the end that was not yet ablaze—and together they tossed it aside. Three men immediately swung water from their buckets to douse the flames.

"Is she all right?" Devon asked, kneeling down.

Vincent pressed his ear to her chest. "Her heart is beating." He took her face in his hands. "Cassandra!" She gave no response. He looked at his brother. "I need to get her to the palace."

"Yes."

He slid his arms under her limp frame and lifted her off the ground.

"I will take care of everything here," Devon assured him. "There is no one else inside the house?"

"They are all here," Vincent replied.

He carried Cassandra to the coach, where Miss Callahan was waiting safely inside with June, along with the other servants and Molly.

"Set her down here," Mrs. Bixby said, reaching out to help bring Cassandra in. Vincent laid her down gently on the seat, then got inside and pounded on the roof. "Go!"

The coach jerked roughly forward as they made off for the palace.

As Vincent carried Cassandra through the front doors, his mother rushed across the candlelit hall in her wrapper to meet him. She took one look at

Cassandra, unconscious and bloody in his arms, and said, "Is she all right?"

"She is alive. She was knocked down by a falling branch." Charlotte came running down the stairs in her nightdress as well. "We'll need the doctor," he said.

His mother nodded. "Charlotte, go and tell Mrs. Callahan what has happened. Have her send for Dr. Thomas, then instruct her to bring bandages and brandy up to the blue guest chamber. Quickly!"

Charlotte hurried toward the servants' wing, while Vincent, still dripping wet and covered in mud, carried Cassandra up the stairs. Aggie Callahan entered the hall with the baby, along with the other servants from the dower house.

Vincent said over his shoulder, "Mother, see to June, if you please."

He was vaguely aware of his mother escorting Miss Callahan up the stairs behind him and turning toward the nursery, while he started down the dimly lit east corridor toward the blue guest chamber.

Turning the corner, he stopped abruptly when he collided with Letitia. Her face was eerily illuminated by the flickering candle she held high in her hand.

Her eyes widened in shock when she beheld

his mistress unconscious in his arms. "What is *she* doing here?"

"She is hurt." Concerned only with getting Cassandra to a warm, safe place, he pushed past his fiancée and continued down the corridor.

Letitia followed. "You shouldn't have brought her here. Why didn't you take her to the village?"

His arms were straining by the time he reached the door. "I told you she is hurt. Now open the door if you please."

"I will not."

He glared at her. "We will speak about this in the morning, Letitia, but right now you will do as I say and open this door." His arms were beginning to shake.

She returned his glare with her own heated ferocity, then did as he instructed. He promptly carried Cassandra inside to the bed and laid her down.

"Is she dead?" Letitia asked. "I hope she is, and I hope she goes straight to Hell."

He looked at her over his shoulder. "I think it would be best for everyone if you left the room."

"No. I will not have you making love to your mistress right under my nose. I told you, this is my domain, not hers. She has no right to be here. Get her out."

He straightened and faced her. "Lady Colchester

is hurt and requires medical attention. She will remain where she is."

"She needs to die, that's what she needs to do."

Vincent regarded the shallow depths of his fiancée's eyes with nauseating clarity, then grabbed hold of her arm and escorted her forcibly to the door. "Go and tell my mother she is needed here. Then go back to your own room and stay there." He shoved her out into the corridor and slammed the door in her face.

Cassandra moaned. Turning quickly, he went to the bedside and brushed her hair off her face. He noted with horror that the pillow was already stained with blood. "Cassandra, darling," he said, laboring to remain calm, "wake up, you were hit on the head."

She did not respond. He gently patted her cheek, willing her eyes to open as the terrifying possibility of her death right there in front of him struck a deep chord in his gut. *Wake up. Please wake up.*

The door burst open then and he jumped, startled by the brash intrusion. He whirled around. "Father."

The duke, wearing only a nightshirt and slippers, was breathing heavily. His white hair was wild about his head, his eyes flashing with fury.

"Who is this woman?" he asked.

"She is Lady Colchester," Vincent replied, his

heart already pounding with anxiety. "She is hurt. There was a fire."

"I know damn well there was a fire. I saw the lightning strike down upon us with my own eyes."

"She needs a doctor."

His father shuffled across the floor to stand over the bed. He looked down at Cassandra, unconscious. "She's bleeding."

"Yes."

"What happened?"

"The lightning struck a tree, and a burning branch fell on her."

Vincent swallowed uneasily as his father bent over Cassandra and sniffed around her head. His face was mere inches from hers as he studied her closely. "She's pretty. Is she alive?"

"Yes," Vincent answered, wondering if his father could hear the sound of his own heart booming like thunder inside his chest.

The duke straightened and stared at him with concern. "A burning branch you say."

The duchess entered the room and stopped in the doorway. "Theodore, what are you doing out of bed?"

He turned. "Brother Salvador woke me. He said something happened. Look, it is the curse."

She went to him, slid an arm around his waist and led him to the door. "There are no monks here, Theodore. You were dreaming."

"No, it wasn't a dream. I told you, it's the curse."

She smiled gently at him and nodded as she continued to usher him out.

"Can't you see it's raining again?" His voice was now quivering with fear.

"Only a little. The sun will shine again in the morning," she said. "I promise."

"But that woman is bleeding."

"Dr. Thomas is on his way."

They left the room. Vincent shut his eyes and cupped his forehead in a hand. He turned to look down at Cassandra, still unconscious on the bed.

How had it come to this? he wondered wretchedly. And why? He had just this night been wishing for a storm in order to help his case, not hinder it. Now he was certain that when his father learned that Cassandra was his mistress and a threat to his marriage to Letitia, he would blame her for the rain and thunder, believe she was provoking the curse upon the palace, and all hell would break loose.

If only there was a way he could bring an end to this insanity. If only there was a way around this curse.

Chapter 19

I wonder what turn of events will bring an end to this wild passion we feel? Surely it cannot go on forever. A mistress is only temporary, after all. Something will eventually snuff it out.

—from the journal of
Cassandra Montrose,
Lady Colchester,
July 8, 1874

By the time the doctor arrived, the first glimmer of dawn had brightened the sky and the rain clouds were moving on. Sunshine poured in through the palace windows—just as the duchess had promised—but Cassandra had not yet regained consciousness.

When the doctor walked into the room at last, Vincent rose from his chair. "Thank God you're here. She is in a bad state."

Dr. Thomas strode to the bed and set his satchel down on a chair. "Good morning, Lord Vincent. How long has she been like this?"

"More than three hours."

The doctor leaned over Cassandra, whose head was wrapped in a bandage tied at the side. He listened to her heart.

Vincent's mother entered the room and closed the door behind her. "Good morning, Doctor," she said, moving silently around the foot of the bed.

The doctor bowed to her, then commented on the bloody pillow. "I understand that the lady was hit by a falling branch."

"That's right."

"And she has not regained consciousness at all?"

"No, but she has been making some sounds," Vincent explained. "She was moaning earlier."

"Was she moving all her limbs?"

"Yes."

"That is a good sign."

"Will she be all right, then?"

The doctor gently lifted her eyelids and examined her pupils. "It is difficult to say. She appears to have a concussion, and head injuries can be unpredictable. The sooner she wakes up, the easier her recovery will be." He untied the bandage and examined the wound at the back of her head. "This isn't bad," he said. "Contrary to how it looks, it's just a small gash. They do tend to bleed rather profusely." He turned to his leather satchel. "It won't take but a moment to rebandage it."

A short time later, Vincent and his mother joined the doctor in the hallway outside the room. "There is not much to be done, I'm afraid," he told them, "though it might help to talk to her." He turned to Vincent. "Sometimes the sound of a familiar voice can work wonders in these situations."

"I will do that. Thank you."

"And when she wakes up, she will likely not feel well. Her head will ache and she might be dizzy or nauseous for a few days."

The doctor turned to the duchess. "I will return this evening to check on her again, Your Grace, though if you need me before then, you know where to find me."

"You have been most helpful, Dr. Thomas. Allow me to accompany you to your carriage."

Vincent shook the doctor's hand and watched them go, then returned to the guest chamber where Cassandra lay sleeping. He sat by the window in the warm sunshine beaming in through the glass and thought about all that had transpired over the past month. He had met his daughter—a beautiful baby girl with the heart-warming light of the sun in her eyes—and had fallen in love with both her and her mother. His life was altered and would remain so forever. Nothing would ever be the same.

And today he was in Hell.

Recalling what the doctor had just told him, he rose from his chair and went to Cassandra's side. "Can you hear me?" he asked.

He took hold of her hand, bent forward and kissed the back of it, and when he straightened, noticed her eyelids fluttering.

"Cassandra," he said, bending forward again, hearing the pathetic desperation in his voice. "It's Vincent. Wake up, darling."

At last her eyes opened. "Vincent," she said groggily. "Is it morning?"

"Yes," he replied, tears filling his eyes as he shook with sobs of laughter. "And the sun is shining."

"Where am I?"

"You're at the palace."

She looked at him with fear. "*June . . .* " She tried to sit up. "Where is she? Is she all right?"

He took hold of her shoulders and gently pushed her back down. "She is fine. Miss Callahan is with her in the nursery. Our little girl slept through the entire ordeal." He narrowed his gaze at her. "Do you remember what happened?"

"Yes, the fire . . . " She relaxed and lowered herself back down onto the pillow. "A tree fell on me."

"It was just a branch."

"Was anyone else hurt? Is the house still standing?"

"Everyone is fine, and Devon has informed me that the house is in good stead as well, except for your room where the tree went through the window. You were wise to close the door. It kept the blaze contained."

She looked uncertainly around the room. "But if you brought me here last night . . . " Wetting her lips, she touched the bandage at her forehead. "Does anyone know I am here?"

"Yes. Most everyone."

"But do they know everything? Do they know who I am? What about your father? And your fiancée? Oh, I cannot bear to think what she must be feeling right now, knowing her fiancée's mistress is under the very same roof."

He hated the sound of distress in her voice. Leaning over her, he kissed her forehead. "Do not concern yourself, Cassandra. All you need to do is recover."

She cupped her forehead in a hand and squeezed her eyes shut. "What must they think of me?"

"They do not think anything. I am not even sure Father understands who you are to me. He is not himself."

Her voice was fraught with concern. "Does he know about June?"

Vincent shook his head. "No."

"Then please let it remain so, Vincent. I think it is best."

"Why?"

"What is the point in telling him? We agreed I would remain a secret. That was the plan from the beginning. I should not even be here. I do not want to be the cause of your ruin."

He was surprised she was so troubled by this, and feared the doubts she was having might overcome the closeness that had at last grown between them.

His temper rose suddenly because of this hellish situation in which he'd become embroiled. His freedom to choose his own future had been taken away from him, and the woman he loved—yes, loved!—was not getting what she deserved.

"You are not a dirty little secret," he assured her, "nor is my daughter. You both deserve more. You will have more."

"But there is no more," she said. "This is our reality. The house you purchased—Langley Hall—I should go there straight away before people begin to gossip. I will be content there, and no one will know about June and me. Your inheritance will be safe."

"I will not have you hiding away from the world like a criminal."

"But I am your mistress. That is my place."

"You are more than that. You have brought me back from the brink of despair. You have given me something to celebrate—a daughter. I owe you everything."

She blinked up at the ceiling. "I think I am going to be sick."

Vincent darted across the room to the wash-stand in the corner and returned to the bed with the bowl, just in time for her to sit forward and retch into it.

"The doctor said you have a concussion," he told her, waiting patiently while she collected herself, "and that you would feel ill for a day or two."

She regained control of her breathing and lay back on the pillows again. "Why do I always end up in a Pembroke Palace bedchamber when I am ill?"

Vincent set the bowl on the floor, poured some water from the pitcher onto a cloth, and wiped her forehead and face. "You'll feel better soon."

Her eyes had fallen closed. "I need to rest."

He retreated to the chair by the window and sat for a long time, watching her until she opened her eyes again.

"You look exhausted," she said. "You did not sleep last night, did you?"

"It was an eventful night."

A knock sounded at the door. Charlotte entered.

"Cassandra . . . " She crossed to the bedside. "I came to see how you are doing. I am so pleased that you are awake."

"Hello, Charlotte," she replied. "Do not fret. I am fine."

Charlotte turned to Vincent with a concerned look. "Have you slept at all? You are still wearing the same clothes you had on yesterday."

"There, you see?" Cassandra said, turning her head on the pillow. "Even your sister agrees with me. You are covered in mud. You do not need to sit here."

He hesitated, then decided he could do with a change of clothes and perhaps a bite to eat while he considered how to handle all of this. But he did not want to leave her.

"Go," she said firmly. "Besides, I cannot sleep with you sitting there, staring at me like that. You make me feel like a fish in a bowl."

Reluctantly, he rose from the chair, approached the bed and whispered in her ear. "I will be back soon. We will work everything out. I promise."

The door opened and a maid entered the room with a bucket and a brush.

"Oh, Iris . . . " Cassandra managed awkwardly to sit up. "Have you come to light me a fire? You always come at just the right time, when a chill is pouring into the room."

"I only came to clean the grate, but a footman

will be along shortly." The maid knelt before the hearth and began to sweep out the ash.

Cassandra looked up at Vincent. "This is Iris, the maid I mentioned when we were coming out of the dower house last night."

He glanced at the woman. "I am pleased to see you were not hurt in the blaze."

The woman kept her eyes lowered and did not meet his gaze, which was not unusual for a servant, but there was something about her . . .

"Thank you, my lord."

He said nothing more as he backed away and left Cassandra alone with Charlotte and the maid, who looked strangely familiar, though he was sure he did not remember ever seeing her clean the grates before.

Letitia curtsied as she entered the library. "Pardon me, Your Grace. I did not know anyone was here."

The duke, who had been asleep and snoring on the sofa, sat up abruptly. "Who's there?"

"It is only I, Letitia, your future daughter-in-law. I came to look for a book about flower gardens. Now that the sun is shining, my interest in horticulture is poking at me."

The truth was, she had no interest in seeds or plants, and especially not dirt. She only liked flowers in vases, and only when they were in full bloom and arranged by someone skillful.

He gestured to her. "Come in, dear. I have many books on the subject." His eyes brightened as he swung his legs to the floor. "Horticulture is my passion. Did you know that?"

Of course she knew. Everyone in England knew of his famous Italian Gardens, though they were hardly worth looking at now. He had dug them all up when the rains first began.

"I had no idea we had so much in common, Your Grace. It appears we are kindred spirits." She smiled and entered the library, closing the door behind her. "Would you be so kind as to select a book that might be of interest to me?"

Not that she had any intention of reading it.

"I would be delighted."

He rose from the sofa, and she made a point not to look down at his ugly bare feet, for fear she might vomit at the sight of them.

"I hope you are not too distressed by what happened last night," she said, following him to the bookshelves. "I, myself, have been dreadfully upset by it. I barely slept at all."

He did not seem to be listening, however. He was distracted by his search for just the right book. "No, no, that's not the one," he said under his breath.

"Your Grace?"

"Yes, dear."

Did he not even know what occurred? she wondered irritably. Did he not know his son was keeping his mistress inside the house at this very moment, and that the woman's presence here was enough to make Letitia want to shoot someone?

"Surely you know about the storm," she said.

"The storm?"

"Yes. Last night there was rain and wind and thunder and lightning. I was in terrible pain." She cupped a hand over her birthmark.

His cheeks flushed with color as he faced her. "Pain, you say?" He looked down at her hand.

"Yes, but thankfully when Vincent's mistress was struck down, the pain went away."

Anxiety flashed in his eyes. "Vincent's mistress?"

"Yes, Your Grace. She has been staying in the dower house, despite my protestations. I thought you knew. I believe she is the reason the rain started again, because I have been having some doubts about my decision to marry your son. That mistress he is keeping—she is most appalling. I do not like her."

Panic contorted the duke's features. "You are not changing your mind, are you? You cannot. You are wearing the Pembroke Sapphire."

"I want very much to do my duty," she told him, "but at times I fear it is impossible when that woman is threatening my position here."

Fear and confusion rattled his expressions. He appeared to be searching his mind for understanding or perhaps a solution, then his bushy eyebrows lifted. "Is it the woman with the bloody head?"

"Yes."

"She is Vincent's mistress?"

"Yes, and I am devastated, Your Grace. My heart is breaking." She raised a handkerchief to her nose and sniffled.

"Oh my dear, do not distress yourself." He put his arm around her shoulder. "Tell me what is wrong."

What is wrong? She had a mind to shake his brains loose. "I just told you, Your Grace. It is that woman with the bloody head—Vincent's mistress. Everything was going so well until she arrived. The sun was shining, everyone was happy. But now she is fanning the flames of the curse."

He frowned. "There was thunder last night, and a bolt of lightning . . . "

"Yes, Your Grace," she replied, pleased that he was grasping her point at last. "The curse tried to strike her down."

The duke squared his shoulders and made for the door.

"Where are you going?"

"I am going to tell my son to get rid of her."

She stepped forward anxiously. "No! Wait!"

He stopped.

"Your son is blinded by lust," she explained, remembering with rancor how he had rejected her the previous morning in his study. "He will not see sense and has not listened to my pleas. I have a much better idea."

He slowly approached.

"Will you sit down, Your Grace?" She took him by the arm and led him to the sofa. "I think that together we can ensure this woman does not continue to stir the wrath of the curse, for I have a plan. Would you like to hear it?"

He followed her unsteadily and sank onto a soft cushion. "Indeed I would."

Chapter 20

There was a time, I believe, that my head was buried in the sand when it came to Vincent's fiancée. I could not bear to think of her when I was falling in love with him. But now I am glad I had the chance to meet her in person.

—from the journal of
Cassandra Montrose,
Lady Colchester,
July 9, 1874

Cassandra woke to the sound of her door creaking open and a throbbing pain in the back of her head. Feeling groggy, she opened her eyes and blinked a few times. Perhaps the maid was returning with another bowl of quail soup. When she managed to turn her head on the pillow, however, she found herself looking up at a tall, dark-haired woman with a flawless, ivory complexion. A cold knot formed in her stomach.

"Good morning," the woman said, lifting a dark eyebrow.

Cassandra looked carefully into her eyes while she fought to suppress a sickening wave of dread, for she had once walked many painful miles in this woman's shoes. She understood the frustration and humiliation she must surely be feeling as Vincent's future wife. She knew the jealousy, the fear, the heartache, and the sense of being completely alone when one's husband was in the arms of his mistress . . .

"Good morning," she replied.

Seconds ticked by like minutes, sluggish and excruciating, while she sat up and inched back against the pillows.

"I assume you know who I am," the woman said.

"Yes," she said with regret.

A muscle twitched at Letitia's jaw. "Just so I am certain that we are clear—I am Lady Letitia Markham, the future Lady Vincent."

Cassandra swallowed uneasily. "I presume you know who I am as well."

"Of course I know who you are. I also know *what* you are."

A black chill rippled down her spine. "I am sorry I was brought here. I did not want that to happen."

She could think of nothing else to say.

"I am not surprised that you did not want it. Women like you prefer to hide away in the shadows, beneath the cover of darkness, so as not to shine too bright a light on your depravity. Isn't that right?"

Cassandra clenched her hands together as she watched Vincent's fiancée slowly circle the foot of the bed.

"Do you think that if your sins are hidden from the world," she said, "they do not exist? That they hurt no one?"

"I never meant to hurt anyone. That was not my intention."

Letitia scoffed. "Pardon my mistake. You have a conscience, do you?"

"I only wanted to be with my daughter," Cassandra explained. "I wanted to provide her with a home. That is why I moved into the dower house. It was supposed to be a temporary arrangement until—"

"I think you wanted more than that, Lady Colchester. You wanted my fiancé's body. Admit it." Her expression flashed with malice. "You wanted your lover close by, so you could have him in your bed whenever you wished, to satisfy your disgusting carnal urges and wicked vices."

Cassandra closed her eyes. This was horrendous, all of it.

Letitia raised a handkerchief to her nose. Her

voice began to quiver. "I am brokenhearted. I beg you to understand that. I love him and I want to make him happy, but how can I do that when you offer your body to him night after night? I can certainly do no such thing, because I am not yet his wife and I must have a care for my virtue."

The overwrought sound of her voice made Cassandra look up.

"I do not blame you completely," Letitia continued. "I understand that Vincent is a very attractive man, and he knows how to seduce women into his bed. Perhaps that is what made you weak. But I had hoped that when I became his wife, he might improve upon himself and give up those wicked ways." She sniffed. "I love him so, Lady Colchester. I will die if I lose him. All I want is a chance to make him happy. I beseech you to understand that."

Cassandra sat very still, looking intently at Letitia and recalling all the times Vincent had claimed his fiancée did not love him or care if he had mistresses. Yet here she was, claiming otherwise.

She began to feel nauseous again, and glanced anxiously at the washbasin across the room.

"Well?" Letitia said. "What do you have to say for yourself?"

Cassandra could only shrug her shoulders, for her stomach was whirling and churning. She was afraid she would be sick right here in front of Vincent's angry fiancée.

"So you have nothing to say?" Letitia moved with impatience to the bedside. "All I want is a chance to win his affections," she went on. "I want our marriage to be a success. Surely you can understand that. Surely you would not wish to stand in the way of it."

It was all Cassandra had ever wanted for herself at one time—to be a good wife and to have a happy marriage, but that had not been possible because her husband had been in love with another woman. He had loved that woman even on the day they were married, though she had not known it at the time.

If only she *had* known. She wished she had. She would have done so many things differently. She would never have married him. She would have set him free.

She looked up at Letitia.

"I want you to give him up," Letitia said. "Leave him and do not ever see him again."

"But we have a daughter together," Cassandra replied, "and he cares for her. I promised I would never keep her from him. We have a legal, binding contract between us."

"Let me worry about that. All you need to do is leave. I don't know what Vincent is paying you, but the duke wants to be rid of you, so he and I have made arrangements for you to have enough money to start a new life elsewhere." She reached into her pocket and withdrew a thick wad of bank notes. "There is twenty thousand pounds here, and if it is not enough, I can get more from the duke. All you have to do is take it." She held it out, directly under Cassandra's nose. "A coach will be waiting out front to take you and your daughter wherever you wish. It is the right thing to do. You know it is."

Cassandra stared at the shocking amount of money. It was indeed more than enough to set herself up comfortably with June. She would not have to rely on anyone. It would put an end to her wicked life as a rogue's mistress. Letitia would be happy. Vincent's brothers would not have to fear the loss of their inheritances.

But what of Vincent?

She felt a wave of sorrow, and lifted her gaze. "Do you know her name?"

"Whose name?" Letitia asked irritably.

"Your fiancé's daughter."

Letitia's mouth tightened into a hard line. "Of course I do not. Why would I want to know that?"

For a long moment Cassandra stared at Letitia, then down at the money she still held out in front of her face. "She looks like him. She has his coloring."

"How lovely." Eyes blazing with determination, Letitia lifted the money again. "Just take this and I will arrange for your servants to go with you. Think of it as a chance to salvage whatever morals and principles you once had when you were a lady. Surely you want your respectability back. You can't possibly want to go through life being a married man's whore."

There it was again—that word that had cut into her heart so deeply a year ago, that shamed her and ravaged what remained of her self-respect. She had sunk to the darkest depths of despair after that. She'd lost everything and given birth to her baby alone in a cold, dirty boardinghouse, without a single shilling to feed herself or her child. It had taken all of her courage and determination to pull herself back up and better her circumstances by finding work in a hat shop.

Swallowing hard, she reached up and wrapped both her hands around Letitia's. She felt the thick wad of money, warm and solid between her hands. It was enough to last her a lifetime. She could start over. She could go anywhere in England with a nest egg like that . . .

Slowly but firmly, however, she pushed it away, hard up against Letitia's chest, and spoke very clearly, to make sure Letitia understood every word.

"Why don't you take this very generous offering, Lady Letitia, and that big, fat shiny ring on your finger, and get out of my sight before I chase you out of here."

Letitia took a step back in shock. A few of the bank notes floated to the floor. "I beg your pardon?"

Cassandra sat forward and spoke viciously. "Just so I am certain that we are clear, Lady Letitia. I love the man you call your fiancé, and I would rather be his whore than a respectable lady like you, who would keep the man she claims she loves from the daughter who means everything to him."

The world seemed to stop spinning for a moment while they glared at each other.

Letitia crouched down to scoop up the money she'd dropped, then rose to her feet, clutching it to her bosom. "It appears you have chosen your future—a most degenerate one."

"Indeed I have."

"Then we have nothing more to say to each other." She turned and walked to the door, but was inclined to spit out one final remark. "The duke will not be pleased."

Cassandra leaned back upon the pillows as the door slammed shut. For a long moment she sat there in silence, staring at the door, blinking in disbelief.

Had she really just done that?

She turned her head toward the washbasin again and noted with a rather perverse swell of pleasure that her nausea had completely passed.

Feeling almost bewildered by the sudden clarity in her heart and mind, she leaned across the bed and picked up her diary on the bedside table. Opening it to the last page, she ripped out a blank sheet of paper and quickly began to write in frantic, messy penmanship.

My dearest Vincent,

I am afraid I must leave the palace. But I now know what I want from the future. I know what is right . . .

Vincent jolted awake with a start and sat bolt upright in bed. His heart was pummeling the inside of his chest. He had been dreaming.

Breathing heavily, drenched in perspiration, he looked around the room. Sunlight was streaming in through the windows. How long had he been asleep? Half an hour? An hour?

Wearily, he swung his legs to the floor and pressed the heels of his hands to his eyes, still burning from lack of sleep. He'd dreamt of that dreadful day with MaryAnn when he rode into the woods in search of her and found her facedown in the mud, dead. In the dream, however, when he turned her over, it was not MaryAnn's face he saw, but Cassandra's—pale and ghostly, devoid of life.

He took a moment to calm his breathing and wait for his heartbeat to slow to a more natural pace. He spent that time reflecting upon the precarious state of his life.

For years now he had been avoiding any kind of deep, emotional involvement with women. He had cared deeply for MaryAnn, and that day in the woods nearly destroyed him. It certainly destroyed his bond with his brother, for Devon had been the sole reason MaryAnn was in the woods then.

It was Devon who made the decision to put her on the horse and take the shorter route home over the hill, which was a river of mud. He was the one holding the reins when the horse slipped and stumbled.

Vincent looked over at the small cedar box on top of his dressing table. The love letter MaryAnn had written to Devon was in it, secure under lock and key.

He stared at the box. Something about the dream was pushing him to get up and retrieve the key from its hiding place in the floor . . .

A moment later he was lifting the lid and withdrawing the letter, which was addressed to Devon in MaryAnn's passionate, scrolling hand. He slowly unfolded the heavy paper and with shaky hands began to read her tear-stained words.

My Dearest Devon,

Please forgive me for what I must make known. If I could conceal it, bury it, I would, but alas, I am helpless, suffering from the pain that lives inside my heart.

Each day when I see you, I must act as your sister, even though I come alive with every look you bestow upon me. Each day I grow weaker against the force of my yearnings, and every morning I awake in agony.

My God, how I fear the disdain that will rage at me when you have read this letter. When I first met you, I was but a girl. How was I to know the passion I would be forced to smother when I became a woman? How was I to know I would fight such a battle with my conscience, after accepting the hand of your brother?

I cannot fight my love for you any longer. I cannot marry Vincent. I must have you, and only you.

Vincent lowered the letter to his side. He remembered dropping to his knees in the mud when he found her, and how violently he had wept by her body. That was when he discovered the letter in her pocket. Later, he'd confronted Devon . . .

You were alone with her. Did you touch her?

Yes.

Did you kiss her? Hold her in your arms? Make love to her?

Yes.

Devon had not denied it. He had lain in his bed, bruised and broken from the accident that cut MaryAnn's precious life short, and openly confessed his betrayal.

That had been the end of their friendship. Devon left for America the following day.

A memory flashed in Vincent's mind—the image of Cassandra lying unconscious under that burning branch. He felt an instinctive urge to run, to flee from the possibility of such heartbreak again if he were to lose her for any reason—whether it was death or anything else. He knew exactly how it felt. He remembered it all too well. It would be unbearable.

For a brief instant he wondered what he would be doing right now if she had not reentered his life. Would he be content in his engagement and ready to accept his fate with Letitia? Would there be no doubts, no pain, no longings?

He glanced down at the letter again. Perhaps he would have been satisfied with a loveless marriage to Letitia. He simply would have continued with his empty life, and continued to nurture the dark hatred he felt toward his brother.

But that was not the hand he'd been dealt, for Cassandra had entered his life, and he had fallen in love again. He'd had need of his brother.

He looked at the letter, admitting to himself at last that it was MaryAnn who instigated their betrayal.

How I fear the disdain that will rage at me when you have read this letter . . .

She knew Devon would be angry. Perhaps he had been.

It was all in the past now, however. Mistakes had been made. He was no stranger to them himself. Now, all he wanted was to forgive. He did not want to go on living his life as an outsider, bitter and alone. He wanted to reclaim the friendship he once shared with his brother—

A knock sounded at his door. He slipped the letter back into the box and went to answer it. "Charlotte."

His sister was standing in the corridor clutching a dirty old letter box in her arms. Her hands were filthy. She looked as if she'd been digging in the garden. "I have something here that I think you should see."

He recognized a look of distress on her face. She appeared almost ready to burst from a secret she was desperate to divulge. "Come in, Charlotte," he said. "What do you have there?"

As soon as she entered the room, he shut the door behind her. She moved to the desk, set the box down, and spoke so fast he had a hard time making out what she was trying to tell him.

"This is full of old letters," she said. "Iris found them ages ago hidden in one of the fireplaces—in the very room where Letitia is staying. She never told anyone else before now."

"Iris? The maid?"

"Yes. She cleans the fireplaces, and we got to talking," Charlotte said excitedly. "Perhaps this is something Father should know about. It is just the sort of madness that would make sense to him."

He looked at her with curiosity, then crossed the room to inspect the contents of the mysterious box. He remembered his earlier conversation with Devon. *We shall have to fight madness with madness.*

Perhaps this would be the key . . .

In the south wing of the palace—at the same time Vincent was reading the letters Charlotte had discovered—quite another letter was being read by the Duchess of Swinburne, who was on her way to her daughter's room with a box of chocolates.

The duchess had just rounded a corner when she spotted Lord Vincent's scandalous mistress sneaking down the same corridor with a bloody bandage wrapped around her head.

Intrigued by the woman's impetuous step, the duchess turned around, found the correct door, and tiptoed into the elusive mistress's room. There, on the pillow, she found a most interesting letter to her own daughter's fiancée, Lord Vincent.

She read every word with dread and alarm, then promptly slipped the note into her pocket. With great haste she left the room and continued down the corridor to speak with her daughter.

Chapter 21

My world makes perfect sense now. I know what I want, and I understand my life and my future.

—from the journal of
Cassandra Montrose,
Lady Colchester,
July 9, 1874

"I beg your pardon?" the duke said, brushing the mud off his knees in the garden and rising to his feet. "What is this you have?"

"Some letters," Vincent replied. "Charlotte found them in Lady Letitia's bedchamber, hidden behind the stones in the fireplace. They are very old."

Vincent set the box down on the fountain wall, which encircled the statue of Venus.

"Who are they from?" his father asked.

"They are from the first Duchess of Pembroke,

written to her sister. They are of a rather personal nature."

Fascinated, the duke sat down on the wall and opened the box. He picked up the first letter on the stack, which was tied together with a black ribbon. "Are they naughty letters?" he asked mischievously.

Vincent felt as if he were addressing a schoolboy. "No, Father, at least not in the way you are thinking."

He began to read one letter, then the next, and the next. By the time he got to the bottom of the stack, he was breathing hard and his eyes were darting back and forth from left to right as he read the private and shocking correspondence between the first Duchess of Pembroke and her older sister.

"The sister tells her not to do it," the duke said. "She warns her that if she does, she will be cursed forever."

Vincent watched his father carefully. "What do you think it means?" he asked, even though he knew very well what it meant and what his father would surmise. But he did not wish to plant any ideas in his head. He wanted the man to decide for himself.

"She hates her husband. She wants to poison him."

Vincent still said nothing. He let his father finish reading.

He came to the last word of the last letter, then went searching inside the box for more. "That is it? There are no more? It doesn't say what happened. What did she do?"

"I do not know."

He looked up at Vincent with fire in his eyes. "The first duke died in his bed. You don't think . . . Is it possible?" He stood up and walked across the ravaged garden, his boots sinking deep into the sticky muck. He read the last letter again, then turned to Vincent. "Brother Salvador led you to these letters, didn't he? He has been waking me at night, always taking me to the gallery to look at the portraits. He always takes me to *her*."

Vincent shook his head. "It was not a ghost, Father. It was one of the maids. The letters are real."

"But Brother Salvador is real. He leads me to the portrait of the first duchess. I am always entranced by her beauty. That is why I was so certain Letitia was destined to be a Pembroke. She is beautiful also, just like the duchess in the portrait." The color drained from his face.

"She doesn't love me," Vincent said. "We won't be happy."

The duke squeezed his eyes shut and cupped

his forehead with both fists. "I always feel like I am forgetting something."

"You often forget things, Father. It is simply your age."

"Is this the origin of the curse?" the duke asked, his expression contorted with distress.

Vincent rose to his feet and strode toward him. "Maybe what needs to happen in order to thwart the curse is not for the sons of Pembroke to marry quickly, but to marry for love. Maybe if we do not, we will be doing exactly what the curse is warning us *not* to do."

The duke frowned. "I still feel like I am forgetting something." He looked at Vincent desperately. "Who do you love?"

"Cassandra Montrose. Lady Colchester."

The duke frantically shook his head. "I don't know her."

"Yes, you do. You saw her last night. She was brought to the palace after the thunder storm."

His father was breathing heavily. He walked around the fountain, then returned to stand before Vincent. "When Lady Letitia came to the palace, and you fastened the Pembroke Sapphire around her neck," he said, "the rain stopped and the clouds parted. That was a good day. It was a sign."

Vincent laid a hand on his father's shoulder.

"Lady Colchester arrived the same day with her baby. She brought your grandchild here."

The duke frowned in confusion.

"Perhaps *she* was the one who stopped the rain, Father," Vincent suggested. "Perhaps it was not Letitia after all."

Even though he knew it was madness, Vincent was beginning to believe it himself—that Cassandra was the cure to all that was wrong in his own life. Everything had changed when she came back to him.

"I have a grandchild?" the duke asked.

"Yes. Her name is June."

His father squinted anxiously. "The woman with the bloody head? The one who was struck by lightning?" His eyes lit up. "Maybe that was a sign. It happened so you would be forced to bring her here to the palace so that I would meet her."

Vincent found himself nodding readily. "I believe you may be right."

All at once his father's eyes filled with panic. "I remember now. The first duchess with the sapphire . . . she came to ask me for money. Your mistress is gone."

"What do you mean, 'gone'?"

"We gave her money to make her leave."

"Who did?"

"The first duchess and I. What is her name? Letitia. She wants to poison her husband. She will poison *you*."

Vincent gently squeezed his father's shoulder. "Did Cassandra accept the money?"

The duke's eyes glazed over in defeat. "She's gone," he moaned. "She got into my coach and drove off with a tiny bundle in her arms. Was that the child?"

Vincent grabbed hold of his father's frail shoulders. "Where? Where did they go?"

Thunder rumbled in the distance. The duke took one look at the rain clouds on the horizon, bowed his head and sobbed.

Vincent pounded his fist against Letitia's door, rattling it in the jamb. When an answer did not come soon enough, he entered without waiting for an invitation, and found her sitting by the window with a plate of chocolates on her lap. "Where the devil is she?"

His fiancée looked up and sneered. "I wonder who you could possibly be referring to?"

"You know exactly who."

Letitia set the chocolates aside and stood up, licking her fingers as she crossed the room toward him. "You should never overestimate the constancy of a whore."

He had no time or patience for her spite. He took three sure and steady strides forward, placed his hands on her tiny corseted waist and pushed her up against the tall mahogany bedpost. She gasped with shock.

"Tell me where she went," he said in a low, dangerous voice, the tip of his nose lightly brushing over hers.

She barely managed to get words out. "I have no idea."

"Yes, you do, darling, and you are going to tell me."

Despite her cool, malicious bravado a moment ago, she was now quivering in the solid grip of his resolve. "She has recognized the error of her ways and left you."

"Not on her own, surely," he replied. "She had nothing but the clothes on her back. Someone must have provided her with some assistance."

Red-hot scorn glimmered in Letitia's eyes. "Your father provided her with funds and a coach to take her to the train station, and rightly so. He knows what is good for you."

"But my father is mad, and I am beginning to think you are, too."

Breathing quickly, she glanced down at his mouth and wet her lips. "Kiss me," she said.

"No."

"But you have pledged yourself to me. Your father will disinherit you if you do not marry me. You have given me your word as a gentleman that I will be your wife."

He smiled sardonically. "I am hardly a gentleman, Letitia. You've always known that. I am a rake and a libertine—a debauched scoundrel, disreputable and depraved. I am famous for my drinking, gambling, and whoring. So surely this will come as no surprise to you or to your mother, or to the whole of London for that matter."

"*What* shall come as no surprise?" she asked, fear igniting in her eyes.

"That I intend to go back on my word, because I would rather slit my wrists than spend a single minute married to you. Print *that* in the papers, darling, and don't forget to mention that I am giving you up for my very wicked but extraordinarily beautiful mistress."

He let go of her and backed away, leaving her panting with fury.

"You are a nobody," she ground out. "The insignificant, irrelevant second son of a lunatic. Even when your father was sane he didn't know who you were, and the only reason he has taken any interest in you now is because of *me*. He adores me and you know it."

"You might discover," Vincent said, "that is no longer the case. I suspect the next time he sees you, he might run screaming out the palace doors."

Her lips fell open in dismay. "You're lying."

"I want you out of this house today," he said, "and if you ever return, thinking you might sink your claws into one of my two younger brothers, I will take you by the hair and throw you out myself."

She sucked in a breath through clenched teeth. "I hope your father denounces you forever."

"What train is she taking?" he asked.

Letitia's shoulders heaved. "All I know is that your second-rate mistress left here in your father's coach in a mad dash for freedom, as if the devil himself were on her heels. That's how badly she wanted to get away from you."

He turned to leave.

"You're a fool," she shouted, following him, "if you give up your inheritance for that whore—who only slept with you for the money—when all you had to do was marry me and keep your father happy."

He was already out the door and halfway down the hall when he said over his shoulder, "I don't care about my inheritance, Letitia. That only ever mattered to you."

He heard the door slam shut behind him, followed by a shrill scream of fury and the violent smashing of glass and china.

Breathing hard after the fast ride across the estate, hoping to stay ahead of the foul weather coming his way, Vincent leaped off his horse to the ground, quickly tethered the animal, and strode into the train station. He perused the room, his gaze frantic at the sight of the empty seats and the horrible, oppressive silence. He was too late.

"Sir," he said to a guard sweeping the floor with a broom. "I take it the train has left. Was there a woman here with an infant? Was she on it?"

"There were a few ladies with babes, my lord, but I believe the one you are referring to was a very fine lady? With fair coloring?"

He strove to suppress his panic. "Yes. Did she get on the train?"

"She did, my lord. About a half hour ago."

"Do you know where she was going?"

"The train was headed for London, my lord. She purchased a second ticket to go on from there, but I don't recall the destination."

Vincent felt the piercing stab of his frustration and anger. "When does the next train depart for London?"

The young guard seemed reluctant to answer. "Not until five, my lord."

"Five, you say." He tried to keep his voice and disposition calm, so as not to frighten the man any more than he had already. "I shall need a ticket, then."

He hoped he would find her in London, waiting for her next departure.

God willing, if he did find her, it would take

every ounce of self-control he possessed not to hate her forever for doing the thing he'd feared most. She had left him and taken June with her, without even saying goodbye.

And she had done it for money.

Chapter 22

He once suggested that there are people in the world who are connected to each other in their hearts and souls. I now believe that is true, and that we are inexplicably drawn to those people. Our souls recognize them the first moment we lay eyes on them, and the connection is both everlasting and indestructible, whether you are together or not.

—from the journal of
Cassandra Montrose,
Lady Colchester,
July 9, 1874

By the time Vincent found Cassandra in a small Newbury inn, it was past midnight. He had spent the past hours traveling across the rain battered English countryside with a brief stop in London, brooding over the fact that she had left him, and in doing so, not only betrayed his trust, but was in breach of their contract as well, for she had taken their daughter away.

Exhausted, he climbed the stairs at the inn, knowing which room was hers thanks to an intoxicated innkeeper who was more interested in accepting a bribe than in protecting his guests' privacy.

Pausing outside her door, Vincent struggled to make sense of the chaos in his mind and wrestled with both his anger and a crippling sense of relief that he'd found her. She had not disappeared from his life completely without a trace.

He remembered his dream about finding MaryAnn in the woods, then turning her body over and seeing Cassandra's lifeless face instead. The sense of loss he felt had been devastating. At least Cassandra was here. Alive. He could speak with her, ask her questions, try to understand . . .

After knocking, he heard the movement from inside. At last the door opened and he found himself staring into Cassandra's surprised eyes. She was holding the collar of her nightdress tight around her neck with a fist. Her golden hair was gleaming, tousled and long about her shoulders. Her rosy lips were parted in dismay. "Vincent, what are you doing here?"

He focused on her face, his body tense with an alarming degree of desire. Evidently, no matter what occurred between them, he would always find her beautiful, especially when she was sleepy and waiflike, fresh out of bed.

"Vincent . . . " Her voice was a quiet whisper.

He strove to keep his head on straight. "Surprised to see me?"

She glanced uneasily over her shoulder into the dark room beyond. "Yes, but June is sleeping. She was tired and fussy from the journey, and I do not wish to wake her. And Miss Callahan is here," she added, letting him know she felt there must be some concern for propriety. As if it mattered at this point.

It certainly did not matter to him. All he felt was a biting need to push past her and see June for himself—if only just to look at her sleeping, to make sure she was there in the flesh, safe and sound.

"Get dressed," he said, "and meet me in the taproom." Without giving her a chance to argue, he turned and went downstairs.

It was a quiet inn. Only a few patrons were seated at the bar. Vincent selected a low table in the corner with two upholstered wing chairs and ordered a tankard of ale. While he waited for Cassandra, he sipped it slowly and contemplated his displeasure.

A few minutes later he sensed her arrival in the taproom. He looked up from his frothy ale and rose to his feet, then waited for her to sit before he sat down again as well.

She looked pale. The bandage on her head was gone but the whites of her eyes were stained with red, as if she had not slept. He suddenly felt a pang of concern for her, but then recalled how he'd been forced to chase after her, not knowing whether he would ever find her. What would he have done then?

"You are in breach of contract," he said in a low, cool voice.

Her pale cheeks flushed with color. "No, I am not."

"Indeed you are. Tell me, was that all you wanted from the beginning? Money?"

"Of course not!" she retorted with obvious shock. "I wanted no such thing!"

"Then why did you leave without a single word to me about it?"

"I *did* leave word," she insisted, her defensiveness almost palpable across the table. "I wrote you a note and left it on the pillow."

He felt curious eyes upon them from the bar, and realized that though she had just sat down ten seconds ago, they were already arguing heatedly about contracts and money and notes on pillows.

When he spoke again, his voice was quieter. "All I know is that my father offered you a generous sum of money today in exchange for your leaving me, and that you accepted it."

Her eyes flashed with fury. "I did *not* accept it. Who told you that? Letitia?"

He blinked at her, seeking to get his bearings and understand what was happening. "Father believed you took it. You left in the coach he provided."

She frowned as she, too, tried to comprehend what had occurred. "You did not find my letter? As I said, I left it on my pillow. Did you not go back to my room?"

"I did. There was no letter."

Cassandra scoffed. "Letitia must have found it and taken it. I assure you, I was not leaving you. I wrote to tell you where I would be, here in Newbury waiting to take up residence in Langley Hall, just as we planned."

He gazed at her in disbelief. He had expected to come here and experience the complete annihilation of their affair. He'd expected to meet a woman whose heart had turned cold, a woman who would tear up the contract in front of his face and tell him the time had come to move on.

She glowered at him. "Did you actually think I would disappear and take June away from you like that?"

He closed his eyes and rubbed his temples, which were now throbbing with pain from the stress of the day. "It has not been easy for me to believe that my life could possibly turn out well. I have not had it happen before."

"Well, neither have I," she replied. "But I have learned a thing or two over the past month. I thought perhaps you might have, too."

"I did," he tried to tell her, still squeezing his forehead. "But then you disappeared."

She sat for a long time saying nothing, then leaned forward and covered his hand with hers on the table. "I did not disappear," she gently assured him. "You simply did not find my letter. If you had, you would not have spent the whole day chasing after me and giving yourself a headache."

The server approached the table. Cassandra leaned back and asked for wine. When they were alone again, he wet his lips. "What did the letter say?"

She sat in silence, just looking at him, then at last began to explain. "I wrote to tell you that I now believe you were right that day in the library at Langley Hall, when you suggested there could be true fidelity of the heart without a written contract or a certificate of marriage. I have decided that I will not spend another minute resisting what is in my heart. I want to be with you, and I shall be brave. My worst fear was that you would break my heart one day, that I would have to share you with other women, but now I am willing to face that possibility. I do not need the contract between us to bind you to me forever. All I need is to love you, to *give* you my love. The passion we have between us, as we are, is enough, for however long it lasts."

He stared at her closely across the table. "However long it lasts?" A deep pang of hurt and disappointment pulsed inside his chest. "I believe, Cassandra, that this is the first time since you came back into my life that you have ever truly sounded like a mistress."

Cassandra's wine arrived and was set down in front of her, but she could not move her hands to touch it.

"Perhaps I sound like a mistress," she told him with a cool air, "because that is what I am. Though I must say, you have never made me feel ashamed of it. Not until now."

He inhaled deeply. "That is because in my eyes you were always above that. And you have become much more than that."

She paused. "Well, that, sir, is news to me."

"I *want* you to be more," he said.

She shifted uneasily. "What are you saying? How can I possibly be more, unless you want to make me your wife. But that cannot be."

"Why not?"

"Because you have told me a dozen times—Letitia is your perfect match. She will allow you to keep your freedom. And also, your father would never accept me. You would lose your inheritance. You would be letting down your brothers."

"First of all, let us be clear. Letitia is not my perfect match. She was once, I suppose, when I was a different man, but she is no longer."

"She is no longer what? Your perfect match?"

"Correct. But she is also no longer my fiancée. We have parted ways."

She stared at him, afraid to believe what he was saying. Or rather, what she *thought* he was saying.

"Even without Letitia as your fiancée," she said, "I cannot be your wife. I could not bear to cause a rift between you and your brothers, nor do I wish for you to lose your inheritance. If that happened, you would resent me. Maybe not now, but one day in the future."

He sat back and folded his arms. "So you want to continue with our contractual arrangement? Is that it? You would be comfortable as my mistress for as long at it lasts, while I choose another woman to be my wife? While I share a bed with her? Have children with her? And of course, the way you describe it, I would leave you eventually for another mistress. That would all be acceptable to you?"

Cassandra wet her lips and tried to hide the fact that she was shaken by the mere mention of him having children with another woman. "I wouldn't like it."

His eyes were dark and determined as he leaned forward again. "What if I told you I don't care what my father says or what my brothers think? Or society for that matter."

"Then I would tell you that you are not thinking rationally because you are blinded by lust."

"Lust?" he angrily retorted. "Do you still think that's what this is about?"

"I don't know."

"Do I feel this more deeply than you?" he asked. "Tell me if that is the case, because if you are not willing to fight for what has become more than just lust between us, I will be grossly disappointed. Especially because all you've ever done before now is fight against it."

She looked down at her glass of wine and finally picked it up to take a sip. Her hands were shaking. "I have been fighting against it because I was afraid I would end up with a broken heart. I still fear that, because there are so many forces against us."

"I have fears, too," he said. "I always will, but it doesn't mean I will not fight against those forces that stand between us. I already have, Cassandra. I have told Letitia I will not marry her, that she can drag me through the papers and the courts and all the mud in England if she is so inclined.

It will not make a bloody difference to me. I will never be her husband."

Cassandra looked at him cautiously. "What about your father? Your brothers?"

"I believe I might have found a way around my father's demands. With Charlotte's help, and that maid . . . what is her name? Iris?"

"Iris? She has become involved in this? How could she possibly be of help?"

"She led Charlotte to some evidence hidden in one of the fireplaces that helped my father stop romanticizing the first duchess—the one who looked like Letitia. It turns out she was a bit of a shrew."

Cassandra was having a difficult time believing all of this. "Does that mean your father's affection for Letitia has diminished?"

"It seems so. He might even be blaming her for the curse, if I have luck on my side. For once."

She placed both hands flat on the table. "Does he know about me?"

"He knows you are my mistress, and that I love you."

She couldn't seem to move. All she could do was fumble frantically in her mind with those words he'd just said to her. *I love you.*

She pushed her glass of wine to the side so she would not spill it. "I am a fallen woman, Vincent. I have birthed your child out of wedlock. I have been your mistress. Surely I am not worthy of—"

"You are the most worthy person I have ever met in my life, Cassandra."

One of the taproom patrons dropped a mug of ale on the floor just then, and it smashed to pieces. Cassandra jumped.

"Let us leave here." Vincent rose to his feet and held out his hand. "The rain has stopped and it is a beautiful night, fresh and sweet-smelling. Come and walk with me?"

Half in a daze, Cassandra placed her hand in his. He escorted her outside onto the empty street, where the air was moist and crickets were chirping in the damp, green grass.

"Which way should we go?" he asked, looking east and west, up and down the street.

"This way," she suggested, turning toward the quiet edge of town and wondering if she was dreaming.

Her arm was linked through his, but he soon slid his hand down and took hold of hers. They walked for a while in silence, stepping around puddles, and the notion that there was hope—that he could love her and be devoted to her—was enough to make her stop in her tracks, close her eyes and say frenzied prayers of gratitude.

He stopped, too, and faced her. "I want to kiss you."

A light gasp floated past her lips as his mouth

touched hers in the darkness, warm and soft, engaging and erotic. His tongue moved with exquisite intimacy, and she was quite sure he was the most amazing kisser in the world.

She moaned softly, sensually, and when he drew back, she spoke with her eyes still closed. "You always make my knees go weak."

"Always?"

"Yes. The first moment I saw you, I melted. I was enraptured. You were the handsomest man I had ever seen. I could not keep my eyes off you. I fell instantly in love. Or lust, whatever it was."

"Is it lust now?" he asked. "Or is there something more?"

She opened her eyes. He was so beautiful, looking down at her intently, she could not bear it.

"But wait," he said. "Before you answer, I must say something to you. You must know this, Cassandra. If you are mine, if we are together, there will never be any other women. I will be yours and no one else's. I will be faithful to you until the day I die, and devoted to both you and June. You are all I will ever want."

She was overcome suddenly by the need to touch him. Laying her palm on his cheek briefly, she glanced down at his hand at his side and took hold of it, stroked it with her thumb, but even that was not enough. She wanted to wrap her arms around him and hold his body close to hers, to feel the beat of his heart against her breast.

"It is so much more, Vincent, my love. I could never be without you."

She melted anew at the light in his eyes when he gave her the devastating smile that always charmed her and aroused her deepest passions.

"Will you be my wife, Cassandra?" he asked. "Please say yes, because I want you forever as my mate, my friend, and my lover."

Even now she was afraid to believe that she could have him for her own, that she could have everything she'd ever wanted—love, passion, devotion. With *him*. With the most incredible man she'd ever known.

"Your father," she said anxiously. "Will he accept me?"

"Will it matter?"

She looked at him for a long moment. "No, I suppose not, if you are certain it is what you want. But what of the scandal? June will always be illegitimate. We may never be accepted back into society."

"We will go our own way for a while," he said. "Together—you, me, and June. We will travel, and spend our time in the country, and eventually, I believe that people will forget. If all else fails, when Devon is duke, it will be a new beginning for all of us. No one would dare to stand against him, and he has given me his word that he will support us."

"You have reconciled with him, then?"

"Yes."

"Oh, Vincent, I am so pleased to hear it. You are brothers again."

He nodded. "And friends."

Warmth flooded her heart.

"But even if June was never accepted in the highest circles," he said, "what would it matter? When the time comes for her to marry, I want her to choose a husband for love, not for duty or position. She can marry the butcher for all I care, as long as he is a good man and treats her well. No matter what, she will always have her family behind her."

"That sounds quite fine, Vincent. More than fine."

He smiled again, then dropped to one knee on the wet street. "Forgive me. I am not doing this properly."

He bowed his head and paused for a moment. She reached down with a hand and almost touched his dark wavy hair, but drew back when he looked up.

"Cassandra Montrose, you are the great love of my life," he said. "You have made me feel whole when I never knew it was possible to feel that way. All the missing pieces of my heart and my life came together inside of me when I met you. I do not ever wish to be without you. Will you do me the great honor of becoming my wife?"

The whole world seemed to burst wide open inside her heart as she looked down at him, and then suddenly she was laughing, throwing her head back as tears spilled from her eyes. "Yes!"

Before she could comprehend anything more, he was on his feet and his lips were upon hers, his arms wrapping around her waist, pulling her to him. Joy flooded through her as she rose up on her toes and threw her arms around his neck. The next thing she knew, she was kissing his cheek and telling him she loved him with all her heart.

It was the happiest moment of her life. He was hers. She was his. She had never dreamed it could truly be possible, that she could be his wife, and yet it was real. He was here. He had followed her across the country to claim her as his own, and now June would be able to call him Father.

All the happiness in the world enveloped her as he swung her around in his arms and promised her everything. Surely life did not get any better than this, for she was going to marry the true mate of her soul.

It was time at last to lay down her shield.

Chapter 23

One year ago he was the cause of my destruction. I only hope that now I will not be the cause of his.

—from the journal of
Cassandra Montrose,
Lady Colchester,
July 14, 1874

Along the drive to Pembroke Palace, the gardens were blooming brightly with color as the coach rolled up the long lane. The soil was rich and dark, nourishing the lush green foliage where sprays of scarlet-crimson nasturtiums and deep pink peonies burst forth in showy, bold blooms. Farther along, thousands of English daisies were crowded together among the larkspur, asters, and hollyhocks in a stunning fusion of color and promise that took Cassandra's breath away.

Ahead of them, Pembroke Palace stood like a

mighty, majestic sentry on the hilltop, protecting its own. She shivered with apprehension, knowing she was about to face that sentry with a baby in her arms, born out of wedlock to a man whose future had already been cast for him by the lord of this palace, the Duke of Pembroke himself.

She thought of the past year of her life, first dashing out of a London ballroom with a handsome, reckless charmer she'd met only hours before, later being tossed out of her home, having nowhere to go, and eventually nothing with which to sustain herself but her skill with a needle. She eventually believed the end of her life had come, and saw no alternative but to give up her child on this very doorstep and skulk away in sorrow. Following that, she had become a rake's mistress.

Now, driving up to the palace with that same wicked rake, she felt like the greatest interloper in the history of the world. What was his family going to say?

She looked at Vincent beside her in the coach. Holding June close to her breast, she wondered if it really mattered, for deep in her heart she knew she was exactly where she was meant to be, that all the grueling events of her life had led her to this moment and to him—and that nothing would ever come between them again. They were connected to each other by some invisible force, and no matter what occurred when they reached the palace gate, that would never change. He was the true mate of her soul, and would remain so until the day she drew her last breath, perhaps even beyond.

At last the coach pulled to a stop. Vincent stepped out and took June in one arm while he offered the other hand to Cassandra. She lifted her face and looked up at the stately front portico, which was crowned by a clock tower, fluttering flags, and stately finials, gargoyles, and lions.

She turned her eyes to meet Vincent's. "My hands are shaking."

"You have nothing to fear," he said, his voice low and comforting.

"What if they do not accept me? What if your father disinherits you?"

"Then we will live with that outcome." He carefully set June back into her arms. "For now, all you have to do is accompany me inside and present our daughter to the family with your usual charm and poise." He gave her a reassuring smile, then escorted her up the wide steps.

His mother appeared at the door. "There you are at last," she said, glancing uncertainly at Cassandra with the baby in her arms. "I thought you would never return." She stepped forward to greet them and kissed Vincent on the cheek. "Lady Colchester, welcome."

She curtsied and glanced uneasily at Vincent. "Thank you, Your Grace."

No one said anything for a few awkward seconds, then the duchess said, "Won't you come in?"

They followed her inside. Cassandra looked up at the high ceiling overhead, the thick, marble columns at all four corners of the hall, and the enormous ancestral portraits on the walls. If she had been intimidated before by the idea of coming here, she was even more so now, knowing she would soon have to face the duke.

"How is father?" Vincent asked.

The duchess stood in the center of the hall. "He is the same, still fixated on the weather, watching the horizon and counting the clouds." She glanced around and lowered her voice. "I must inform you, Vincent, that he does not remember what you told him in the garden or the letters you showed him. He believes Letitia is still here and that nothing has changed, that you are still engaged to her. He says he sees her at night."

Vincent glanced at Cassandra. "He must be looking at the portrait of the first duchess."

"That is what we have concluded."

"Where is he?"

"In the drawing room."

Cassandra, still holding their sleeping baby in her arms, felt a surge of apprehension. "Perhaps you should go and see him first, on your own."

"No, we will go together."

The duchess nodded and led the way to the drawing room, where they found the duke, along with Devon and Rebecca, who were drinking tea on the opposite side of the room.

"Theodore?" the duchess said, entering first and approaching the duke carefully. "I have good news. Vincent is home."

The duke's hair was wild about his head, his expression anxious as he turned from the window to face them. He wore no shoes.

Cassandra stopped just inside the door.

"Hello Father," Vincent said, giving him a moment to take in their presence. "Devon, Rebecca." They all greeted him. "There is someone here I wish you to meet."

"Who is this?" the duke asked.

Vincent gestured toward Cassandra and June. "First of all, I want you to meet your granddaughter, June Marie Sinclair."

The duke stared, bewildered, then padded across the room toward them. He stood before Cassandra, looking into her eyes. "This is not the first duchess."

"No, Father. This is the woman I love." Vincent looked across the room at Devon, who gave him an encouraging nod.

The duke's surprisingly calm gaze dropped to

June, who was wrapped in a blanket, awake now and wiggling happily in Cassandra's arms. "This is your child?" he asked her.

"Yes, Your Grace," she said.

"May I hold her?"

"Of course." Not knowing what to expect, Cassandra placed her baby daughter into his arms. Vincent was watching his father carefully.

The duke carried June to the center of the room. He swung back and forth, rocking her, murmuring quiet words Cassandra could not hear, nor could she see his face, for he had turned his back on them.

At last he faced them. "This is my grandchild?" he said to Vincent.

"Yes, Father."

Cassandra braced herself for the worst, but then the duke threw his head back and laughed out loud. Seconds later his laughter turned to sobbing. "Vincent, my son, she looks like you when you were this age. She has the same dark, intelligent expression."

Vincent's voice was quiet. "Do you even remember what I looked like?"

Tears filled the duke's clear eyes. "I remember everything. You were a beautiful child. I wept when I first held you."

Cassandra looked across at Vincent and felt the most wonderful joy at his astonishment.

The duke looked back down at June in his arms and spoke playfully, bouncing at the knees. "What a remarkable girl you are, just like your father. You have his eyes. Will you be a fast runner like he was? He used to win all the races against his brothers."

Vincent's gaze rushed to meet Cassandra's. It was as if his joy and hers were mingling and humming between them. He knew she understood everything. She understood all that existed in the wondrous depths of his heart and soul.

Just then the duke seemed to remember that she was still standing there. He approached and placed June back in her arms.

"You're the mother?"

"Yes."

He nodded and took a step back, studying her with intense scrutiny. Vincent came to stand beside her.

"What happened to the other one?" the duke asked pointedly. "The one I picked out for you?"

"She left," Vincent replied.

He frowned, trying to understand. "Was she the fairy?"

"Yes, she was dressed as a fairy when she first came to Mother's birthday ball."

The duke narrowed his eyes, as if seeking to understand. "She didn't love you, did she? She wanted to poison you in your bed."

"You are thinking of the first duchess, Father. But you are correct about Lady Letitia. She did not love me."

Cassandra noticed that Devon and Rebecca had risen to their feet and were watching and listening intently.

The duke looked at Cassandra again. "Do *you* love him?"

"With all my heart and soul, Your Grace. I would give my life for him, and for our child."

She met Rebecca's gaze across the room. Rebecca smiled warmly.

Stepping forward, the duke touched June's little cheek with the back of a finger. "She is a lovely child. I've never been a grandfather before."

Cassandra smiled at him. "Then today is a very special day."

The duke nudged Vincent. "You have not yet introduced me to this beauty."

Vincent slid his arm around Cassandra's waist. "No, Father, I have not yet done so. Please allow me to present, to all of you, Cassandra Sinclair, Lady Vincent. My wife, as of yesterday."

Adelaide gasped and covered her face with both hands.

Vincent met his brother's gaze. Devon nodded at him with approval.

The duke's eyebrows lifted. "We have another bride of Pembroke?"

"We do," Vincent said, smiling.

The duke's mouth fell open. "That is why the sun has been shining."

"I believe so."

The duke looked at Cassandra with the cheerful, magnanimous innocence of a child. "I am so pleased."

"As am I, Your Grace," she replied, laughing uncontrollably as tears of joy filled her eyes.

"The curse is thwarted again," he said simply, his bushy eyebrows lifting.

"It seems so, Father," Devon said, approaching.

The duchess hugged Vincent and Cassandra. "Congratulations to you both. I couldn't be happier."

While the others were fussing over June, Vincent approached his brother. "May I have a word with you?" he asked.

"Of course," Devon replied.

They moved to the other side of the room where they could speak in private.

"I cannot begin to pretend that we have not had our differences over the past few years," Vincent said.

"We have," Devon agreed.

"What happened between you and MaryAnn caused me great pain—a pain that I did not even want to put behind me. I preferred wallowing in my bitterness."

"Vincent—"

He put up a hand. "Let me finish." He met his brother's clear blue eyes. "I know that you suffered, too, Devon. It could not have been easy, receiving that letter from the woman your brother intended to marry, and then having to tell us all that she was dead. I know you did not encourage her affections, and it was wrong of me to punish you for so long afterward. I should have forgiven you. I am deeply sorry."

His brother closed his eyes and bowed his head. "If you only knew how I have longed to hear you say those words. I have suffered from my guilt, more than you could ever know. I have wished I could go back in time and do it all differently. I would never have gone to see her. I would have ignored her letter. I would have gone away—anything to change the way it turned out. Perhaps then MaryAnn would still be alive and you would have had your wedding day."

Vincent shook his head. "We would not have been happy. She did not love me, and that was what I wanted most of all—to marry a woman who truly loved me."

"And now you have."

"Yes."

"I hope we can be friends again . . . "

Vincent held out his hand. "Friends *and* brothers. Loyal to the end."

"Loyal to the end." They looked meaningfully into each other's eyes and shook on it.

Vincent noticed their mother watching them, so he and Devon returned to where the others were gathered in a circle around June.

The duchess took hold of her husband's hand. "I hope you will sleep well tonight, Theodore."

"I dare say I will," he replied. "A lovely bride and a grandchild all in the same day." He laughed out loud and threw his arms up into the air. "Now all we need is for the other two to come home. Where the devil is Blake, anyway? Does anyone know? The man has bloody well disappeared into thin air. I dare say, he best get himself back here dressed in wedding attire, or he'll face my wrath."

"Indeed," Vincent said, meeting Devon's gaze with a hint of amusement. "It's time he and Garrett both learned how truly wonderful a wedding day can be." He touched Cassandra's cheek. "When one is marrying the right woman, of course."

Devon moved to stand beside Rebecca, and smiled. "You are a wise man, Vincent, for more insightful words were never spoken."

Chapter 24

I have been making love for forty-eight hours straight, and have hardly slept a wink. One would think I'd be exhausted.

I suppose, when one is in love, amazing things are possible.

—from the journal of
Cassandra Sinclair,
Lady Vincent,
July 16, 1874

I am eager to move into Langley Hall," Vincent said to Cassandra two days later, slipping his arm around her waist as they strolled through the palace gallery at sunrise. They had been up all night making up for lost time, and were on their way to the breakfast room for some much needed sustenance.

"As am I," she replied. "I have spent many hours

daydreaming about the library and the grounds and the lake. You told me once that you intend to teach June to fish one day. Do you still wish to do that?"

"Of course. I will take her digging for worms and show her how to row a boat."

"That sounds perfectly lovely."

"You can come, too," he said. "Do you know how to cast a line?"

Cassandra stopped suddenly in the gallery. "Good heavens, is this the first duchess?"

Vincent looked up. "Yes. The resemblance to my former fiancée is rather hair-raising, don't you think?"

"Disturbingly so," she replied. "This woman has the same ruthless look in her eyes."

They stood hand in hand, staring at it.

"I should count myself lucky that you saved me from the fate of becoming her husband," he said. "I would have been miserable."

Cassandra squeezed his hand. "I cannot bear to think of it."

They moved on, walking past the other family portraits.

"That is the first duke," Vincent said, stopping again under an impressive painting of a heavily bearded aristocrat. "Remember I told you about him? He was a trusted friend of King

Henry VIII, who awarded him the dukedom in the 1500s."

"And he chose this site to build his palace on the ruins of an old abbey," she said, "where his father, the prior, was murdered."

"Yes." Vincent pulled her close. "Because he committed the terrible sin of falling in love with a woman who was forbidden to him."

"A monk with a mistress," she said with a sigh, "murdered as a punishment for his passions. It is not exactly the stuff of fairy tales."

"No, certainly not."

They continued on, but Cassandra stopped again. "My word, this looks like Iris." She strode toward a tiny oval miniature of a woman, framed and hanging next to the larger portrait of the duke.

"That is the mother of the first duke, the prior's mistress. We know so little about her life. This is all we have left of her. Even her name is a mystery."

For a long time Cassandra stared at the small portrait, marveling at the resemblance to the maid who had been so kind to her. "Another remarkable similarity," she said, "don't you think?"

Vincent took a step forward. "Yes, you are right, my darling. Perhaps that is why Iris looked so familiar to me when she came to your room that day. She looks like my ancestor."

They joined hands and continued on to the breakfast room, unaware of Iris sweeping the ash out of the grate at the far end of the gallery, watching them and smiling at the sight of their happiness. She finished her job, brushed her hands together to dust off the ash, then turned and disappeared into the corridor.

"Do you think there will ever be a day," Cassandra asked, as they began to eagerly inhale the aroma of coffee and bacon, eggs and toast, "when we will not be completely besotted with each other?"

Vincent stopped her in the corridor and backed her up against the wall. "Not a chance in heaven, my angel," he replied, and then pressed his lips to hers and gave her the most perfect kiss. It was deep and wet and erotic, and before breakfast no less.

"You have always made me weak in the knees," she sighed breathlessly, her eyes still closed as he stepped back. "And I suspect you always will."

"Then you have answered your own question, darling. The rapture will go on."

With a smile, she took his hand. "In that case, we are absolutely obligated to get some breakfast, if we are to sustain ourselves for the everlasting, undying rapture—which will continue on throughout the day, I hope?"

He grinned wolfishly. "Indeed. Will you let me serve you up a plate?"

"I would be most obliged if you would. I shall sit myself down and conserve my strength for later."

And together they strolled blissfully into the breakfast room.

Epilogue

The scandal over Lord Vincent Sinclair's secret marriage to his mistress, Lady Colchester, was, in a word, colossal. For years it was talked about in every fashionable drawing room from London to France, and all the young, marriageable daughters of good families were firmly reminded to never, under any circumstances, dash out of a ballroom with a stranger, no matter how handsome or charming he proved himself to be. The couple was criticized, rejected, openly excluded from every respectable guest list for five seasons straight, and it mattered not one bit that they were out of the country. They were added to the lists regardless, just so the host or hostess could have the pleasure of striking them off.

And so, the lovers traveled. They rode camels over Egyptian deserts, fed elephants in India, sailed the seven seas, and steamed their way across America by train, first class all the way. They were as happy as anyone could ever be.

By the tenth season, the details of the scandalous affair and Lady Colchester's terrible fall from grace began to grow somewhat sketchy, and soon, stories began to circulate about the unparalleled beauty of the illegitimate daughter of the affair, who possessed all the exquisite features of her mother—the golden hair, the entrancing blue eyes, and the captivating, mysterious allure that had, by some miracle, tamed a wild, black lion.

Back at Pembroke Palace, the duke, in his seventy-ninth year, passed away peacefully in his sleep, and a new age began for the Pembrokes. His Grace, Devon Sinclair, along with his wife, Rebecca, Duchess of Pembroke and Countess of Creighton, a peeress in her own right, held a ball to welcome their brother and sister-in-law home from their world travels, along with their four children—two boys and two girls, who became fast friends with the duke's many children. They amused themselves by searching for ghosts in the subterranean passages of the palace, where the boys howled in the dark corners to frighten the girls.

The ball held in their honor was an enormous success, and Lord and Lady Vincent's names were immediately added back to every relevant guest list that season.

Eight years later, Lady June, widely regarded as the most beautiful young woman to enter society in half a century, was presented at court, and two years after that, she married a handsome young viscount—for love—and they, like their parents, lived a long and prosperous life blessed with many children, and much joy and laughter.